The Gamble

Robert Cort

Clink Street

Published by Clink Street Publishing 2023

Copyright © 2023

First edition.

The author asserts the moral right under the Copyright, Designs and Patents Act 1988 to be identified as the author of this work.

All rights reserved. No part of this publication may be reproduced, stored in a retrieval system or transmitted, in any form or by any means without the prior consent of the author, nor be otherwise circulated in any form of binding or cover other than that with which it is published and without a similar condition being imposed on the subsequent purchaser.

ISBN
978-1-915785-15-2 – paperback
978-1-915785-16-9 – ebook

To Waldemar Januszczak,
for unravelling many of the mysteries and hidden stories
about famous artists and their paintings.

*"There are a million stories in the world of art…
this has been just one of them."*

ALSO WRITTEN BY ROBERT CORT

THE IAN CAXTON THRILLER SERIES
    Volume 1 – The Opportunity
    Volume 2 – The Challenge
    Volume 3 – The Decision

www.robertcort.net

'The Gamble'

'The Gamble' is the fourth volume in the Ian Caxton Thriller series.

Ian Caxton has committed to a major change in his career, but will the gamble prove to be a success?

Fresh challenges face Ian and his colleagues as they attempt to unravel more mysteries in the art world. Are the paintings of 'Sir Edgar Brookfield' and 'Mademoiselle Chad' worth millions of pounds? Who's the famous artist hidden behind the signature, 'Madeleine B' and why does Ian think an identical painting, currently on display in the Musée des BeauxArts d'Orléans, is really a fake?

Is Gladstone's association with his boyhood hero connected to the murder of Millie Hobbie and why is Ian's nemesis, Jonathan Northgate, back in his life?

All is revealed in the continuing page-turning tales of adventure, risks and rewards, where paintings once considered lost are now worth millions of pounds.

Chapter 1

It was late on a Sunday afternoon and both Ian and Emma were still discussing the two options concerning their future. They'd analysed all the pros and cons but were still not 100% certain which was the right choice to make. It really was a tough decision.

How things could seriously change in just a few days, Emma thought. Her understanding was that everything had been sorted and agreed about Ian's job at Sotheby's. Ian was going to resign and they'd both concentrate on building up their art business and be able to spend more time using the apartment in Monaco. Now, with the offer of the Managing Director's job at Sotheby's, all this, potentially, was in jeopardy.

Ian had previously explained to Emma all the benefits of taking the Managing Director's role. A much improved and secure salary, larger eventual pension, more benefits and enhanced personal prestige. Yet, despite all these attractions, Ian still could not convince himself, never mind Emma, that this new option was the right decision. Indeed the serious warning words of Michael Hopkins, his boss and the current MD, continued to bounce around in his head. He could almost remember Michael's serious words exactly:

'This is a big opportunity, but it is also very demanding on all your talents… and especially on your time and family life. It's not for everyone, so you really need to get Emma's full support and commitment too. Without that everything, and I mean everything, could easily fail.'

Emma could feel Ian's frustrations and anxiety. They had both experienced broken nights' sleep since Ian's last meeting with his boss… and the tempting offer of the top job. It was a big decision, a huge decision! Even she was starting to have second thoughts. After all, there were no guarantees when you stepped away from a secure employed role and into the world of self-employment. No more regular income that they'd become used to… and had certainly taken for granted! Robert's school fees and a large mortgage would still have to be paid. The usual domestic bills, food, two cars, entertainment, the list went on and on! They would have to be very, very successful in the art world to get even close to the income and benefits that were currently enjoyed by Sotheby's Managing Director. Maybe we are being too adventurous. Are we really cut out for this uncertain existence? Yes, we are reasonably financially secure… well, yes, at the moment, but what about illness, another world financial crisis, that could well see the bottom fall out of the art market once again. Where would we be then?

Ian knew he had about 16 hours left in which to make his final decision. The biggest decision of his life. The decision that he might eventually live to regret? His excitement and enthusiasm, just a few days ago, had now changed to anguish and apprehension. How was he going to finally decide?

When Ian and Emma finally fell asleep just after midnight, it was due to exhaustion, not a gentle drifting off to sleep. They had gone to bed at 10.45pm with the final decision still in the air. Emma had suggested they try to summarise their many discussions by listing all the benefits and downsides they had decided before.

It was just before midnight when they'd finally, yes finally, come to a joint decision. Both Ian and Emma were definitely as one. They kissed and snuggled down under the duvet. Ian hoped he would now finally get a good night's sleep.

At 6.45am the next morning, the bedside alarm clock rang. Ian switched it off but Emma hadn't stirred. He got out of bed, showered and shaved. He then put on his best suit and his lucky blue tie. A quick bowl of cereal and he was then on his way, walking towards Esher railway station. Again, he recognised a number of the 'regulars' standing on the platform, waiting for the same train to London as him. But, again, he didn't know any names, no occupations, nothing about their individual lives... he only recognised their faces.

It was 8.35am when Ian walked into his outer office. Penny, his PA, was usually the first to arrive, but then he remembered she had mentioned on Friday that she would not be in the office until about ten o'clock as she had a dental check up.

Ian walked through Penny's area and into his own office, stopping in front of his desk. He placed his briefcase down on the polished oak surface and looked around the room. It was a nice and comfortable size, with space for a small table and four chairs for meetings and two more cushioned seats facing the desk.

This was not going to be his office for much longer, he thought... whatever his final decision! He walked over to the far wall and hung up his overcoat. On the cream painted wall immediately next to him was the large colour photograph he had taken some years ago. It was the view across Victoria Harbour from Kowloon to Hong Kong

Island. Such a lot had changed in his life since the time he'd been working there. Great times, so many happy memories.

He checked his wristwatch. 8.40am. Twenty minutes to go. He took a deep breath and wished this was all over and done with. But, of course, it wasn't, not just yet. Suddenly he smiled and remembered the old black and white cowboy movie, *High Noon*. Yes, his meeting with his boss in a few minutes' time, was going to be his own *High Noon*. He could now feel the 'butterflies' fluttering in his stomach. His breathing was deeper and his heartbeat was much more rapid. He also began to perspire.

He walked over to his window and looked out. The earlier drizzle had now stopped and the street was busy with commuters hurrying to their offices, shops and elsewhere. Like ants going about their daily business, Ian thought. He checked his watch once again. 8.44am. He decided not to waste any more time and strode out of his office and walked along the familiar corridors. His mind was trying to focus on what the right words he was about to deliver to his boss would be. His stomach was still churning; the palms of his hands felt nervously damp. He hoped the tenseness he was feeling in his body would not develop into a horrible headache. As he passed the men's lavatory he quickly popped in and washed his hands and perspiring brow. He dried both on a paper towel and then rechecked his watch. 8.52am. He looked in the mirror and brushed his hair with his hand. Four minutes later he walked into his boss's outer office where he found Michael Hopkins, the MD, standing near his office door talking to his PA.

"Ah, Ian," cried Michael, looking across and a little surprised. "A little early, but come on... into my office."

Ian smiled and nodded at Michael's PA. She briefly smiled back. He followed his boss into his office, gently closing the door behind him. He took a deep breath.

"Sit down, Ian. Did you have a good weekend?" asked Michael, sitting down behind his large walnut desk. He removed his reading glasses and placed them on the side of his desk.

Ian smiled. If only he knew. He sat down opposite his boss and said, "I've had a lot to think about, Michael, and, of course, I've also had numerous discussions with Emma. We really didn't have much time to do anything else."

"Yes, of course," said Michael, more seriously. "A big decision. So then, what have you both decided?"

This was it, thought Ian. He shuffled a little in his seat and nervously rubbed his hands together. Finally, he looked across to his boss, and started to speak, "Michael, your offer of the Managing Director's position, last week, came as a total surprise. I had no idea you were planning to retire so soon or that I was being considered by you and the chairman to be your preferred successor. Your wise words advising me to discuss all the implications with Emma before I made my final decision were very astute. A strong warning that the role was not for everybody, whatever their qualities and skills. As I mentioned earlier, Emma and I have discussed nothing else all weekend. Emma did, however, confirm that she would support me in whatever decision I finally made." Ian took another deep breath before he continued.

"However, I have to tell you, Michael, it's not my ambition to become Sotheby's Managing Director. Over the last few days, I've found it very difficult to change that view. I accept that, careerwise, it's a massive opportunity and you're also paying me an enormous compliment, but... I'm sorry to say, Michael, I'm refusing your offer."

"I see," said his boss, a little shocked, but not totally surprised. "And that's your final decision?"

"I'm afraid it is, Michael. As I say, it is a wonderful compliment you pay me, but your job isn't what I want to do over the next five, ten or whatever, years. When I was in New York and Hong Kong I was single and very ambitious. Now I have a wonderful wife and a lovely son. My life has changed, my priorities and ambitions have similarly changed. My family is my future, not the Managing Director's role. As you rightly warned me, it's almost impossible to do both without sacrificing something. I don't want to risk the possibility of losing Emma, or feeling that I'm not being fully committed to the MD's role. That wouldn't be fair to Sotheby's, me, you or, indeed, anyone."

"Okay, Ian, you've made your decision and I respect your reasons," replied Michael. He pondered on his next words. "We'll just have to look for an alternative candidate, which, of course, may or may not be good news for you in your long-term career."

Ian smiled. He had been expecting something along these lines. "I know. If I was the new MD, I'd want to make my own mark at Sotheby's and review the whole set up. And, of course, that would include all of the staff as well."

Ian put his hand into his inside jacket pocket and pulled out a white sealed envelope.

"When I came to the meeting with you last week, I had this letter in my pocket. However, when you announced you wanted me to succeed you as the Managing Director, I decided it was only fair and proper to give your offer the full and serious consideration it deserved. As I said, it was an enormous compliment. This serious consideration now done: I'm giving you notice that I wish to resign from Sotheby's."

Ian leaned forward and placed the envelope on his boss's desk.

Michael picked up the letter, looked at the envelope and then back at Ian. After a few seconds, he placed the letter, still unopened, into the top left drawer of his desk.

Chapter 2

When Ian left Michael Hopkins' office, he was still shaking and sweating. He returned to the men's lavatory and washed his face and hands in cold water. He looked in the mirror. He was worried and wondered if he'd made the right decision. Too late now, he thought, but he was curious to understand why his boss had not opened the letter. Why did he just place it into the top drawer of his desk?

Drying his face and hands and taking two deep breaths, Ian realised that his increased heart rate was now returning to normal and his trembling body reaction was much calmer now.

After leaving the lavatory, he slowly walked back towards his office. However, he suddenly stopped and diverted out through an exit doorway and into the side courtyard to take a deep breath of cool, fresh air. On the far side of the courtyard three members of staff were talking and having a smoking break. Ian looked across, but he didn't recognise any of their faces. He took some more deep breaths of the cool air, but then shivered briefly and decided to head back to the confines of his much warmer office.

When he arrived back into his outer office, he noticed Penny had still not appeared. He walked through to his own office, picked up his mobile phone and telephoned

The Gamble

Emma. When she answered he confirmed he'd declined the MD's job and had handed in his notice. Emma started to ask questions about his boss's reaction, but Ian stopped her when he heard activity in the outer office. He said he would tell her the full details that evening. When he'd finished the call, he wandered over to the doorway between the two offices to investigate. He saw Penny hanging up her coat.

"Good morning, Penny. All okay at the dentist's?" he asked.

"Oh hi, Ian. Yes, fine, thanks," replied Penny, turning around to face her boss. "All okay." She gave Ian a slightly exaggerated smile.

"Will you come into my office? I've got some news to tell you." Ian wandered back to his desk and sat down.

When Penny walked into his office, Ian asked her to close the door.

Penny gently closed the door, walked over and sat down on her usual seat opposite her boss. Shutting the door was a rarity for Ian, so Penny was immediately concerned with what he was about to say. It was obviously going to be serious. Was it going to be bad news?

"First of all, Penny, what I'm about to tell you is for your ears only."

Penny nodded, but remained focused on Ian.

"At least for the next two or three days."

Again, Penny nodded, but still didn't say a word.

Ian continued, "This morning I had a follow-up meeting with Michael Hopkins. Last week Michael told me, in confidence, that he would be retiring at the end of the current financial year." Penny's eyes suddenly became wide open in surprise. Ian continued. "The bombshell that came next was that he told me that both he and the chairman wanted me to replace him as the new MD."

"Goodness!" exclaimed Penny. "Wow."

"Michael gave me the weekend to talk it all over with Emma. Needless to say, we didn't talk about anything else all weekend. We weighed up all the pros and cons and I've just told Michael my decision. I also gave him my letter of resignation."

"Oh, my goodness, Ian. Really!" exclaimed Penny. She was totally stunned and shocked.

"You knew from our conversation some months ago that this was my intention, but I've decided the time's now right to take this next step in my career. There's more to tell you, but now's not the time. Michael and I didn't talk about the timescales before I leave Sotheby's so, at the moment, I'm continuing on the basis that I'll still be doing this job for the next six months… as per my contract."

Again, Penny nodded. She wanted to ask him some questions, but decided to just sit and listen to what more he was going to tell her.

"Obviously things could change much more quickly. The appointment of the new MD may have a serious bearing on the matter. Sotheby's may decide to pay me off and get rid of me, as soon as possible, but history shows that's not their usual style. In the meantime, and if you're still keen, I'll continue to make every effort to push for you to be promoted to head of this department. You won't pick up my director's role, but the head of the department is a nice career step. So, are you still keen?"

Penny was still somewhat shell-shocked from Ian's earlier news. "Well, yes. Yes, of course, but… you, resigning! Wow, Ian, it's a massive step."

"I've spent the last 18 months planning this move, Penny. Needless to say, both Emma and I have had many sleepless nights. But now? The decision has finally been made."

"I remember you saying that tomorrow is the first day of the rest of our lives."

The Gamble

"I said that? Well, yes, it's true. This next year will be a massive change for both of us."

Yes, thought Penny, and even bigger changes for me than you currently know... at the moment.

It was two days later when Penny stood at the entrance to Ian's office. She looked across and saw Ian was peering at his computer screen.

"Ian?" she said quietly. Ian looked up. "I've just had Mr. Hopkins' PA on the telephone. Mr. Hopkins would like to see you at 4pm."

"Did he say what about?"

"No, sorry."

"Okay." Ian looked at his watch, 3.35pm. "I'll be there."

Penny smiled and then walked back to her desk. She really hoped he knew what he was doing. Was this the moment he would change his mind?

Ian considered Penny's message. He assumed the directive from his boss was to finalise his employment situation, in particular, to tell him when he would be leaving Sotheby's. At least Sotheby's, he thought, were not the sort of company who would give him just one hour's notice to clear his desk before security marched him, unceremoniously, off the premises.

At 3.50pm Ian logged off his computer and headed across the office. As he passed by Penny's desk she looked up. Ian gave her a tentative smile.

"Good luck," she said. Her worrying eyes followed him until he'd disappeared into the corridor.

As Ian headed towards his boss's office, he was wondering what Michael was planning to say. Since the meeting on Monday, he'd not heard anything more from his boss. He also wondered whether Michael had now opened his letter of resignation.

When Ian entered Michael's outer office, his boss's PA gave him a smile and indicated, by the wave of her hand, that he should go straight through. "He's waiting for you," she said.

Ian smiled back, nodded and walked towards his boss's door. Although it was open Ian still knocked politely and waited.

"Ah, Ian. Come in," said Michael, taking off his reading glasses and pointing to a seat in front of his desk. "Please, sit down."

Ian quietly closed the door behind him. He was thinking that this was all too friendly. Two days ago, he'd turned down the Managing Director's job and handed in his notice. Why wasn't Michael biting his head off?

Ian sat down and waited for his boss to speak.

Michael opened the top left drawer of his desk and pulled out an unopened envelope. He placed it on his desk and then looked across at Ian.

Ian wondered what the hell was going on! He recognised his writing on the envelope. It was his letter of resignation and it was obviously still unopened. Michael was not renowned for playing psychological games, but what was he trying to achieve?

A few seconds passed then Michael broke the silence. "Had any further thoughts?"

"Further thoughts?" queried Ian, somewhat surprised. "Further thoughts about what, Michael?"

"The Managing Director's role, of course," said his boss, pushing the envelope further across his desk so that it was directly in front of Ian.

Ian smiled a little. So that's his game. He sat back in his chair, moving away from the envelope.

"No, Michael. Sorry, but my decision is still the same… and for all the same reasons."

The Gamble

"That's a shame, Ian. It means we'll have to appoint Jonathan Northgate."

You are kidding me, Michael, surely, thought Ian. He had worked with Jonathan Northgate in New York and knew the man was just hot air. Good presentation skills, but totally lacking in substance. "Well, I must admit, Michael, that is a surprise. And to be honest, a very big... and disappointing surprise," replied Ian.

"He has big ideas for Sotheby's and has a few immediate changes already planned."

"In that case, Michael, I'm even more pleased to be leaving. I don't rate the guy and I think the company's making a huge mistake. You've been an excellent MD, Michael, and this man is certainly nowhere near your calibre... or indeed your class."

Michael smiled and nodded at Ian's compliment. "We wanted you, Ian, remember? But you've turned us down."

"Michael, Sotheby's are making a huge mistake with Northgate."

Michael Hopkins leaned forward, still looking directly at Ian, and put both arms on his desk. He then released his right hand and slowly pushed the envelope further towards Ian.

Chapter 3

Earlier that day in Antigua, Oscar had visited the 'Shell Gallery' in St John's. Wesley Fredericks, the owner, was keen to get Oscar's opinion on a number of new paintings he'd recently acquired. Oscar had explained his immediate thoughts and ideas and had promised he'd speak with his connections to see if he could generate some interest.

After he left the gallery Oscar walked towards Redcliffe Quay, situated close to the waterfront promenade. This area was one of Oscar's favourite parts of St John's. He enjoyed walking among the old alleys and passages, glancing into the various shop front windows. The area, he knew, dated back over a hundred years and it still contained many preserved buildings of a bygone age. Occasionally he would enter a small art gallery or antiques shop, to see if there were any pictures that might just be worth buying. Today, however, nothing was grabbing his attention.

After about an hour, he was feeling hungry and so headed towards the waterfront and, in particular, to 'Jake's Bar'. This was a bar he often frequented when he was in the area. He liked the colourful and rustic feel of the decor and the Caribbean food. It was very popular with the locals and therefore there was always something extra to the bar's character and atmosphere.

The Gamble

To start with, Oscar ordered a beer and then, from the food menu, a portion of jerk chicken and fries. He sat down at a vacant table with his beer and waited for his food to arrive. Looking all around him, he guessed that the bar was probably about half full. Immediately behind him a group of four black men were sitting on the next table. They were talking quite loudly so Oscar had no difficulty in following their conversation.

When his food arrived, Oscar forgot about the neighbouring chatter and concentrated on his meal. He pulled away a portion of the chicken with his fork and placed it into his mouth. As he was savouring the hot and spicy piece of food, one of the men behind him mentioned the name of Millie Hobbie. The announcement of this name quickly grabbed Oscar's attention. He knew her killer had still not been apprehended, so he leaned back on his seat and listened more intently to their conversation.

After a few general comments, it was then that he heard one of the men say, "Of course, nu'ting will ever be proved against Clancy. Besides, whether 'e was involved or not, 'ardly anyone in the Caribbean would find dat man guilty. Along with Bob Marley, we all know, 'e's a big reggae hero."

"Me brother, Charlie, 'e's a policeman, and 'e says the case is slowly being wound down."

"Clancy has donated a lot of his time and money to a number of Caribbean kids' charities. De' guy's an 'ero. I agree. No jury would find 'im guilty. Besides I gather Millie was a gold digger. I really don't know what Clancy saw in dat wuman."

At that moment one of the men stood up and picked up the empty beer glasses. "Same again, guys?"

Suddenly the topic of conversation changed and Oscar returned to his food. He put another piece of chicken into his mouth and thought that maybe his colleague, Gladstone, would be interested in this bit of news.

Viktor had decided it was time to make some changes to the window display at the 'Taylor Fine Art Gallery'. He looked through his stock and wondered whether he should have a new theme or just put what he thought were currently his best paintings on display.

The gallery had two large windows facing onto the street and Viktor wanted to make a new and strong statement. He tried different permutations and finally decided on a 19th century landscape theme. After placing the paintings in their new positions, he went outside and stood on the pavement to inspect both of the window displays.

He was still pondering on the new arrangement, when a female voice behind spoke to him.

"I preferred the previous display."

Viktor turned and looked into the smiling face of Penny, his fiancée. "Oh, you think so?" he replied, slightly alarmed.

"Just kidding," replied Penny, still smiling. "It looks very good. You've chosen a nice set of landscapes."

Viktor turned back to re-inspect the new display. "You don't think it looks a bit… twee?"

"Twee?" replied Penny, somewhat surprised. She stepped forward to look more closely. "No, I think it's well thought out and gives a good suggestion of what the customer's going to find once they step inside."

"Okay… are you coming in?" asked Viktor, now feeling a little happier as he moved towards the door.

"Just for a few minutes. I've just been to look at two paintings that might be auctioned. I told Ian I'd be back by one o'clock."

Viktor and Penny entered the gallery and he offered Penny a cup of coffee.

"No, I'm okay for the moment. Anyway, have you thought of any dates for the wedding?" asked Penny, reminding Viktor of their conversation of two evenings ago.

The Gamble

"No, sorry, Penny. I need to speak to my parents and they're away until tomorrow. Do you have any suggestions I can give them?"

"I'm thinking of the beginning of September."

"Seems okay for me, but, as I say, I'll have to discuss it with my parents."

"I've also been thinking, Vic. You'll need to sort out a best man and I need someone to walk me down the aisle. As you know, there's only me and my mum now."

"Can't we just elope to Gretna Green or Las Vegas? It'd be so much simpler."

"No, we cannot!" responded Penny emphatically. "I only intend to get married once and I want a proper wedding."

"Okay, okay. Just a thought."

"Well, you can put that thought out of your mind."

They both looked at each other for a few seconds, then Penny said, "What do you think about Ian?"

"What, as my best man?"

"No, no. I was wondering if I should ask him if he would walk me down the aisle."

"Oh. Right. Err…"

"You don't like the idea?"

"No, hang on. I didn't say that. I just wanted to think."

"And?"

Viktor walked over to his desk and sat on the edge. He looked up from the floor and across to Penny. Then he said, "I think it would be an excellent choice. But will he agree to do it?"

"Well, we'll have to see, won't we? I'll ask him this afternoon." At this point Penny walked over and gave Viktor a kiss, a smile and then left the gallery.

Viktor watched her walk away, heading in the direction of Sotheby's. He decided he would love to be a fly on the wall when that conversation took place!

When Penny arrived back at her desk there was a note from Ian waiting for her. It just said that he would be back in the office just after two o'clock.

Penny put her mug of coffee on her desk and opened the packet of sandwiches she'd bought after leaving Viktor. She decided to have a quiet lunch and plan on what she was going to say when Ian returned to the office.

It was 20 minutes later when Ian reappeared.

"Oh, hi, Penny. Any luck with the Hendersons?"

"You were right. Their paintings are good examples of Cezanne's work. Mr. Henderson said he'd ask Christie's for a quotation too, but I'm still optimistic we'll get the business."

"Well done," said Ian, walking towards his office. "Let me know how it goes."

Penny rose from her desk and, before Ian had disappeared, she asked him, "Ian, can I have a word, please?"

"Please, eh?" said Ian, teasing. He stopped at the doorway and looked back at Penny. "Sounds important. You'd better come in."

Penny followed Ian into his office. He sat behind his desk and Penny sat on her usual seat.

"Okay. I'm all ears," said Ian. He leaned back in his chair and waited for Penny to speak.

Penny smiled. It was a phrase her boss often used, especially when he was in a good mood.

"It's personal, Ian," said Penny.

Ian now sat upright in his chair. His face was more serious. He waited for the probable bombshell.

"Vic and I want to get married this year…"

"Hey, that's great news, Penny," interrupted Ian. But he then realised what he'd just done – interrupted. So, he decided to hear Penny out without any further comments.

"…but we've not decided on a date yet," continued Penny.

"I'm thinking of early September. I want a proper, traditional, church wedding." Ian nodded. "However, I do have a problem. You probably remember my father died four years ago and so I've not got anyone to walk me down the aisle. I was wondering if you would do me a great honour and be my 'father of the bride'?"

Suddenly Ian's eyes were wide open and a large smile appeared on his face. He couldn't keep quiet now. "Oh, wow, Penny. What a fabulous honour. Yes, of course I'll do that for you." Ian began to feel quite emotional.

Immediately Penny leapt from her seat and ran round to Ian's side of his desk and gave him a kiss on the cheek. Then she realised what she'd just done. She quickly stepped back and looked aghast at her boss.

Ian just laughed. "Does that mean I have to adopt you now?"

Penny still stared at Ian and slowly a tear began to trickle down her cheek.

Ian stood up and gave Penny a gentle hug. What would HR think about this? he wondered.

He then let her go and Penny wiped the tear from her cheek. They stood facing each other.

"I'll really miss you, Ian, when you leave Sotheby's. You're a great boss and a lovely man."

Ian smiled. "Vic's the lucky man and you'll benefit from me moving on. Speaking of which, I have some more news. You'd better sit back down."

Chapter 4

Penny sat back down on her chair and Ian returned to his own seat.

"I've not had a chance to tell you about my meeting with Michael yesterday. He was still trying to persuade me to reconsider my decision about turning down the MD's job, but, as you know, I've made my career choice and it no longer includes Sotheby's."

Penny nodded and concentrated on every word Ian was saying.

"This next bit of news is for you alone, Penny. Can you just pop over and close the door please."

Penny swiftly did as she was asked and returned to her seat just as quickly.

"I know I'm out of order for telling you this, but I also know you'll keep it to yourself until it's all officially announced. Michael Hopkins is going to reveal his retirement plans at tomorrow's press announcement and it looks like Sotheby's will also be declaring the appointment of Jonathan Northgate as the new MD."

Penny tried to recall the name, but then decided she had never heard of the man.

Ian continued. "I worked with Northgate in New York. He's British and about four years older than I am. To be

The Gamble

honest, Penny, I wasn't impressed then and I'm even less impressed now. The guy won't last six months in the role. He really hasn't got the talent, intelligence, or any of the other skills needed to push the company forward and to be successful."

"Then why is the management appointing him?"

"Good question. I challenged Michael, but he wouldn't give me a satisfactory answer. What he did hint, however, was that one of the first things Jonathan Northgate would do would be to get rid of me!"

"You've resigned anyway. What's the point?"

"You don't know Jonathan. He knows I have a poor opinion of his abilities and that I'd be a threat to his authority from day one. He just wants me out of the way."

"As I say, you've resigned. He can't do that. He can't sack you, surely?"

"Officially, Michael Hopkins has still not opened my letter of resignation. He's still hoping I'll change my mind before tomorrow's announcement."

"And will you?"

Ian smiled at Penny. "It's tempting, just to keep Northgate from taking over, but, no. I've made my decision. Michael knows that… and he knows my reasons. I really don't think he wants Northgate either. However, the chairman and the board have made that decision."

"So, what are you going to do now?"

"Another good question, Penny." Penny smiled. "I've agreed with Michael that I'll leave Sotheby's at the end of the month. According to the terms of my contract, Sotheby's still have to pay me six months' salary. However, I've agreed with Michael that, as long as he announces my resignation before Northgate's appointment, I'll only take three months' compensation."

"At the end of the month! This month? That's just, what?"

exclaimed Penny, and she calculated in her head, "ten days' time!"

"That's right. But now the much better news." Ian opened his briefcase, pulled out an envelope and pushed it across his desk towards Penny. "That, young lady, is a letter from Michael Hopkins. It's your formal notice of promotion to head of this department. With effect from the first of next month."

Penny leaned forward, with eyes wide open. She hesitantly picked up the letter and immediately saw her name written on the envelope. She then looked back at Ian and decided she had at least a hundred questions she wanted to ask.

Ian continued, "Have a really good read of the terms and conditions. If you're happy everything is okay, then fine. If you have any queries, talk to me tomorrow. You'll have three months before Michael actually retires and Northgate takes up the role of MD, so that'll give you a good period to get your feet under this desk. Michael also wants to see you tomorrow afternoon at four o'clock to personally congratulate you."

Penny looked at Ian, then to the envelope and back to Ian again. She was not, at that very moment, very excited at all. "You know, Ian, the department is not going to be the same without you."

Oscar had arranged to meet up with Gladstone at their usual bar. It had been three days since they'd last met and Oscar was keen to see Gladstone's reaction to the news he'd overheard whilst lunching at 'Jake's Bar'.

Oscar was the first to arrive and purchased two glasses of lager. However, when he wandered over towards their usual table, he was disappointed to see that it was already occupied. He decided to walk a little further along the balcony when he saw two empty chairs. He placed the drinks on the table and sat down. He could still get a glimpse of the beach area, but quickly concluded that the view was much better from where they usually sat. He looked at his watch. Gladstone was ten minutes late, but Oscar had become used to that. Even after nearly two years of living in Antigua, Oscar still couldn't get used to the Caribbean people never being on time. He pulled out his mobile phone and started to check on his emails.

"Why you hiding here, man?" It was Gladstone who had crept up behind Oscar.

"Our normal table's occupied. Anyway, you're late," said Oscar, putting his phone back into his pocket.

Gladstone looked at his watch, shrugged his shoulders and sat down. He picked up the full glass of lager. "Cheers, man." And before Oscar could respond, Gladstone drank about a quarter of the glass. "I needed that."

"I've got some news for you," said Oscar, adjusting his sitting position so he could see Gladstone's face more fully. He then went on to summarise the conversation he'd overheard in 'Jake's Bar'. After he'd finished, he waited for Gladstone to respond.

Gladstone shrugged his shoulders. "I've told you before, it's nothing to do with me, man. You have to remember, Clancy… he's a hero in these parts. I agree, no jury would ever convict him here… even if he was guilty!"

Gladstone had not flinched a muscle in response to Oscar's revelation.

"Are you not bothered that a murderer could be let off scot-free?"

"As far as I know, the police haven't charged Clancy and, from what you say, they're unlikely to do so now… or in the future. So, the guy's innocent. Anyway, I'm on his side, he's paid my bill for my correct valuations. Come on, man, lighten up. Let's change the subject. What you been doing in the art world recently?"

Oscar decided he'd said enough about Clancy. It was obvious Gladstone was not going to admit to anything about any involvement in Millie's murder. However, he did just wonder how much Clancy had actually paid Gladstone for his so-called 'valuation fee'!

Chapter 5

In Tokyo, Yuki had become more content with his new business life. His involvement in the business partnership with Ian Caxton's group had meant less travelling around the world to achieve the same level of painting sales and purchases. He was also pleased that Ian, and to a lesser extent, Viktor, were now becoming more the UK contact and the 'local face', to his British clients. And in China, a market he had not tried to expand into before, he was both surprised and encouraged to achieve a number of sales via May Ling.

As a result, Yuki was now almost totally based in Japan and had more time to discuss and develop possible ideas with his partner, Yoshi. In particular, they were now mulling over Yuki's latest suggestion of expanding and setting up a new gallery in Osaka.

"So, Yoshi, do you think now is the right time to open a new gallery?" asked Yuki.

The two men were sitting in Yoshi's main office situated above the 'Cherry Blossom' gallery. This was just one of the three galleries owned by the two men in Tokyo and which were managed on a daily basis by Yoshi.

Yoshi was pouring himself a top up from the bottle of mineral water.

"I'm not totally sure, Yuki. Yes, we've moved on quite a

bit over these last two years, but with you wanting to retire soon and Osaka being many kilometres away from Tokyo, I'm not convinced we can manage a new gallery properly from this far away. We'll need to take on either a good local manager or an additional partner. I certainly don't have the time to oversee it as the three galleries here in Tokyo take up all of my time. It would also be a large capital outlay."

Yuki sat back in his chair, sipped his coffee and pondered on what Yoshi had said. Yes, Yoshi's comments did make some sense, he thought, but Yuki was still keen to see the business expand. He didn't want their business to stand still. "Okay, maybe you're right. Let's just keep the option open for the time being," responded Yuki. "However, I have more time available now and it would be a shame not to take full advantage of it."

"What about May Ling in Beijing? There must be bigger opportunities in China and Hong Kong. Maybe you should have a conversation with her and see if we can sell more of our stock into her market. That's where all the new money is."

"You're right," replied Yuki. "We've just been responding to May's requests to date. Yes, I'll speak to her. I need to be more proactive as we might be missing out on a much bigger market there than in Osaka."

Yuki was as good as his word and sent a detailed email to May. In summary, he wanted to know what paintings and artists the Chinese market was particularly looking for at the moment.

Once he'd sent his email, Yuki looked at the lengthy spreadsheet of all the paintings they currently held both on display at their galleries and also in their storerooms. He started to make a number of notes and comments. After two hours he decided to have a break and switched his attention to his existing clients, especially those he knew already had paintings for sale. Again, he added these details to his notes.

The Gamble

Once he'd finished updating the spreadsheet, he sat back and thought about his findings. He hadn't realised the volume and range of pictures he had immediate access to. And, of course, there was also the Singapore Freeport paintings opportunity to take into consideration.

When May Ling received Yuki's email she was intrigued. To date, Yuki had been a useful member of the partnership and had volunteered four pictures painted by the Japanese artists that she had been searching for. Now it appeared Yuki wanted to be more enterprising. May Ling replied listing all the Far Eastern artists that were currently in fashion in China. She concluded by saying that she was eager to hear Yuki's thoughts and any suggestions he might have.

Viktor decided it was now time to appoint an assistant manager at the 'Taylor Fine Art Gallery'. The footfall had been increasing, but so too was the time he spent on making visits to new and existing clients. Each time he had to leave the gallery the 'closed' sign was placed in the entrance door's window. This meant there were two major issues to resolve. Firstly, he didn't know how many potential customers he was missing and, secondly, the gallery was closed at random times and on different days. He was determined to overcome these problems and get back to offering a better and more focused customer service.

It was during a quiet period on Thursday afternoon that Viktor drafted a detailed email to his senior partner, Bob Taylor, in Monaco. He outlined the problems that were occurring when the gallery was closed and the potential opportunities being missed. He then suggested an answer and included a cost–benefit analysis of employing an extra member of staff.

It was just three hours later that Bob replied. He'd agreed to Viktor's request and suggested he should immediately advertise for an assistant.

Viktor had kept a copy of the original advertisement that Bob Taylor had created when he was looking to recruit the gallery manager. He now used this for the basis of his own advertisement and placed it in two art magazines, an employment agency and on their own gallery's website. He now eagerly awaited the results of his efforts.

In Monaco, Zoe and Bob were expanding their client base significantly. The enthusiasm of Zoe, Bob's greater freedom with the running of the gallery since Antoine had stepped back from direct involvement, plus the success of Ian Caxton's partnership, had each made a contribution.

Bob totalled up their turnover and profit for the last nine months and, later that evening, he was explaining all the details to Zoe. "It's quite amazing. We've increased our turnover by an average of 4% each month over the last 15 months. That compares really well against the time before you came back to work in the gallery and prior to the commencement of Ian's partnership group. Turnover was largely flat then, or even slightly negative."

"My father was stopping us from developing as well. You were right to join Ian's partnership. The extra buying power's made such a difference. I can talk to many more wealthy clients than I could before," replied Zoe. She was really pleased with all the changes.

"Our London gallery is working well too. Viktor's doing a really good job. So much so that I've agreed he should employ an assistant. A lot more of his business is now generated outside the gallery premises and he has to close the gallery each time he goes out. That's not really how it should work. Anyway, we can now afford the extra cost and, hopefully, it should pay for itself in the long run."

The Gamble

It was Ian's last day of his employment at Sotheby's and he wanted to keep everything very low key. He'd spent a large part of the last three days with Penny, explaining the details of the extra tasks and demands of her new role. She was a quick learner and Ian knew she'd be a success.

For Penny, however, it was an emotional time. She had worked with Ian since leaving university and she was apprehensive about her new role, especially without Ian's presence and leadership to guide her. She had really enjoyed the last few years at Sotheby's and had learned so much from Ian's management style and experience. It was now all about to change, and, despite her promotion, she was not looking forward to the next few months at all.

Over the last week fellow colleagues had spoken to Ian and wished him well. However, when they'd asked what he planned to do in the future, his reply was always along the lines that he was going to take a break and review the situation in a few months' time.

Earlier that morning, Michael Hopkins had asked Ian to join him in his office. Michael wished him well and thanked him for the success he had brought to Sotheby's. He reiterated how disappointed he was that Ian was not replacing him, but he was nevertheless determined to make sure Ian's departure was on the best of terms.

Ian thanked him for his kind words and wished Michael well in his retirement.

"So, what are your plans then, Ian?" asked Michael. Despite probing over the last two weeks without success, he hoped Ian would now be a little more forthcoming… and specific.

Ian wondered if he should explain his intentions, but finally decided to keep the matter still somewhat vague. "I just want to take a break for a while, Michael. Emma and I have holiday plans to go to the Mediterranean again. After that… then we'll decide on what we want to do next."

Michael just smiled. He knew Ian too well. He never did anything without considerable thought and detailed planning.

As Ian was about to leave Michael's office, he was surprised when Michael stopped him and quietly said, "I want us to keep in touch, Ian. I have some plans for myself after I leave here and I'd be interested in your thoughts and opinions. Now's not the time to discuss this matter, but I'll telephone you later in the year."

Ian was caught a little off guard, but immediately agreed that they should keep in touch.

As he walked along the corridors and back towards his office, Ian wondered what exactly Michael's plans were and in what way they could possibly involve him?

Chapter 6

Ian deliberately left Sotheby's offices early on this, his final day. He certainly didn't want to draw out the last few hours. He'd already said goodbye to his team and wished them well, but he knew his personal farewell to Penny would be a much more emotional moment. He promised her that he would always be just a telephone call or an email away if she needed any help or advice. Or, indeed, if she just wanted to discuss any issue. Finally, he stressed how much he was looking forward to being her 'father of the bride' later in the year. His last picture of Penny, as he left his office, was seeing her trying to smile but also wiping her eyes at the same time.

On the train journey home to Esher, Ian had mixed emotions. He was pleased to be moving on with his life, but knew he would still miss Penny, and a few other colleagues, on a day-to-day basis. Whilst the job had paid him his salary, he also knew it was the people, his colleagues, that had made his work so much more enjoyable. He wondered how many would still be working at Sotheby's after experiencing the first six months of Jonathan Northgate's reign.

When Ian walked into his house it was just after 3pm. A much earlier time than he usually arrived home from work. All was quiet as Emma hadn't returned from collecting

Robert from school. After changing his shoes, he strolled into the home office and placed his briefcase down on his desk. He looked all around the room and took a deep breath. Gradually a smile appeared on his face as he realised this room, in future, was going to be his main place of work. No more commuting, train delays or fighting for the last seat in the carriage. It was all going to be wonderful and perfect… he hoped.

A few seconds later Ian sat down behind his desk and stared out of the window. He wasn't looking at anything in particular but his mind started to wander back on his Sotheby's career. Fresh out of university, he'd arrived in London with lots of enthusiasm and ambitious goals. Hardworking, quick-witted and energetic, he soon made an impact and his career accelerated when he was rewarded with promotion to Sotheby's auction house in New York. But there he came up against the first big challenge of his career and the subsequent frictional conflicts with 'the clown', Jonathan Northgate. The man, he quickly realised, was a cheat and a liar. Totally self-centred and jealous of others' abilities. Northgate couldn't compete with colleagues' competence and talents, so his only answer was to get rid of such competition… and quickly.

Ian now recalled how he'd slowly realised that Northgate was gunning for him when a number of minor incidents began to occur which had put Ian under suspicion. Although he was able to prove each case was unfounded, it was Northgate that always gave him the knowing smile. In every other way, Ian knew he was doing very well and enjoying his first experience of working abroad. However, the Northgate situation finally came to a head when a valuable painting he was handling was found damaged. Ian was responsible for arranging for the picture to be valued, cleaned and catalogued ready for auction, but overnight,

The Gamble

whilst the painting was securely deposited in a protected storeroom, the canvas had somehow acquired two small knife cuts.

Ian, Northgate and two other Sotheby's staff were questioned. Nobody had any knowledge, or information, other than Northgate, who'd said he'd seen Ian with a knife earlier in the day. Ian was adamant that he'd neither seen nor used such a knife.

The painting was subsequently repaired with the previous damage being invisible to most people's eyes. The owner eventually accepted Sotheby's compensation settlement after the picture had been successfully sold, but Ian's reputation had taken another, and more serious, knock.

Ian began to think of different ideas for revenge and retribution towards Northgate, but then fate took an intervening hand. Not that Ian knew anything about it at the time, but Michael Hopkins was watching his career from afar. He had plans for Ian and they didn't include this Northgate / Caxton feud.

Within a matter of 20 days, Ian was on the plane to Hong Kong. A promotion opportunity had surprisingly become available and Ian was keen to relocate to this exciting and vibrant former British colony.

Ian continued to sit in his quiet home office and thought about his time in Hong Kong. It still seemed like just yesterday but, in reality, it was many years ago. There was no Northgate in Hong Kong and Ian was able to progress in his career properly again. Although, with a sly grin on his face, he also remembered several experiences with Oscar and other colleagues that he would still prefer to keep a secret from Emma.

Unfortunately, his future in Hong Kong was not going to be long term. They say you should never go back, but he did. Back to London for a second time. A move he never really wanted, but always believed it had been forced upon him by career pressures… and, of course, by Emma. She, in particular, had made it very clear right from the start of their relationship that she had no intention of living in Hong Kong… even for just a short while.

Ian now began to wonder what might have happened if… but then, turning around, he looked back at the contents laid out on his desk. A framed photograph of the apartment block in Monaco reminded him of Andrei, the time when Andrei had first come into his life and how quickly his world had become enlivened again. His eyes sparkled at the memories of his introduction into a different art world. The money, the excitement, different types of challenges and a new opportunity… a new future. But now there was no Andrei. That, too, was all in the past.

Bringing his mind back to the present, Ian opened up his briefcase and removed the few personal items he'd kept on his desk at Sotheby's. Two of the items were framed photographs, one of Emma that he'd taken on their honeymoon and one of Robert, dressed in his first school uniform. He now placed them, pride of place, on his new, full-time business desk. Finally, he removed the large photograph that had been hanging on his office wall, the night view of Hong Kong Island from Kowloon. He looked closely at the picture's details and, in particular, the Star Ferry slowly crossing the dark waters of Victoria Harbour. He smiled and imagined himself now sitting on that same boat. Was the boat's journey symbolic of his career to date? Kowloon being the start of his voyage and the boat's distance covering his life and career to date? The remaining journey to Hong Kong Island, did this represent his fresh start? The future with all its new challenges and unknowns?

He placed the picture down on his desk, closed his briefcase and then leaned back in his chair. Linking his hands together behind his head he smiled at the thought that he was now free of the Sotheby's shackles. It was both he and Emma, together, who had decided on their new future, their new direction... nobody else. He was convinced it was all going to work, it had to work. Yes, it was a gamble, a big gamble, but the art world would be fun, exciting and challenging once again... and, yes, definitely rewarding. More rewarding than my wildest dreams? Just as Andrei had predicted.

Ian's reminiscing was suddenly broken when he heard a car draw up in the driveway, the banging of car doors and then the familiar voice of his son, Robert. He smiled and walked into the hallway to greet them. These two people, he thought, were his future... his full-time future from now on.

Ian opened the front door, to the surprise of both Emma and Robert. Robert ran over and gave him a hug and then carried on through and ran up the stairs. Emma followed and gave Ian a smile and a kiss.

"So that's it, is it, Ian? You've finally left?" asked Emma, standing back to look at his face.

"Yes, that's it, Emma. All finished at Sotheby's," replied Ian. He took a deep breath, feeling a little emotional.

Emma moved in closer again and gave Ian a hug. Ian responded and pulled Emma into a deep embrace. After a few seconds Emma broke away and said, "Come on, I'll make us both a cup of tea. You can tell me all about your final day at Sotheby's."

Ian closed the front door and followed Emma into the kitchen.

Later that evening, after Robert had gone to bed, Ian and Emma were sitting on the sofa in the lounge. Ian had topped up their wine glasses. They were both winding down at the end of a very memorable... and emotional day.

"The reason I was late coming home from picking Robert up was because his teacher, Mrs. Barnsdale, wanted to speak to me," said Emma, picking up her refreshed glass of wine. "She told me that the headmistress, Miss Wardley, was wondering if you do valuations of paintings. Apparently, the school's insurer had commented that their art collection was last reviewed ten years ago and it's now in need of an up-to-date valuation. During this period the cover's automatically increased with inflation, but there are now some concerns the collection might be underinsured. I told her you did do valuations and I've set up a meeting for you. It's with Miss Wardley, on Monday morning at 9.30am."

"I see," replied Ian. "So, this means I'll also be doing the school run with Robert that morning too."

Emma smiled. "You'll enjoy meeting all the other mothers. Welcome to your new world."

"Oh," replied Ian. He'd forgotten about meeting all the mothers. "I'm not so keen on that idea."

"They won't eat you. Besides, they'll all be interested in seeing you," teased Emma.

"I think I'll take Robert into school a little later. Blame it on the traffic."

"Chicken."

Chapter 7

This particular Monday morning was unusual for Robert. He was used to his mother calling him and chasing him up. Had he got this, had he got that? Today it was all so different. Dad was taking him to school and there was no rushing, chasing or hassling. He liked that. In fact, he was ready to depart before his dad. That never happened with Mum.

Ian drove leisurely to the school. Robert noticed there was no cursing at fellow drivers or taking a chance on the red lights. He knew he would be late for school, but Dad didn't seem to mind. When they arrived at the school car park theirs was the only visitor's car still there.

It was then that Robert became alarmed. He realised he'd be the last one in class and everyone would be staring at him as he sneaked into the room.

When Ian stopped the car, Robert opened the door, grabbed his two bags, shouted "thanks" and ran around to the front entrance.

Ian, meanwhile, looked at his watch. 9.12am. He slowly got out of the car, retrieved his briefcase from the back seat and locked the door. It was a nice warm day as he strolled along the path through the short alley of trees and around to the front of the large red brick building. He briefly stood and stared at the view across the playing fields. His mind wandered back to his previous Monday mornings. The hassle of the commute and the sheer volume of people arriving in London for their working day.

After taking a deep breath of the lovely fresh air, all he could hear was a subtle rustle of leaves in the trees, created by the warm breeze, and a number of bird sounds. He could already feel his heart pumping at a much slower rate due to the much calmer surroundings, the cleaner air and his more relaxing pace of life. He began to wish he'd made this decision 12 months ago.

Ian walked over towards the building's main entrance and tried to remember the last time he'd stood in front of these two old wooden doors. He decided it must have been when he and Emma had first visited the school to assess whether this was going to be the right school for their son. That's ridiculous, he thought. Why have I not been here since then? Maybe work had something to do with it.

He was just about to turn the metal door handle when the door suddenly began to open from the inside.

"Hello, Mr. Caxton, welcome back to 'Brookfield School'," said a female voice.

Seconds later Ian recognised the features of the headmistress, Miss Wardley, as she stepped from the shadows and into his view. In her early fifties, slim with short black hair, she definitely had a voice of authority. Someone not to get on the wrong side of for sure, he decided. "Hello, Miss Wardley, I was just admiring the setting. Lovely, isn't it?"

"Yes, I feel very privileged to be working here." They both shook hands and Miss Wardley stepped aside to let Ian enter the hallway. "Come in. We'll go up to my office and I'll explain our situation."

Ian followed Miss Wardley along the oak-panelled corridor, up the old wooden stairs and glanced at the various pictures that were covering the walls. Not serious art, but

The Gamble

drawings and paintings by pupils, and photographs of past classes and members of staff.

Eventually they arrived at a door displaying a brass plaque with the word 'Headmistress' on it. Miss Wardley opened the door and they walked into a bright reception area. A fair-haired lady was sitting behind a desk, typing on the keyboard of her computer.

"This is Mrs. Bailey, Mr. Caxton. My 'Man Friday', or should it be 'Woman Friday'? I'm never really sure nowadays."

Ian and Mrs. Bailey exchanged smiles. Mrs. Bailey was about his age, Ian guessed, of medium build and with a friendly face. He followed Miss Wardley into the adjoining office.

"We'll sit over there," announced Miss Wardley, pointing at a small table and two chairs in the far corner. "Please sit down and I'll bring the paperwork to the table."

Ian duly sat down whilst Miss Wardley walked over to her desk. He looked around the room. Again, there were lots of photographs, but also a large oil painting hanging on the wall above Miss Wardley's desk. A portrait of a grand and serious looking gentleman. He remembered the picture from the last time he'd been in this room.

How interesting, he thought.

Miss Wardley gathered up the pile of papers and a large red book from her desk and carried them over to the table. She placed them down in the middle and sat down.

"Now then, Mr. Caxton..."

"I'd prefer Ian," interrupted Ian.

"I would prefer Mr. Caxton," countered Miss Wardley. "This is business. Now then... ah yes. This red book contains all the history of the pictures and paintings. We have 86 in total. Mrs. Bailey checked again on Friday and they're all still on the premises."

Ian nodded, but dared not interrupt again.

"These papers are a mixture of receipts, old valuations and insurance policies. I expect you'll want to take them home with you, to read at your leisure. The paintings are spread all around the school. Most are on display but some are in our storerooms. Mrs. Bailey will give you a guided tour and you can make your notes, or whatever you normally do, with her. Now then, any questions so far?"

Ian was a little afraid to open his mouth, but did ask about the painting on the wall. He pointed to the portrait.

"Ah, I see you have a good eye. Yes, that's a portrait of the school's founder, Sir Edgar Brookfield. An amazing man. Most of the paintings you'll see in the school were donated by him. He hoped they'd remind pupils of scenes from major events in British history. There are some portraits too. All the portraits are of famous people who lived in that same era. There are no restrictions on us selling any of the collection, if we need to but, I'm happy to say, none have been sold to date."

Ian nodded again. "Thank you for that background information. Can I suggest I borrow Mrs. Bailey and we can get started?"

"I'll leave all these papers on the table for you to take away with you when you've completed your viewing. I'll be very interested to hear your initial thoughts before you leave. Now then, let us speak to Mrs. Bailey."

Over the next two and a half hours, Mrs. Bailey led Ian to the various locations where the paintings were hanging and, also, to the three storerooms. During this time, Ian made a number of notes on all the paintings he was shown, some notes being more detailed than others. He also took some photographs using his mobile phone.

When they arrived back in the headmistress's outer office, Mrs. Bailey tapped on the open door to Miss Wardley's

The Gamble

domain. She explained that Mr. Caxton had been shown all the paintings. Miss Wardley asked for Mr. Caxton to be sent into her room.

Mrs. Bailey turned around and said to Ian, "Miss Wardley will see you now."

"Thank you… and also for all your time this morning," replied Ian. He smiled at Mrs. Bailey and walked hesitantly into the main headmistress's office. It reminded him of one of the times when he'd been 'frog-marched' into the head's office during his own younger schooldays… after one of his demeanours!

"So, Mr. Caxton, what have you got to tell me? Come over here and sit down."

Miss Wardley was sitting behind her desk and pointed to the seat opposite her.

Ian sat down and started to speak. "You have a fine collection. There are a number of valuable paintings by some important artists and I need to do some further research on those. It's a shame you have some pictures in the storeroom. They're going to deteriorate in those conditions, so, I suggest you either store them properly or sell them."

"Thank you. Yes, we need to make a decision on a number of the collection. Our insurers, as well as insisting on up-to-date valuations, want us to install a more modern burglar alarm system. That will cost the school money, so we may have to sell some of the paintings to pay for that expenditure."

Ian nodded. "A bit of a 'Catch 22' situation."

Miss Wardley ignored Ian's comparison. "Please take the red book and those papers on the table. How long do you think you will need to complete your report?"

"I can prepare a document for you in about 14 days," replied Ian, although he knew he would be pushing it a bit to achieve that deadline.

"Right. Then I'll inform our insurers that you have the matter in hand. Our renewal isn't for another month, but I want to get this problem sorted as soon as possible."

Ian smiled and rose up from his seat. He collected the papers from the table and placed them in his briefcase. The red book he tucked under his arm. He was just about to walk out of the office when Miss Wardley said, "By the way, Mr. Caxton, I've been hearing lots of positive reports about Robert."

Ian smiled and said, "I know he's enjoying his time here. Both Emma and I are pleased with our choice for his schooling."

A brief smile appeared on Miss Wardley's face before she replied. "Goodbye, Mr. Caxton. I look forward to reading your report in two weeks' time."

Ian left the main office and, as he passed by Mrs. Bailey's desk, he thanked her again and made his way through the building and back out into the warm sunshine. He stopped and looked back admiringly at the old red brick facade. He suddenly spotted Miss Wardley looking down at him from one of the upstairs windows. He smiled and slowly walked back towards his car.

After he'd unlocked the doors, he placed his briefcase and the red book in the car's boot. He shut the boot door and looked back at the rear of the large school building. Mmm, he thought, maybe I might just have a problem with Miss Wardley.

When Ian arrived home, he found Emma in their home office. As Ian joined her, she immediately looked up from her computer and asked, "How did it go?"

"Bit of a tyrant is Miss Wardley. She obviously runs a very strict school."

Emma smiled. "What did you think of the art collection?"

Ian placed his briefcase and the red book on his desk.

The Gamble

"I've got a number of papers in there, which I need to read. The school has 86 pictures in total, some are interesting, but not worth a lot of money, but there are a few valuable paintings of the 19th century era. It will be interesting to compare my views with the last set of valuations."

"When have you got to report back?"

"I said it would probably take me about 14 days. It may be pushing it a bit, but I'll certainly be able to produce my initial findings, if not my full report, in that timescale."

"I've made some sandwiches, are you ready for lunch?"

"You know, Emma," said Ian smiling, "I could certainly get used to this lifestyle."

Chapter 8

Sheldon Murray was worried. His client, Clancy Hobbie, was, in his personal opinion, a very, very lucky man. Whilst a large proportion of the population of Antigua, and the wider Caribbean, could never see their Clancy as anything other than a local hero, Sheldon's professional opinion was that Clancy's involvement with his wife's murder was a very grey area. Clancy had previously made several outbursts announcing 'having his wife rubbed out' or 'dealt with'. Not only had he been present on these occasions, but several other people were witnesses as well. It wouldn't look very good for Clancy if the case ever did come to court as such outbursts would be extremely difficult to defend.

Nevertheless, thought Sheldon, Clancy still seemed to have the perfect alibi. He was in Kingston, Jamaica, attending a reunion party at the time of the murder. But, of course, being a very wealthy man and now avoiding a very unpleasant and expensive divorce, the easiest and cheapest option would be to hire a professional killer to 'deal with the problem'. Especially if Clancy had employed a professional killer who was from another country, or indeed, the other side of the world. So far, the police hadn't established any direct connection to the killing. All the evidence was

The Gamble

just circumstantial. He just hoped, for Clancy's sake, this would remain the situation.

It was not the first time that Sheldon was doubtful about one of his clients' innocence. Occasionally he knew his client was guilty, but it was still up to the prosecution to prove their case. It was not Sheldon's job to prove his client was innocent, he just had to make sure his client had a fair trial and that he argued successfully against the evidence being thrown at his client. It would then be up to the jury to come to their own conclusions.

Sheldon had few scruples when it came to his clientele. He was paid very handsomely to defend each person properly and he used the full weight of the law to assist him. For these wealthy individuals he was available 24 hours a day and regularly managed to keep his clients away from prosecution or prison.

With Clancy it was much easier to achieve this sort of result as many of the Antiguan police force were either fans of his music or thankful for all the valuable charity work he'd done that had benefited a large proportion of the island's population. The only serious problem that Sheldon could see was whether Millie's killer would either be identified and arrested or come forward of their own accord and then admit the offence and implicate Clancy. However, he felt neither was that likely to happen. Nevertheless, he was still worried. Clancy could still do, or say, the stupidest of things and suddenly all local sympathy would be lost. He needed to remind Clancy to keep his mouth firmly shut.

Gladstone, meanwhile, was also a worried man. He had helped his boyhood hero, Clancy Hobbie, and as a result he'd been very well rewarded. Nevertheless, he too was concerned that new evidence may yet still come to light that could implicate him with Millie's killer. He too had been in Jamaica at the time of the murder, but many miles away from Kingston where Clancy was staying. He'd been at his son's home in Montego Bay and was there to celebrate the birth of his very first grandchild.

So far, the police had no reason to interview Gladstone and, as the days slowly passed by, he hoped this situation would continue. He was certainly relieved when he'd noticed the police's attention on the case was gradually reducing. Nevertheless, he was still privately worried about Clancy and his occasional outbursts or stupid remarks which could reawaken the police's interest and investigations into the murder of Millie Hobbie. Gladstone decided he needed to speak to Clancy… and quickly.

In the UK, Viktor had invited three of the six applicants for the role of assistant manager to attend an interview. Following these, he'd now narrowed his selection down to two possibilities. Both were completely different and offered contrasting qualities. John was 21 years of age, fresh out of art college, keen, enthusiastic, but maybe a little too flash and confident. Mary, however, was much older and at 46 she wanted to return to full-time work. She'd explained to Viktor that her two teenage children were now able to stand on their own two feet and it wouldn't be too long before they both went on to university. Mary also had previous experience working part time at Christie's and, prior to that, full time at a well-respected London gallery.

That evening, Viktor discussed the two candidates with Penny. He listed all the pros and cons of each candidate and the needs and requirements of his gallery. In summary, Viktor could see the potential in John and liked his keenness and enthusiasm. On the other hand, Mary was a more stable option and would bring a good level of experience to the role.

Penny read both CVs and had listened to Viktor's

descriptions of each candidate. She quickly decided that Mary would be her selection and started to explain why. "I think Mary would be my choice, especially for the role you want to be filled. She has the right level of experience, has worked in a gallery before, although some years ago, and sounds as though she'd be a reliable cover for you when you're away visiting clients. John would require a lot more training and therefore you wouldn't gain the same benefit for quite some time."

"I think you're right," replied Viktor. "I guess I looked at John and saw a little of me in him. The same sort of keenness and ambition, but what I really need is someone more experienced, steady and reliable. Someone who's maybe just happy to do the job I want done without being too ambitious."

"Would you be okay being the boss of a woman a lot older than you?"

Viktor smiled. "Do you think she might mother me?"

This time it was Penny's turn to smile. "No. What I meant was, she might be too experienced and tell you what and how things should be done."

"Well, I'm still learning the ropes anyway," replied Viktor. "So maybe a bit of mature competence would be a bonus."

Penny laughed. "That's the decision then, is it?"

Viktor nodded. "I'll sleep on it, but I'm sure you're right."

Next morning, after Viktor had opened up the 'Taylor Fine Arts Gallery' for business, the first thing he did was switch on his computer. He then typed an email to Mary Turnbull and offered her the position of assistant manager.

Chapter 9

It was 13 days since Ian had had his meeting with Miss Wardley. He'd spent much of this period researching the history of the school's 86 pictures. 62 were oil paintings, 19 were watercolours and five pencil sketch drawings. He was impressed with the collection as a record of 19th century Britain's history and could see why the school's founder, Sir Edgar Brookfield, had decided on this particular group of pictures. Ian had also researched a little into Sir Edgar's life and noticed there were often crossovers between the individual's background and the type of art that he appreciated and bought.

Ian had established that Sir Edgar had grown up during the reign of Queen Victoria. It was a time when Britain was a dominant force on the world scene. It had a very strong navy and many colonies spread across the globe. Any country or person trying to challenge that position was swiftly dealt with by the British government. Hence a number of portraits in Sir Edgar's collection were of the Duke of Wellington, Sir Robert Peel, Disraeli, Gladstone and Viscount Palmerston. The industrial revolution was also well represented with portraits of Isambard Kingdom Brunel, Robert Stephenson, Andrew Carnegie and Thomas Telford.

The Gamble

The other paintings were a mixture of the new growing cities and the old countryside practices. Here, Ian assumed, Sir Edgar was trying to show the development and benefits of the industrial revolution and contrasting these with the changing, yet still important, farming practices. After all, these farms were still producing most of the food the British people had come to rely upon.

Ian could see the important message Sir Edgar wanted to convey to young and impressionable male minds, that being the essential qualities of hard work, respect and, above all, achievement. Sir Edgar was well known for these in his own career.

Unfortunately, whilst a number of the pictures were an excellent representation of their time, Ian decided they were probably only purchased for the vision and inspiration Sir Edgar wanted them to convey. They were not bought as a long-term financial investment. If they had been, then Sir Edgar would have purchased work by some of the more acclaimed artists of that time.

The portrait of Sir Edgar, hanging in the headmistress's office, however, did still intrigue him. It was a painting of real quality and the artist had certainly captured Sir Edgar's confident character in his facial features. Located either side of Sir Edgar in the painting's background were a number of clues that implied this man had had a very successful career. However, Ian had also identified two key problems with the picture. Firstly, the painting had not been signed and, secondly, he couldn't establish a provenance before the school obtained the picture in 1912.

When Ian examined the last valuation report, he found he now only really needed to allow for inflation over the last ten years. The portrait of Sir Edgar, however, was still causing some uncertainty and confusion. The collection of valuations had all stated the unsigned painting was attributed to the artist William Arthur Breakspeare and the last report valued it at £50,000… but Ian wasn't so sure this was correct.

In his office, Ian was looking again at the photograph he'd taken of Sir Edgar's painting. On his computer he was able to zoom in on different areas of the picture to get a much closer look. Yes, he had to agree, it had something of the style of Breakspeare's work but, no, it just wasn't quite right. He stared at the computer screen, rubbed his chin and then said to himself, "This is… I'm sure, is more likely to be by Wa… mmm." He sat back in his chair and pondered again. Finally, he decided he needed to do some more research. If the picture was really painted by the artist he was thinking of, then the current value would certainly be well over the £50,000 mark, before allowing for inflation – more likely at least £1 million!

In Japan, Yuki and Yoshi were discussing May Ling's reply to Yuki's latest email. They had earlier listed the latest batch of paintings they had for sale. Included were paintings owned by clients and 'possibilities' from the Singapore Freeport. May's reply said that she had five possible buyers for seven of the paintings listed. She also stated the buyer's offer prices.

"So," said Yuki, looking across Yoshi's desk to his partner, "what do you think?"

Yoshi, always the more pragmatic half of the partnership, was still mulling over the offers and was comparing them against the prices their galleries were currently advertising them for. He did some calculations on his calculator.

"If May takes all seven pictures, and we accept her offer prices, we'll be about 10% down on our suggested sale prices. However…" Yoshi did some more pressing of the calculator's keys. "…I calculate we'll still make a profit of

The Gamble

about 22% on what we paid for them. About 48 million yen if we sell all seven pictures together. Not bad for stock we've been struggling to get rid of."

Yuki smiled. "So, should I tell May that the offers are accepted?"

Yoshi put his calculator aside, looked at Yuki and nodded. "You know, Yuki, we're selling our stock so fast now, your retirement could easily occur a little earlier than you previously planned."

"That wouldn't be a bad thing, especially after the offer we've just received for the whole of the business."

Yoshi smiled and nodded.

At the 'Taylor Fine Arts Gallery' premises, Viktor had just opened up the gallery and was making himself his first mug of coffee of the day. Once completed, he wandered towards the front desk, sat down and placed the mug on a desk mat. He opened up his laptop computer to read his new emails. His attention was immediately drawn to the email from Mrs. Mary Turnbull. He read the contents slowly and carefully. Gradually a broad smile appeared on his face. Yes, he exclaimed to himself, she had accepted the offer. Her starting date? He checked the email again. Yes, she had also agreed to his suggested date. Starting at the beginning of next month. In just nine days' time.

At last, thought Viktor, now I'll be able to develop the business properly. He sat back in his chair and slowly sipped his coffee. He decided he'd needed to do some very serious planning… and also some tidying up.

Emma was driving her car back towards home after dropping Robert off at his school. She was not in any hurry and had decided to take a slightly different route this time. Instead of ploughing along the main 'A' road, she'd opted to take advantage of the warm sunny late March morning and was slowly travelling along the quieter 'B' roads.

She was definitely feeling far more relaxed than at any time she could remember. She was certainly still busy but, with Ian at home more often, she could now spread her time more easily between their new business venture and the usual domestic activities.

As she drove along the country lanes, she was enjoying the open views across the countryside. Spring was definitely her favourite time of the year. It was the time for new life, hope and optimism for the good times ahead. The different green tints of young leaves on the trees and hedgerows raised her spirits and contributed to her cheerful mood. The gloomy cold, dark and dormant winter months were long gone and it was now time to take a deep breath of fresh air and listen to the happy songbirds sending out their own positive messages. Yes, she thought, it really is going to be a fabulous spring and summertime.

Chapter 10

Ian was sitting in front of Miss Wardley in the headmistress's office. He'd completed his valuation of the school's collection of 86 pictures and was explaining how he'd calculated each picture's individual value. When he came to the final painting, the oil painting of the school's founder, Sir Edgar Brookfield, Ian's relaxed mood suddenly changed.

"This picture was a bit more of a challenge," Ian explained, waving his hand generally in the direction of the portrait hanging on the wall close to where they were both sitting. "Past valuations have attributed the picture to the artist William Arthur Breakspeare. A good artist in his own right, certainly. However, we both know the portrait is not signed and there's no record of this artist ever meeting Sir Edgar. So, if it was not painted by Breakspeare, then who did it?"

Miss Wardley raised her eyelids slightly, but still sat quietly and waited.

Ian continued. "When I first saw this picture, it was at the time of our first meeting when my wife and I discussed with you the possibility of Robert attending this school. I particularly took notice of this painting. It's a quality piece of work. I thought at the time that I recognised the artist. Then, when I was able to make a closer inspection at our last meeting, I was even more convinced. Despite it lacking a signature and your old valuations all stating it was by Breakspeare, I actually think it was painted by someone else – George Frederic Watts."

"Oh!" exclaimed Miss Wardley, somewhat surprised. "Are you saying that all the previous valuers have been incorrect?"

"That is my opinion, yes," replied Ian, flatly. "I can explain."

"I'm intrigued. Please, Mr. Caxton, continue. I'm anxious to hear your explanation."

Ian took a deep breath. "Firstly Breakspeare, although he did paint some head and shoulder portraits, this was not the area he was most renowned for. He also mainly only worked in the Birmingham area and I would doubt Sir Edgar ever visited that part of the country. After all, he only made infrequent trips back to England from South Africa. If you recall, Sir Edgar's family home was in London. Nevertheless, it's not impossible. But, of course, the picture has never been formally authenticated as having been painted by Breakspeare."

"But the valuations," interjected Miss Wardley.

"Just one man's opinion from many years ago. There are five sets of valuations with the first one dated 1912. This 1912 valuation stated that Sir Edgar's portrait was painted by Breakspeare. My guess is that all the subsequent valuers have done is just increased the value of each picture for inflation, without actually challenging any of the original report. Furthermore, I could not find any trace of this portrait being included in any authorised collection of Breakspeare's work."

"I see," interrupted Miss Wardley, now alarmed and a little disheartened. She swivelled in her chair and looked questioningly up at the picture on the wall.

The Gamble

"The lack of provenance before 1912," continued Ian, "doesn't help us either. There's no record, or paperwork, in the folder you gave me prior to 1912."

Miss Wardley swivelled her seat back and was looking directly at Ian. "All I know is the painting was donated to the school by Sir Edgar's family after he died. Does this mean the painting is worthless?"

"On the contrary. If we can prove the portrait was painted by Watts, it could be worth, maybe, well certainly over one million pounds."

"Oh my goodness!" exclaimed Miss Wardley, with a surprised voice. "Are you sure?"

"We cannot get too excited just yet. It's not going to be easy to find evidence that will conclusively prove this picture was painted by the hand of George Watts. Perversely, the painting doesn't appear in any authorised collection of George Watts' work either. But, of course, we both know the picture's not been signed… so it still could still have been painted by someone else."

"So, what makes you think it was painted by this… Mr. Watts?"

"It definitely has his style, and the palette of colours being used is typical of his work. It's about the right time and Watts also lived in London for a large part of his life. On the downside, however, he rarely painted portraits and when he did they tended to be commissions for select individuals or as an historical record of the great men of his time which he preferred to keep in his own possession. But, the main point is, and this is crucial, my guess is that he agreed to paint Sir Edgar, partly because Sir Edgar had been so influential with his mining businesses in South Africa and maybe because Sir Edgar was prepared to pay him well. All conjecture, I know, but definitely more likely than Breakspeare."

"But not actual proof, is it?" commented Miss Wardley,

with a deep sigh. This was all somewhat confusing to her and she was now wondering if Mr. Caxton was actually correct.

"No, I accept that. As I say, it's just my opinion."

"So, what happens now?"

"Well, there are different options to consider. You could get a second opinion as, of course, I could be wrong. But one way or another you need to establish who the correct artist is. In the event of any damage to this painting, your insurers would certainly want to see full documentation that proves who the correct artist is and a correct valuation. A thorough investigation to establish these, I'm afraid, is going to cost the school money."

"I see," Miss Wardley pondered on Ian's comments. "So, are you saying the picture, as it currently stands, has little value?"

"It may be worth a few thousand pounds without formal authentication. It's still a good painting but, of course, it could still be a fake or a good copy. But if it is a Breakspeare, which at the moment is what everybody has accepted it is, then it's probably worth about £100,000. That's the sort of valuation I've put on it. But, as I said earlier, if it is proved to be by George Watts, then we're definitely talking above one million pounds."

"What am I going to tell our insurers?"

"That's a tricky one. They've accepted the picture as a piece of work by Breakspeare to date, but, as I say, they're not going to pay out £100,000 without full proof and the right documentation. You could be paying premiums for nothing."

"It's part of the school's history, and, indeed, feels part of the fabric of the school. Its monetary value is obviously important, but the picture is priceless to the school."

"Then I think you have three options. One, get a second

The Gamble

opinion, which I certainly recommend, and use that report for the insurance valuation. Two, take it off the insurance schedule and keep it in its current place here in your office, or… three, try to sell it."

"But nobody's going to pay money for it without the same proof and the correct documentation that you mentioned earlier."

"I would," responded Ian, to Miss Wardley's astonishment.

"Now why would you do a thing like that, Mr. Caxton?" Miss Wardley had a slight smile on her face. What, she wondered, is Mr. Caxton up to?

"As I say, I think it was painted by George Watts and I would be prepared to put my professional judgement on the line and, of course, my money. I would also arrange for you to receive a similar copy replacement."

Miss Wardley sat back in her chair and looked directly at Ian. "How much would you offer the school for this painting then?"

"I would be prepared to pay double the current valuation of it as a Breakspeare, i.e. £200,000."

"I see," said Miss Wardley. "This is all very interesting. The problem is, I have the school governors to consider. They would have to be informed and, of course, their opinions canvassed."

"Of course. But before you do that, I urge you to get a second… or even a third, opinion."

Miss Wardley arose from sitting on her chair and walked around to the front of her desk. Ian immediately stood up as well.

"Mr. Caxton, it has been a fascinating meeting. Thank you." Miss Wardley held out her hand. Ian looked down and grasped it gently. "Please send me your invoice for the valuation. I'll let you know how the school intends to handle Sir Edgar's portrait."

Ian picked up his briefcase and looked back at Miss Wardley. "Thank you." He turned away and walked towards the outer office.

After she heard the outer door to her office close, Miss Wardley walked over to the window that gave a view of the gravel entrance in front of the building and also the playing fields in the distance. After a few seconds she spotted Ian after he'd exited the building. She watched him saunter away until he was out of sight. Under her breath, she whispered to herself, "Goodbye, Mr. Caxton."

Chapter 11

Ian arrived home and found Emma in the rear garden. As he walked across the patio, he could see she was bending down and pulling up the first sprouting weeds in the flower beds. The dormant cycle of winter was obviously coming to an end.

When Emma heard Ian's footsteps she stood up and walked over the lawn to join him. They kissed.

"So," said Emma, smiling, "I see Miss Wardley didn't bite your head off."

Ian smiled back. "No, it was an interesting meeting. Let me make us both a cup of coffee and we can drink it out here as it's pleasantly warm."

"I know, I'm even sweating just doing a bit of weeding."

"Let me get the drinks and then I'll tell you all the details. As I said, it was an interesting meeting."

Ten minutes later Ian had made and delivered the two mugs of coffee. They sat next to each other on the garden bench where the spring sunshine was warming their faces. Ian explained how the valuation and his comments about the Sir Edgar Brookfield portrait had been received.

"What do you think Miss Wardley's going to do now?" asked Emma.

"I'm hoping she'll do as I recommended and get a second opinion. I'm as intrigued as she is to hear that result."

"I don't understand. Why are you so keen for her to get a second opinion?"

"Well, from a professional point of view, I could still be wrong. It could yet be a picture painted by Breakspeare, or a fake, or just a good copy. But I'd bet money it'll be none of these. Also, I didn't want to be seen as being too pushy. I just wanted to sow some seeds of curiosity and a little doubt."

"You are devious, Mr. Caxton," replied Emma, with a smile on her face.

Ian laughed. "Look, there's a balancing act here between maybe obtaining a valuable painting for a good price and not upsetting the school Robert attends."

"You sound more and more like Andrei every day," responded Emma. It was not meant to be a compliment.

Again, Ian laughed, but privately that was what he was hoping to hear.

After they'd both finished drinking their coffees, Emma went back to her weeding and Ian returned the mugs back to the kitchen. He then strolled into the home office and switched on his laptop computer. He accessed and read through his new emails and was curious about the email from Yuki in Japan. He clicked on the entry and read the following contents:

Hello Ian,

I thought I had better tell you that Yoshi and I have sold our three galleries in Tokyo. I will still be part of the partnership until the end of the financial year, but after that I will be stepping down and retiring from the art world.

The success of your partnership has meant that I can now retire much sooner than I had originally anticipated. Also, the proposition we received for the galleries was just too good an offer for us to turn down.

The Gamble

I have thoroughly enjoyed our profitable adventure and I know the partnership will continue to grow and be a success. I only wish I was 20 years younger.
Many thanks,
Yuki.

Well, thought Ian, now there's a surprise. Or, maybe not. He remembered back to his early meetings with Yuki. He'd indicated that he was ready to ease down on his business, especially his globetrotting. The surprise, however, and Ian was now reflecting on this, was how quickly the situation had changed. Ian didn't blame Yuki. He'd obviously had a great offer for his and Yoshi's business, so good luck to them. Time to enjoy the fruits of all their hard work over the years.

Ian leaned back in his chair and began to consider the implications and the effect this decision could have on the future of the partnership. Obviously, the partnership will be paying off Yuki for his share of the business, but what do we do going forward? Find a replacement? Carry on with one less partner or wind the partnership up altogether? Our next annual meeting will be an interesting one and I need to make sure I have all my own answers to the inevitable questions.

Oscar didn't own a television. Even in Hong Kong it had been some years since he'd seen a live television programme. He tended to get all his news and entertainment from his computer, via the internet. So, when his neighbour, Garfield, leaned on their adjoining fence and asked Oscar if he had seen the news on TV, Oscar, who was sitting on his lounger enjoying the late afternoon sunshine and a can of beer, said, "No." Then truthfully added, "Because I don't own a television."

"Man, you have no TV! What do you do in the evenings?"

Oscar was a little surprised at Garfield's question. "Most of the time I'm on my computer or reading. Why, what have I missed?"

"One of our island heroes has been arrested, that's what the TV news just said. Heard of Clancy Hobbie? Used to be a big reggae performer back in the 1970s and '80s."

What! exclaimed Oscar to himself and immediately sat up. "Yes, I've heard of him. What's he been arrested for?"

"Murdering his wife, that's what!"

"Wow," responded Oscar, but his mind was thinking more about Gladstone. Was he implicated? Had he been arrested as well?

"His wife was murdered some months ago in St John's, whilst Clancy was in Jamaica."

"How's he supposed to have murdered her then?"

"The police always figured it was a professional job. They've obviously got some more information that connects Clancy with a professional killer. That's my guess, anyway."

"Oh," said Oscar. He couldn't think of what else to say.

"What you doing Saturday?" asked Garfield. "I'm having a barbecue. Want to join us, man?"

Oscar was still thinking about Clancy and Gladstone, but after a few seconds he said, "Don't think I've got anything planned. What time are you suggesting?"

"About four o'clock. Okay? Bring some beers."

"Thanks." Oscar got up from his lounger and picked up his half-finished can of beer. "See you on Saturday then."

Garfield waved and then stepped back into his garden.

Oscar went into his villa and immediately telephoned Gladstone's mobile number. However, he only got the answerphone. Oscar left a message and told Gladstone to ring him as soon as possible. He also then sent him an email.

Over the next few days Oscar accessed his computer for all the local Antiguan news. He wanted to see if there'd

The Gamble

been any further developments concerning the arrest. Frustratingly, there was no additional information published, other than that Clancy was still 'helping the police with their enquiries'.

Oscar had to wait another couple of days before he got a response from Gladstone. Gladstone had sent Oscar a reply to his earlier email, saying that he was back in Jamaica again and staying with his son and family. He would be back in Antigua in about ten days' time.

Oscar quickly responded and asked Gladstone if he had heard the news about Clancy?

Another day passed before Gladstone replied saying, yes, he had heard that Clancy had been arrested, but no, he didn't know any more details.

Oh well, thought Oscar, I guess he's not too worried about the situation.

It was another two days before any further public news was announced. This time the headline on the website report read, *'Clancy Hobbie Released on Bail'*. Further on in the report it was stated that bail was conditional on Clancy surrendering his passport and him agreeing not to leave the island of Antigua.

The report also contained a short video of Sheldon Murray, Clancy's lawyer, standing in front of the main entrance to the police station. He was making a brief statement for the benefit of the press. He told them, "My client denies all knowledge of the circumstances behind his wife's murder. As you all know, he was in Jamaica at the time of the murder and the police are wasting everybody's time trying to prove Mr. Hobbie was in any way involved."

After Oscar finished watching the report, he switched off his computer, sat back in his chair and wondered why Clancy had been arrested in the first place.

Chapter 12

Mary Turnbull had been working at the 'Taylor Fine Arts Gallery' for ten days. She'd already improved a number of the office administrative functions, had suggested minor improvements to the gallery's display area and the re-siting of the manager's desk.

When Viktor had subsequently shown Mary the gallery's website, she was quick to point out two obvious errors. From that moment onwards Viktor was happy to leave the website monitoring and maintenance to her. He was really pleased with Mary's knowledge and positivity and knew he'd made the right choice. She was going to be a very competent and positive asset to the business. Enquiry numbers had already marginally increased and he was confident the gallery would soon be seeing a corresponding increase in the business turnover.

Viktor was also much happier now that he didn't have the irritation of having to temporarily close the gallery when he made his calls on clients. Something he had been yearning to do since he'd first left Sotheby's.

In his first report to Bob Taylor since Mary had been employed, he'd raved about her and, in Bob's email back, he congratulated Viktor on his successful recruit and was looking forward to seeing the positive results from Viktor's greater freedom.

The Gamble

Now, thought Viktor, time for me to show what I'm really worth!

Emma was working in the kitchen when she'd taken the telephone call. The call was from the headmistress at Brookfield School, Miss Wardley. She told Emma that she wanted to make a further appointment with Mr. Caxton to discuss the Sir Edgar Brookfield painting. Emma agreed that Ian would meet with her at 9.15 tomorrow morning.

When Ian came in from the garage, Emma met him in the utility room and told him of the planned meeting for the following morning.

"Well, that should be interesting," replied Ian. He was washing his hands in the sink. "I wonder what she's managed to find out?"

"It must be good news for you, don't you think? Otherwise, why would she ask for another meeting?" replied Emma, trying to think of any other reason why the headmistress should ring about the painting.

"I guess we'll just have to wait until tomorrow. Do you want me to take Robert into school first, or should we both go together?"

"Maybe we should both go together. I can do some shopping and pick you up after your meeting."

Next morning Ian, Emma and Robert travelled in Emma's car to Brookfield School. They arrived in the school's car park at 8.50am and Emma walked with Robert around to the front of the building. Robert then saw one of his friends, said goodbye to his mother and ran off. Both boys then entered through the main entrance together. As Emma slowly walked back towards the car, she took the opportunity to speak to one of the other mothers.

Ian, meanwhile, had remained in Emma's car catching up on emails and rereading two websites about George

Frederic Watts. He checked his watch, 9.07, so he closed down his laptop and put it, with his notes and papers, back into his briefcase. After getting out of the car and closing the door, he spotted Emma chatting to a woman he didn't know. He checked his watch again and decided it was now time for him to make his way to his meeting. Passing by the two chatting women, Emma and Ian briefly exchanged smiles and Emma called out, "Good luck".

A few minutes later Ian arrived at the main door to the school and pressed the buzzer. Mrs. Bailey responded, via the intercom system, and told him to come in as the door was now unlocked. Ian pushed on the old oak door and entered the large entrance hallway. He spotted Mrs. Bailey waiting for him at the top of the stairs. Ian joined her and they both walked into the headmistress's outer office. There they met Miss Wardley who was refiling some papers into one of the cabinets.

"Good morning, Mr. Caxton," announced Miss Wardley. "Please, come into my office."

Ian said good morning in reply and followed her into her office. He smiled at Mrs. Bailey and said, "thank you."

"Please sit here, Mr. Caxton."

Ian smiled a little to himself and he did exactly as Miss Wardley had instructed, sitting on the chair directly in front of Miss Wardley's desk. He carefully placed his briefcase on the floor at the side of his chair.

"Following your advice," said Miss Wardley, preventing the possibility of any small talk and now sitting in her usual place behind the desk, "we've had three further valuations of Sir Edgar's painting."

Ian raised his eyebrows slightly in surprise and then he and Miss Wardley looked up at the picture still hanging in its usual place on the wall.

Miss Wardley continued, "One valuer thought it was a

The Gamble

copy by an unknown artist, another thought it might be by Mr. Breakspeare and the third valuer listed a number of artists that it could have been painted by. All in all, I'm afraid they weren't very helpful."

"I see," replied Ian, not totally surprised. He knew valuers today were far more reticent to give definitive opinions than previous valuers had done in the past. That is, unless provenances and scientific evidence had already been well proven. Indeed, the buying public were also now much more likely to sue for any incorrect pronouncements, especially where many thousands, if not millions, of pounds were involved.

Miss Wardley continued, "I put this information, plus your offer, to the school governors two days ago. There was quite a heated discussion and several wondered why you would offer such an attractive figure for this painting." Miss Wardley looked up at Sir Edgar's portrait.

"As I said before," responded Ian, "I don't think it was painted by Breakspeare. But I do think it might have been painted by George Watts and I still stand by my earlier opinion… and my original offer."

Miss Wardley didn't smile very often, but she did at that very moment. "Mr. Caxton, you are either a very clever man… or a fool. I very much doubt it is the latter."

Ian laughed.

"The governors have decided that if your offer still stands, and subject to our painting being replaced by an excellent copy, then the £200,000 is accepted."

"I know a specialist artist who'll be prepared to produce an excellent copy."

"In which case, Mr. Caxton, you may take this picture with you and arrange for the copy to be produced. If the governors are satisfied with the replacement, then the sale can definitely go ahead."

"Thank you. I'll make sure the original is well cared for

whilst it's being copied. Do you want me to take it down from the wall?"

"Yes please."

Ian stood up and lifted the picture of Sir Edgar off the wall. He inspected it in detail. Satisfied it still appeared to be the same picture he'd inspected three weeks ago, he laid it down on the nearby table and, with the use of his mobile phone, he took several photographs of both the front and the rear. He wanted to compare these with the photographs he'd previously taken. From his briefcase he then removed and unfolded a strong canvas bag, purposely made for carrying paintings. Moments later the painting had been placed into the bag and secured by three Velcro fasteners.

Miss Wardley got up from her seat and joined him, standing at his side at the table. "How long will it take to complete the copy?"

"I'll bring both paintings back here in about two weeks. You can then decide which you think is the copy."

Miss Wardley smiled again. "Mr. Caxton, I look forward to seeing them both together. Goodbye, and thank you."

Miss Wardley held out her hand and Ian grasped it with his own. For a second they both held each other's gaze. Ian then broke eye contact and pulled his hand away. Picking up his briefcase and the canvas bag by its handle, he said goodbye and headed towards the outer office. He smiled and nodded at Mrs. Bailey and then exited the room.

Miss Wardley stood at the communicating doorway between her office and the outer office. She watched Ian leave and then looked at Mrs. Bailey. They both smiled. Miss Wardley's third smile of the day.

As Ian arrived back in the car park, he saw Emma's car approaching along the driveway. When the car stopped Ian put both the canvas bag and his briefcase in the boot next to a bag of various vegetables. He then opened the passenger's front door and climbed in.

"I see you've got the painting," said Emma, looking across at her husband.

Ian smiled. "But I've now got to speak to Peter Walker and get him to produce a good copy. He's a super talent and will be up for that. Then all I've got to do is prove the original was really painted by George Watts. No pressure then."

Emma smiled. "£200,000. Yes, no pressure."

She engaged first gear and drove the car away.

Chapter 13

When Gladstone arrived back in Antigua, his first telephone call was to Oscar. Oscar was pleased to finally hear from his colleague, but he was still annoyed that Gladstone hadn't been in contact with him much earlier. Oscar was still learning that everything moved at a much slower pace in the Caribbean than the breakneck speed he'd been used to in Hong Kong. They agreed to meet up at their usual bar at seven o'clock.

Oscar was the first to arrive and ordered their usual two beers. He paid the barman and carried the two glasses over to their regular table, which Oscar was pleased to see was vacant this time. It had been another hot day and even now the air temperature was still around 30 degrees centigrade. Oscar sipped his beer, stared at the view and waited for Gladstone to appear.

At 7.10 Gladstone joined his colleague, sat down and took a long draught of his beer.

"Wow," said Gladstone, "I needed that, man. Cheers."

Oscar smiled and replied, "Cheers to you. So, you've been to see your granddaughter again. How is she?"

Gladstone continued smiling and removed his mobile phone from his pocket. He flicked through the aps until he came to 'photos', whereupon he showed Oscar eight photos of a tiny baby.

The Gamble

"She's got a little bit more hair than the last photo you showed me," observed Oscar.

"She's beautiful, man. My son's such a lucky boy. So, what have I missed in the art world?"

"It's all been very quiet. I did some work for Wesley, at the 'Shell Gallery', but otherwise it's just been quiet."

"What about the partnership?"

"Yuki and May have been doing quite a bit of business together and I gather Yuki's retiring shortly. They've sold their business in Japan. Apparently, he's told Ian he's going to leave the partnership at the end of our year. Pity that, I like Yuki."

Gladstone nodded. "Yea, Yuki's okay."

"Anyway, coming back here, the main news is the arrest, and then bail, of Clancy," said Oscar, trying to stimulate any extra information and gauge Gladstone's reaction.

"I spoke to Clancy about a week before he was arrested," said Gladstone, much to Oscar's surprise.

"You did! Why did you do that? What did you say?"

"Sheldon Murray, his lawyer, telephoned me. He was concerned about Clancy's outburst in front of me at Clancy's house. He wanted to know if I'd been contacted by the police, or if I had any intentions of contacting them. Anyway, I told him that Clancy was a fool, and no, I had no intention of telling the police."

Oscar sipped his beer and waited for the next revelation.

Gladstone continued. "Sheldon seemed happy with my comments, but I wasn't. I decided to speak to Clancy myself. He had paid me handsomely for my valuations, but I was worried another one of his outbursts might implicate me in some way. I telephoned him and told him I wouldn't say anything to the police so long as he didn't involve me. If he did, then I'd have to tell the police the truth. Clancy told me he was totally innocent and was determined not to say anything to anyone. He also told me Sheldon had advised him to keep his mouth tightly shut."

"But he was subsequently arrested anyway. Did someone else come forward?" asked Oscar.

"Don't know, man. It all happened whilst I was in Jamaica, staying with my son. I've heard nothing and, as I said before, it's got nothing to do with me. Someone once said, 'never meet your heroes' and they were right. I wish I'd never accepted the job of valuing Clancy's painting collection."

Oscar nodded and then sipped his beer. Gladstone's explanation seemed plausible but he still wondered if he really was telling him the full story.

"Drink up, man, and I'll buy you another," said Gladstone, standing up and holding out his hand for Oscar's glass.

Oscar drained the last of the contents in his glass and passed it to Gladstone. He watched Gladstone walk slowly towards the bar and then turned his head to look in the direction of the beach. All he could see now was the moon's broken white reflections lighting up a narrow strip of the otherwise serene, black Caribbean Sea. Towards the horizon he could just make out three partially illuminated fishing boats. All seemed very peaceful and calm. He wondered if this was just another lull before the next Clancy storm!

Penny was finding her new role at Sotheby's very challenging. With no Ian to bounce her questions and ideas off, she felt uncomfortable and exposed. She'd enjoyed her time working with Ian, but now… well, it was all very different. Indeed, with the imminent departure of Michael Hopkins, the current MD, a lot was already changing at Sotheby's. There were also rumours about further changes still to come over the next few months once the new MD took charge. She was seriously wondering if this was really the career she now wanted. Also, the planning for her wedding to Viktor was taking up a considerable amount of her free time. Being the only daughter, her mother, a widow, was stressed and anxious that everything was properly planned and only the 'right people' would be invited. Without the presence of her father to assist her mother, this was putting more and more strain on Penny. She was beginning to think Viktor's suggestion of an elopement to Gretna Green, or a quiet tropical island wedding, was not such a bad idea after all. Nevertheless, she was still in regular telephone contact with Ian, who had agreed to 'walk her down the aisle'. He'd now become her tower of strength. Cool, calm and practical, as ever, he kept supporting and uplifting her during the many doubtful moments she was currently experiencing.

It was almost two months to the day since Ian had left Sotheby's, when he'd suggested to Penny that he'd like to take her out for a relaxing evening meal. Just the two of them… to discuss the wedding arrangements. Penny was more than pleased with his suggestion and said she was available any evening. They duly met in a quiet London bistro close to Covent Garden.

After meeting outside the restaurant and exchanging an affectionate embrace, Ian could see this was not the usual Penny. Her face looked strained and she had lost some weight. A lot had happened in her life since they'd last met, face to face, on Ian's last day at Sotheby's… and there were obviously more challenges still to come.

Over apéritifs they mainly talked about her new role at Sotheby's, but also a little bit about Viktor and Ian's new career. Then, over the main course, Penny explained her mother's idea of the perfect wedding. Ian could see it was all becoming a bit much for Penny. He knew she had dreamed of a 'proper wedding', but the reality of all the hard work seemed to be overwhelming her… and probably her mother too.

Ian knew Penny was competent and, in time, would prove to be sufficiently talented to progress in her new business role, but with the wedding, her promotion and the new MD shortly starting, a lot of pressures were certainly building up on her.

The plates for the main course were taken away and they waited for their deserts. Ian continued the discussion. "Okay, let's concentrate on the wedding. What exactly do you want me to do?"

Penny explained her mother's list of requirements. Ian never flinched a muscle, other than nodding his head to indicate his understanding and acceptance of his role.

"That sounds all okay to me," said Ian, trying to give an air of relaxed confidence and hoping to calm Penny… at least with his part and involvement in her wedding.

"After I'm married, I'm not sure I want to stay at Sotheby's, Ian. I know you have so much confidence in me, but I don't feel the same way. You'd hardly recognise the company now and the new MD, apparently, has all sorts of new plans and ideas when he starts shortly."

"I know I probably shouldn't say this but the incoming MD, Jonathan Northgate, is a dangerous idiot. I've told you before that I knew him in New York. I also know Michael wasn't keen on him either, but the chairman and the board are the ones in favour. I feel partly guilty as Michael really wanted me to take on the role. But honestly, Penny, it's not the job I wanted. To do the role properly, well it's 24/7, full on. That's not for me. Emma and Robert are far too important to ignore. Have you chatted through your thoughts and concerns with Vic?"

"Vic's so wrapped up with the gallery and especially the outside calls. He's doing well and he's just taken on a manager to run the gallery. This is freeing up more time for him to develop the business opportunities away from the gallery."

The Gamble

"Vic's very ambitious. I love his enthusiasm, but it's dangerous to be too self-centred, especially when you're in a serious relationship. I was like that in New York and Hong Kong. It's great until reality kicks in. In my case it was Emma. I wanted to stay in Hong Kong, I loved it. But Emma would have none of it. Life changes so quickly and what was once so important suddenly isn't anymore. Vic will realise this and then he'll have to make a big decision."

"I don't want to put any obstacles in his way, Ian. I want to be able to support all his ambitions."

"But what about you, Penny? What do you want from this marriage?"

Penny smiled. "Me? I suppose I want a loving husband, a nice house and eventually children."

"Are you sure? Is that it? Where does your career come into that scenario?"

"It doesn't, does it? I thoroughly enjoyed working with you, Ian. You've always been so nice and confident in my abilities. Now? Well, you're not there anymore."

Not for the first time, Ian felt he'd let Penny down, and maybe Sotheby's as well. He certainly wanted to make amends with Penny... and try to prepare her, the best he could, for the imminent arrival of the menacing Jonathan Northgate.

Chapter 14

Ian returned to Brookfield School with the original painting of Sir Edgar Brookfield and the copy recently painted by Peter Walker. Ian had originally met Peter whilst he was still at art college. A colleague at Sotheby's had mentioned this young man's talents and, when Ian met him, he was impressed with Peter's abilities to be able to copy the styles of various different artists. Unfortunately, Ian quickly realised that Peter's talents lay almost entirely in copying. He seemed to lack both the direction, interest and imagination to develop a style of his own. When copying, he was brilliant. His own style? Average at best.

For various reasons clients often needed additional copies of their masterpieces and gradually Ian used Peter's talents more and more. Indeed, he'd employed Peter to copy the Gainsborough picture he'd eventually sold at auction a year ago. Peter thoroughly enjoyed the challenges of copying the various artists' styles and his reputation spread quickly. He'd become wealthy, well known and his abilities were used by many people in the art world. He deliberately never painted exact reproductions or copies for illegal purposes. They were always certified as not originals and nothing more.

Mrs. Bailey showed Ian into the headmistress's office and Miss Wardley greeted him with a "good morning" and a shake of his hand. She then pointed to the table and Ian walked over and laid his two canvas bags down on the table top. He then proceeded to remove one painting from each bag and laid them side by side.

Miss Wardley put on her reading spectacles and walked over to join him. Ian stepped aside to give her more room for the inspection. Firstly she compared each painting as they faced her side by side, then individually and finally front and rear. After a few moments she lifted each picture and stood them together leaning against the back wall.

"Mr. Caxton, these two paintings might be twins. I do hope you know which one is which."

Ian smiled as he looked at the face of Miss Wardley. "Yes, I know which is which. Like human twins there's a subtle difference, but I'm hoping you and the governors will be satisfied to hang the copy on your wall."

"I really cannot see a difference." Miss Wardley looked closely at both paintings again. "Even the frames have similar chips and age marks. The copier has done an excellent job."

"Peter is a talented copier. I've used him several times before and he always produces an excellent piece of work. Now then, have you worked out which one's the copy? It's more difficult, I agree, because the original's had a really good clean."

Miss Wardley looked closely at both pictures one more time. "I think this one is the copy." She finally decided, pointing to the painting on her right-hand side.

Ian smiled. "So, what made you decide on that painting?"

"It, well… it looks newer. If that makes any sense."

"Well, I'm sorry to tell you, but it's the other painting that's the copy. You picked out the original. It may be newer in your eyes because it's had a thorough professional clean."

"So, what's the difference?"

Ian leaned over to the original and pointed to a few grey hairs just above Sir Edgar's left ear.

Miss Wardley leaned down to see where he was pointing. She adjusted her spectacles and then looked at the same area on the copy. It was still difficult to spot, but eventually Miss Wardley could just see the faintest of differences. "I would never have spotted that in a hundred years. Mr. Caxton, it looks as though you have bought yourself a painting."

Ian smiled again. "Do you want me to put the copy on the wall for you?"

"Yes please. You know, Mr. Caxton, I really do hope you're able to establish that this original picture was painted by Mr. Watts."

Ian lifted the copied painting of Sir Edgar and placed it onto the hook on the wall above Miss Wardley's desk. He stood back, looked at the alignment and then stepped forward and adjusted it again. "I hope you're right, Miss Wardley, because if it is, I promise I'll pay the balance of Robert's school fees in one single payment."

Ten days later Ian made his first visit back to Sotheby's premises in Bond Street since his final day of employment there. He was taking up the invitation to attend his former boss's retirement gathering and formal send off.

Ian found it strange to re-enter the premises. Arthur, the front desk security guard, was still there and gave Ian a nod and a smile. He then said quietly, "Welcome back, Mr. Caxton. You've been missed." Ian acknowledged the compliment and thanked Arthur. He then walked along the corridor, heading for the main conference room, wondering why Arthur had made such a comment.

As he approached the conference room Ian could already hear the chattering noises coming from inside. He took a deep breath, pushed the door open and confidently walked in. There were about forty people, Ian guessed, spread around the room. They were talking in small groups. Ian

The Gamble

picked up a glass of champagne and looked to see how many faces he immediately recognised.

Jonathan Northgate, the newly appointed MD, spotted Ian when he entered the room, so he immediately left the group he was talking to and walked over towards him, determined to get the first wound into his old adversary. "Hello, Caxton, long time no see, as they say."

"Congratulations, Jonathan. I never dreamed you'd achieve this level of promotion," responded Ian, with the same intended barbed comment.

Jonathan smiled. "Evidence of your poor judgement of people's abilities."

It was now Ian's turn to smile. "More to do with other people's inexplicable opinion of you I think."

"Hello, Ian, so good to see you again. Thank you for coming to my last supper." It was Michael Hopkins who had stepped in between the two sparring egos.

Jonathan slowly backed away and rejoined the people he'd been talking to previously.

"Thank you for inviting me, Michael. However, I do feel a bit of a trespasser."

Michael laughed, but then more seriously said, "Oh, Ian, I do wish it was you who was replacing me. Northgate is a fool."

It was Ian's time to laugh and slowly shake his head from side to side. He then briefly looked around the room before leaning closer to his former boss. He whispered, "Pity the board didn't agree with your, and my, view."

"But they did, Ian. When I proposed your name for the role nobody objected. They all supported me."

"Sorry, Michael. It was just too big a commitment. Emma and Robert will always come first."

Michael, showing a despondent smile, gently patted Ian on the shoulder. "You made that very plain when we discussed it before."

Ian didn't know what to say. He still felt part of him had let his boss down.

"Now, I've got to move around and say my goodbyes," continued Michael, but before moving away he put his hand into his pocket and pulled out a sealed envelope. "Put that in your pocket. Read it later."

Ian did as he was told and put the envelope into his inside jacket pocket as Michael walked away and joined another group of guests.

Ian looked across at the other faces in the room and then spotted Penny looking in his direction. She gave him an affectionate smile, made her excuses to the colleagues she was talking to and walked over to join him. They briefly embraced and then Penny stood back and said, "I noticed you were talking to our new MD." She remembered that he and Jonathan Northgate didn't get on.

"The man's still the same arrogant and menacing idiot," replied Ian. "Much, much more interestingly, how are you?"

"Outside of work, things are fine. All the wedding plans finally appear to be in good shape and my mother's finally calmed down. Well, a bit anyway."

Ian smiled and sipped his champagne. He looked at Penny. She still had the strained look on her face, but seemed to have put on a little more weight.

"There's one bit of really good news though," said Penny, her voice pitched a little higher with excitement. "Vic and I have chosen where we're going to live."

"Oh, that's great. Where are you moving to?"

"We've exchanged contracts on a three-bedroom penthouse apartment in Docklands. Vic's persuaded the bank to lend us most of the purchase price money against his inheritance from his father's friend, Andrei. I'm planning to move in as soon as possible. Vic's parents are a bit old fashioned, so Vic's decided not to move in until after the wedding."

"That's very gallant of him. Still, you've only got a few weeks to wait."

"By then, Ian, I'll also have made up my mind about my future at Sotheby's."

Chapter 15

The day after Michael Hopkins' retirement send off, Ian resumed his investigations into his new purchase, the portrait of Sir Edgar Brookfield. He spent the next two days in his office, on his computer, looking at numerous websites, many of which he'd looked at before. He'd also explored his collection of art books and catalogues and had even been to the local library. Unfortunately, he still couldn't find any further information that was going to help his cause. A little part of him now wondered if he had made a bad financial decision, but with his professional hat on, he was still convinced that the picture had been painted by George Frederic Watts. After all, it had all the hallmarks of the man's work. More important though, was his 'sixth' sense' – the itchy scalp or sweaty palm of his left hand rarely let him down. In Sir Edgar's case, it was the itchy scalp! Okay, so HE was convinced, but he still had the task of persuading others to agree to his opinion in order to justify the extravagant investment he'd made. He needed something, just something, more significant and authentic to emerge. Anything to get the ball rolling.

It was late morning when Ian left the office. Feeling a little frustrated, he wandered into the kitchen where Emma had just finished preparing the evening's casserole and was washing her hands.

The Gamble

"Fancy a coffee?" asked Ian, collecting the kettle and filling it with water.

"That would be nice. Thank you."

Ian started to boil the kettle and prepare the cafetiere.

Emma was drying her hands when she said, "Ian, I was wondering. It'll be Robert's school holiday in three weeks' time and your mum was asking if we wanted him to stay with them for a few days. I said I'd talk to you. We have no plans, so I was wondering if we should take up her offer and then we could have a few days in Monaco… on our own?"

"What a great idea. It's been a while since we were last there," replied Ian, pouring the boiling hot water into the cafetiere. He then picked up the tray containing the cafetiere of coffee, milk and two mugs.

They both walked out onto the patio and sat down next to the table. It was nearly midday and the sun was warming, but not burning. The air temperature was being cooled by a gentle breeze.

"I'm still having problems with the Brookfield painting," announced Ian, with a hint of frustration in his voice.

"Is there anything you want me to do?"

Ian pondered on Emma's question. "I'm not sure," he said finally. "I've exhausted all my usual avenues. I might have to give Penny a ring and ask her to look in Sotheby's library. Their collection's much bigger than mine."

"Should you be doing that? After all, you don't work there anymore. Have you thought about asking the partnership?"

"Hey! That's a great idea. I'll send them all an email this afternoon. Well done."

Emma looked back with a smug smile of satisfaction on her face.

That afternoon Ian drafted his 'help' email to the partnership, asking if anyone could provide him with information about George Frederic Watts and his connection with the Sir Edgar Brookfield portrait.

Two days later he'd received a reply from all the partners, but only one, Bob Taylor, had any positive news. He'd emailed Ian to say his father-in-law, Antoine, had dealt with three George Watts pictures several years ago. As a result Antoine had purchased four publications covering both Watts' work and his professional life. Bob also gave Ian the titles of each publication and said that if Ian couldn't obtain similar copies in England, then he could borrow Antoine's four editions next time he visited Monaco.

Ian immediately emailed Bob back and thanked him for the information. He also mentioned his and Emma's plans to return to Monaco in three weeks' time and added, yes, he would be grateful if he could borrow Antoine's books, that is, if he couldn't track down the same publications in the UK himself. Ian also took the opportunity to ask if he and Zoe would join them, as their guests one evening, for a meal at a local restaurant.

In Antigua, the big social media gossip was all about Clancy Hobbie. Rumour was now widespread that the Miami police in Florida had, three weeks ago, arrested a man named Jack Binder, a known professional killer. He'd been arrested for the murder of an important government official in the Miami Beach area. Amongst Binder's papers, telephone and computer records, the police had found the names of Clancy Hobbie and his wife Millie Hobbie. From Binder's passport and airline flight records, the police had also established that Binder had been in Antigua at the time of the murder of Millie Hobbie. They had also identified that two days before Millie's murder, US$1 million had been deposited into his bank account. Two days after the murder, a further

The Gamble

US$1 million had been transferred into the same account from a bank account in Switzerland.

When the Miami police informed the Antiguan police force of Binder's arrest and their findings, two Antiguan detectives were immediately dispatched to Miami. They wanted to interview Mr. Jack Binder... urgently! However, when they arrived, they were warned that Binder was not just any old 'run of the mill' criminal. He had been interviewed and arrested several times before, but the evidence was never strong enough to charge him and get him into court. Binder never admitted anything and his stock answer to any questioning was always, 'no comment'.

Sheldon Murray and Clancy were back and forth to the St John's main police station as and when the police required Clancy to be interviewed. Clancy was still on bail and Sheldon announced to the reporters waiting outside the police station that Clancy was continuing to cooperate fully with all the police inquiries.

The Antiguan detectives, who had visited Miami, now questioned Clancy about this new information. They asked him specifically about his and Millie's name being on Jack Binder's computer and also about the money that had been deposited in Binder's bank account two days before and two days after the murder. Clancy said he had no idea why Binder should have both their names on his computer and categorically denied the bank account deposits had anything to do with him. He even offered the officers access to his bank account. These accounts would confirm he'd not transferred these levels of money in a long time.

The Miami police had already tried to track the route of the money into Binder's bank account, but they had eventually given up. They traced the first deposit back as far as Panama and the second one to Switzerland. That was where the trails had come to an end.

After each of Clancy's and Sheldon's visits to the police station, newspaper reporters continued to gather outside, waiting for Sheldon to give them his latest update.

Sheldon, conscious of the presence of television cameras and newspaper reporters, always dressed for the part. In his light grey $2,000 suit, white cotton shirt and blue silk tie, he intended to be noticed. The television coverage was better than thousands of dollars spent on advertisements.

Sheldon's comments were deliberately short, one or two sentences at the most, and he never answered any of the barrage of questions he always received. Today was no exception. As he stood outside the front of the police station, he looked directly at the television cameras and simply said, "My client is innocent of all allegations made against him and continues to fully cooperate with the police inquiries. He has not been charged and continues to remain on bail. Thank you." At that, and despite the crescendo of questions, Sheldon said no more, got into the passenger seat of a waiting car and was driven away.

Gladstone had just been watching this latest television coverage and smiled at Sheldon's performance. However, his smile quickly disappeared when he started to reflect on what a complete idiot Clancy Hobbie had been.

For several days, Gladstone read all the social media gossip about Clancy and had purchased copies of the *Antiguan Observer* newspaper for any fresh information. In addition, he also studied the gossip articles and alleged insider information about Jack Binder. Gladstone was still not a happy man. If he was implicated by Clancy in any way, then, as he'd already warned Clancy before, he would tell the police all that he knew. In the meantime, he would just carry on as usual and wait to see what eventually transpired. To Oscar, and anybody else who asked him, he would continue to say that he knew absolutely nothing about the circumstances leading to Millie's death. 'None of it had anything to do with him'.

Chapter 16

Emma sat down next to Ian in their home office and watched as Ian logged on to his computer. Ian had arranged with all members of the partnership that today would be the date for the annual meeting. In addition to the general review of the previous year's business activity, he also wanted to gauge everyone's opinion as to how they saw the partnership going forward now that Yuki was stepping down.

Again, the meeting was a video conference and once all the partners had finally logged in, Ian greeted everybody and presented a summary of the partnership's activities over the past 12 months. He then went on and advised that the bank account now had a cash balance of US$278 million. All the partners were pleased with this balance and it was unanimously agreed that a 10% dividend would be paid this time, based on each individual's original contribution.

Ian, and then all the other individual partners, thanked Yuki for his valuable contribution and it was proposed that he should be repaid his initial investment plus his share of the fund's increase in value, as well as his dividend. The proposal was unanimously agreed.

At this point Yuki thanked everyone and emphasised how much he'd 'enjoyed the journey'. He was sad to be stepping down, but reminded everyone that he was older than

The Gamble

they were and wanted to enjoy his money now. He said his goodbyes, smiled, waved and switched off his computer.

Ian now raised the next item on their agenda. The next 12 months. He said that he thought the partnership had three options to consider going forward. One, the partnership could just carry on as now, but without Yuki's connections and the resultant reduced fund following Yuki's departure. Two, any of them could offer to increase their percentage by purchasing all, or part, of Yuki's share. Three, close the partnership down completely with each partner taking all of their benefits, similar to what Yuki had just done. Ian then suggested, because this was a major decision, that they should all have time to think about their personal preference. He recommended that another meeting should take place in one week's time.

Oscar then mentioned a possible fourth option. Namely to seek an additional partner, or partners, to replace Yuki's share.

There were some initial thoughts and comments about all four options but Ian emphasised that it was important for each partner to take their time before making any quick, and maybe, rash decisions. It was then finally agreed that the next meeting would take place at the same time in seven days' time. At that meeting they would then make the definitive decision on the partnership's future. There was no other business and Ian brought the meeting to a close and switched off his computer.

"So, how do you think that went?" he asked Emma, sitting back in his chair and looking directly across at his wife.

"I thought you handled it very well. Everyone has a lot to consider. With Yuki leaving, I'm sure some will think that maybe now is the right time to cash in too."

"That's my feeling. Do you think we ought to cash in as well?"

Emma smiled at Ian. "As you said to the others, Ian, we have a week to make that decision."

Following the end of the partnership's meeting, Viktor closed down his computer. He was sitting in the office at the gallery. Okay, he thought, so I have a week to make up my mind. He started to reflect on all the things that had happened since he, and initially, his father, had first decided to invest in the partnership. He had made a nice return on his investment and he'd learned quite a lot about the art market from the expertise of the others. Now, however, he wondered if he should just concentrate on continuing to develop his own client base. Getting married, and very shortly moving into their new home, was going to be a lot more demanding on his 'free' time. Lots to consider.

In Antigua, Oscar and Gladstone were sitting in Oscar's kitchen discussing the partnership options. Oscar said he was still very keen to carry on with his involvement in the partnership. Indeed, he was even thinking about increasing his investment by buying a share of Yuki's holding. Gladstone, however, was not so sure. He knew he was not getting any younger and the Clancy Hobbie situation had dampened his enthusiasm. For a few weeks he'd been thinking about relocating to Jamaica to be closer to his son's family. Becoming a grandfather had seriously changed his outlook on life and now he wondered whether it was time to finally retire himself. After all, he'd built up a much larger pension fund than he'd thought was possible before the partnership and now he also wanted to financially help his son and family. He'd listened to Yuki's explanation as to why he was leaving the partnership and, as Yuki was only two years older than him, he decided it certainly made sense to consider pulling out and enjoying his money now... before it was all too late!

Oscar was definite, but Gladstone still had much to consider.

The Gamble

In Hong Kong, May Ling was also wondering what her decision was going to be. She thought that Ian had given a big hint that maybe it was now time for the partnership to wind up their activities. Was that what she wanted? She had recently completed a lot of business with Yuki and now that supply would be drying up. Her Chinese client base was slowly increasing each month meaning she had less time to devote to the partnership. Also, Ian had often grumbled that she was always the last to reply to requests and decisions. Sometimes that was due to her presence in Beijing, but often due to overwork. Nevertheless, she knew her investment had increased substantially since the commencement of the partnership and this extra money, held in her Swiss bank account, was a very useful 'extra' on top of her main income from China and Hong Kong. This is not going to be an easy decision, she thought.

Meanwhile, in Monaco, Bob and Zoe Taylor agreed that their own business was much bigger now because of the weight of the partnership funds. It was these funds that had enabled them to buy and sell much higher value paintings than they would have been able to do in the past. However, without Yuki's access to the Singapore Freeport, Bob realised that a large portion of their normal supply chain had now ended. Going forward, he wondered if their investments would be better utilised by moving them directly to their galleries, both in Monaco and London. Their turnover may reduce slightly if they pulled out of the partnership but they would, once again, be able to keep 100% of the business profit they personally generated in Monaco.

It was three days later and Oscar had just returned to his villa from his usual early morning swim in the Caribbean Sea. Whilst he dried himself and prepared his first cup of coffee of the day, he switched on his computer and accessed the latest stories on the Antiguan news website. He nearly dropped his coffee cup, however, when he read the headlines. 'Jack Binder Killed!' He quickly sat down and carefully read through the whole report. In summary, the article stated that Jack Binder and three policemen had been surrounded by a group of about 12 men whilst Binder was being transferred from the Miami police station to the local court. In the ensuing melee, Jack Binder was shot in the head four times and died immediately at the scene. All 12 attackers had disappeared as quickly as they'd arrived. A further police report stated that this was a deliberate, and a very well organised, murder of Jack Binder. The three policemen had minor injuries but were mainly suffering from shock. The police believed the attack was solely directed at murdering Jack Binder.

Oscar just stared at the computer screen. "What the...? Oh, my goodness," he said to himself. He sipped his coffee and then read a further article which tried to tie in Jack Binder's murder with Clancy. The article was solely sensationalist and didn't add any more facts, but it did make Oscar think about Clancy. Was he behind this killing too? After all, Jack Binder was probably the only person who knew if he had a connection with Clancy or not. Now that he was dead, would this mean all possible charges would be dropped against Clancy or was there more evidence still to come?

A little later that same morning, Gladstone read the same report on his own computer and watched the brief CCTV video of the attack. He just shook his head in disbelief. He thought it all looked like a Hollywood thriller film. Surely this was not real life. What was going on? He then switched to his usual social media website and read the various comments and opinions on the situation. The general feeling was that Clancy Hobbie was a very, very lucky man!

Gladstone was making a late fruit and cereal breakfast

The Gamble

when his mobile phone rang. He checked on the phone's screen to see who the caller was. It was Oscar.

"Hi, Oscar. I guess you're ringing about Jack Binder?"

"You've heard the news then."

"Just this minute. Amazing, isn't it? Just like a Hollywood film."

"You know what this means. Clancy will be a free man."

"I guess so."

"Is that all you've got to say?" asked Oscar, a little exasperated.

"There's nothing else for me to say. It doesn't involve me as I've told you before. What I have got to say, however, is that I've made up my mind. I'm stepping away from the partnership and moving closer to my son in Jamaica."

"Oh," replied Oscar, suddenly shocked and very surprised. "Is that because of Clancy?"

"No, man," shouted Gladstone, down the phone. Then with a calmer voice he said, "Been thinking about it for a few weeks. I've decided now is the right time. I want to retire and see my granddaughter growing up."

"I see," replied Oscar. "When are you going to move?"

"As soon as possible. I spoke to the rental people yesterday and told them I want to rent out my home."

"Yesterday? Before…"

"Yes!" interrupted Gladstone, "before Jack Binder was killed."

"Well, I'm going to miss you, Gladstone. We've worked well together."

"I'm only moving to another Caribbean island, man, not to the moon. We can still be friends. Anyway, must go, things to do. What about a drink this evening, seven o'clock?"

"Yes, fine, okay," said Oscar, still a little shocked with all this latest news.

Chapter 17

Seven days after the last partnership meeting, Ian was now switching on his computer for the follow-up meeting. Whilst he was logging into the video conference link, Emma joined him in their home office. They had discussed the various options and, depending upon each of the partners' individual decisions, Ian now had four choices he was prepared to take.

Over the next five minutes, all the remaining partners also logged on to the link and Ian started to speak. He welcomed everyone back and firstly asked if anyone had any questions. There were no verbal responses so he continued and summarised the position as he currently saw it. After he'd finished, he again asked if there were any questions and did everybody understand the situation. All the partners responded this time, saying they understood.

Ian then proposed that each partner should have the opportunity to speak and say which option they preferred, or wanted to take. And, if they desired, to explain the reasons for their decision.

Over the next 30 minutes each of the partners stated which option they wanted to take and why they had come to that decision. In summary, Viktor wanted option three and to take the balance of his investment. Gladstone also

The Gamble

said option three and gave the same reasons he had given to Oscar some days earlier. Oscar said option two and declared that he was prepared to purchase Gladstone's share. May Ling said she had very mixed feelings, but her personal view was that they had all had a very successful run, so concluded by saying she preferred to vote for option three. Bob Taylor said he also preferred option three and gave his reasons.

Finally, it came to Ian, the instigator of the partnership. He looked at the votes so far and said that he would follow the majority vote and go for option three. He explained both his personal and business reasons for this decision and concluded by stating that there was only one vote for continuing the partnership. He therefore agreed the partnership should be disbanded forthwith and promised all partners would receive their share of the fund. It would be transferred to their bank accounts over the next two days.

A general discussion then ensued, which at times became a little emotional, but everyone agreed that they'd had a lot of fun and made a significant profit. They all wanted to stay in touch, but agreed the partnership was now formally dissolved.

Ian had the final word saying, "It's all been a successful adventure and I hope you have gained greater knowledge of the art world as well as a larger bank balance. Good luck to everyone and I hope we'll all keep in touch... as friends."

The meeting ended and Ian switched off the video link.

"The end of another era," pronounced Emma, with just a touch of emotion in her voice.

"Indeed, it is. At least we managed to finish on a high," replied Ian, even though he was also feeling a little emotional himself.

"We all made the right decision, Ian. With Yuki stepping aside, it wouldn't have been quite the same," said Emma, trying to be reasonable and hoping to lift a little of Ian's despondency.

"I need to chat with Oscar. He's the one who's truly disappointed. He really wanted the partnership to continue."

"Maybe give him a couple of days."

"Mmm. Okay. It's been a fabulous adventure. I know we've made a lot of money, but the freedom and the challenge… it's all been just what I wanted."

"I know, Ian," said Emma. She could feel his emotion. "We've got many more adventures still to come."

Again, Ian smiled. "Yes, Emma. Lots… I hope."

Emma stood up, leaned down and kissed Ian on his forehead. "I'll make us a cup of coffee."

When Emma had left the office, Ian remembered the letter his former boss had given him at Michael's retirement 'send off'. He'd already read it twice. He opened the top right drawer of his desk and removed and unfolded the one sheet of A4 paper. He read the contents once again. Interesting proposition, he thought. Now the partnership is all over, I think I'll give Michael a call when we get back from Monaco.

Less than two weeks later, Ian and Emma arrived at their penthouse apartment in Monaco. The weather was lovely and warm, just like they'd hoped. As soon as they'd both unpacked their cases, Ian opened the large glass doors and stepped out onto the balcony. He walked across to the railings and looked down and around the harbour area. He could feel the late afternoon sunshine warming his face and the gentle breeze ruffling his hair. There he watched the usual comings and goings of yachts and boats and people strolling along the esplanade. He took some deep breaths, sucking the fresh sea air deep into his lungs.

A couple of minutes later Emma joined him. She had a glass of cold Chablis in each hand. Ian took one of the glasses and proposed a toast. "Cheers, Emma. Here's to a relaxing and enjoyable few days."

"Cheers, Ian," replied Emma, and they both chinked their glasses.

Emma stood next to Ian against the railings and they both looked down and then out into the Mediterranean Sea. They so loved this view and discussed what was happening in the harbour and along the esplanade. Ian pointed to a large white-hulled yacht that was slowly backing away from its mooring. There was very little room to manoeuvre, but inch by inch, the yacht had eventually moved clear.

Emma laughed and said she thought the captain must be good at 'threading a camel through the eye of a needle'.

After a further ten minutes, they sat down on the two balcony chairs and placed their wine glasses on the small wooden table. On the horizon, out into the Mediterranean Sea, the sun was just beginning to set. There were no clouds to help create the perfect sunset, but they still enjoyed watching the sun slowly disappear. The end of daylight but not quite the end of the day.

"Which restaurant do you fancy tonight?" asked Ian, looking at his watch, conscious of the time.

"I don't really mind… but I think I fancy eating seafood."

"In that case we'll go to 'Pierre's Fish Bar'. It will be nice to stroll along the esplanade again."

"I had better get ready then," said Emma, standing up, collecting her wine glass and walking back into the apartment.

Ian picked up his own glass and then raised it in the air as though proffering a toast. He then whispered, "Na Zdorovie, Andrei! Thank you, my friend." Ian knew he would never ever forget Andrei. He still missed him… just like the elder brother he'd never had.

Chapter 18

It was just after 6pm in Antigua and Oscar was having a drink with his colleague, Wesley Fredericks. They were sitting on the terrace of the bar opposite Wesley's premises, the 'Shell Gallery'. Oscar was feeling sorry for himself. He'd so enjoyed the partnership and wanted to increase his investment, but that had now stopped trading and he was feeling a little lost. Also, his friend and business colleague, Gladstone, had now moved to Montego Bay in Jamaica. To top it all, the local art market had become very quiet.

"We've had spells like this before, man," explained Wesley. He took a sip of his beer. "It will pick up again soon. Maybe you need to investigate what's happening in the US, Asia and the UK."

Oscar didn't fancy investigating anything, never mind the US, or indeed, the UK. He nodded his head reluctantly and sipped his own beer. His sulky and unsmiling face said it all.

"Might be missing something big!" Wesley was trying his best to lift the spirits of his colleague.

"I'll do a bit of exploring tomorrow," replied Oscar, but thinking, maybe he would, but more likely, he wouldn't.

"Are you still happy in Antigua, man?"

"Of course," responded Oscar, positively. "It's, well... it's just the sudden change to a number of things. Otherwise, yes, I'm really happy here."

"Well, that's good. I like you Oscar, man. We've done a lot of business together and I know we'll do lots more in the future. Cheer up, man… and drink up your beer. It's my round."

Ian's earlier invitation to Bob and Zoe to take them out for a meal had been welcomed. Bob had responded saying Zoe was looking forward to meeting up with Emma once more and it would be good for him and Ian to chat again, 'face to face'. He also reported that Zoe had recently visited her parents and had obtained the four George Watts publications from her father that he wanted.

The two couples met up at a restaurant on the harbour front, just a short walk from both of their properties. Zoe and Emma talked about fashion and children, whilst Bob and Ian discussed old times at university and the current art market. However, when the subject turned to the winding up of the partnership, all four of them took part in the discussion.

"You know, Ian, it was a difficult decision to step away from the partnership. It was such a great time. We were able to expand our client base because we could trade in higher value paintings which is obviously a really important factor here in Monaco. But, of course, we weren't getting the full profit, just a percentage, and that in the end was the deciding factor."

"I know," replied Ian. "It was a difficult decision for everyone. We all had our personal reasons. Oscar, unfortunately, has taken it quite badly. I telephoned him a few days after the last meeting. The problem is, he was on his own as the rest of us had decided the partnership had run its course. It's far better to get out whilst you're ahead. Oscar's view was that we were only halfway there."

Emma now interjected. "With Yuki deciding to retire, well, that seemed to make people think a little deeper. It obviously helped Gladstone to make his decision."

"I liked Yuki," said Zoe. "He was very professional and considerate… a really nice man."

The conversation continued until they were the last group still remaining in the restaurant. Ian paid the bill and Zoe insisted Ian and Emma came back to their apartment for a 'nightcap'.

Both Ian and Emma laughed at Zoe for using a very English phrase, but they both agreed it would be a nice way to finish a lovely evening.

As they walked towards Bob and Zoe's gallery, Bob reminded Ian that he could take his father-in-law's copies of the George Watts books when he left their apartment.

It was nearly 1am when Ian and Emma returned to their penthouse apartment. They were both very tired and definitely not used to such a late evening. Ian placed the four borrowed publications on the dining table and decided he would read them sometime tomorrow.

Next morning, Ian woke up much later than usual. Emma was still fast asleep, so Ian quietly crept out of bed and into the bathroom. Twenty minutes later, he was sitting on the balcony with a mug of tea reading the first of the George Watts publications. It was a biography about Watts, but with an emphasis on his style of painting. Unfortunately, Ian could not find any reference or photograph connected with his own painting, or the name, 'Sir Edgar Brookfield'. He was just about to pick up the second book, when Emma appeared on the balcony in her dressing gown.

"Ah, so you're out here," said Emma, shielding her eyes from the sun. "It's lovely and warm again."

"Mmm, just a nice temperature," replied Ian, putting down the book and standing up. "Do you want a cup of tea?"

"Not at the moment. I'm just going to have a shower."

They both walked back into the apartment. Emma went off to the bedroom and Ian helped himself to another mug of tea. He then wandered back out onto the balcony and picked up the second book. He quickly established that this publication concentrated on the various individuals who'd had their portraits painted by Watts. As a result, he became excited at the prospect of finally finding some reference to Sir Edgar. However, after about five minutes of checking both the index and by flicking through some of the pages, he still couldn't find anything useful. He was just about to give up on this book when, suddenly, on page 84, there it was! The picture of Sir Edgar. A colour photograph of his painting. Ian immediately read the details written underneath the picture, but quickly became confused. The reference stated that the picture was not of Sir Edgar, but a portrait of 'Lord Rye and Rother'!

Well, well, well, thought Ian. Now what have we got here? Lord Rye? He quickly put this book down and flicked through the pages of the third publication. But no, there was no reference to either Sir Edgar Brookfield or Lord Rye. He disappointedly cast that book aside and picked up the fourth one. Quickly scanning the index, he established there was again no Sir Edgar, but, happily, there was a reference to Lord Rye. It was located on page 125, according to the index, so Ian eagerly turned over the pages and there he found a black and white photograph of his painting, but again, the written details below the picture referred to Lord Rye and Rother.

Ian put the book down and went into the apartment. He quickly walked over to the study area and sat down at the desk. He opened the lid of his laptop computer and after signing in, he googled 'Lord Rye and Rother' and 'George Watts'. Immediately a number of websites appeared so he clicked on the first one. He anxiously read the contents and then tried another suggested website. Again, he read the contents. Finally, he leaned back in his chair and stared at the far wall… thinking and then smiling.

It was at this moment that Emma joined him. "So, you've moved in here now. I was just about to join you on the balcony."

"Emma, you're not going to believe this." Ian pointed to the screen of his computer.

Emma sat down next to Ian and he explained his findings from the morning's investigations.

When Ian had finished, Emma expressed some surprise. "So, the school's painting was not of Sir Edgar after all. Miss Wardley's going to be in for a very big surprise."

"I know, but the best thing is, it looks as though my hunch was right. It was painted by George Watts all along. Hopefully that means it still could be worth somewhere between one and two million pounds."

"Wow! Well done you," exclaimed Emma.

"Well, we're not completely there yet, of course. I still need to prove that the painting is the original and not just a very good copy."

"What about its provenance?" asked Emma, thinking about Ian's comment.

"Quite," responded Ian. "We have just over the last 100 years covered. It has, as you know, been the property of the school during that time. It's now vitally important that we find out the full history, particularly what happened to it before it was donated to the school. This could still all be very tricky."

Emma looked at Ian and nodded. She'd already decided this would be her personal challenge once they'd arrived back in the UK.

Chapter 19

Penny and Viktor were checking and double checking all the arrangements for their wedding. Penny's mother, meanwhile, was still irritating Viktor. On several occasions he'd had to bite his lip rather than explode in frustration at his future mother-in-law's comments. Despite Viktor assuring her, several times each week, that the jobs he had been delegated with were either completed or fully in hand, she still insisted on checking what he'd actually done.

Penny, feeling she was placed 'between a rock and a hard place', explained to Viktor that her mother was like that with everyone. Just try to keep calm.

That was easier said than done, thought Viktor. Especially as he, at the same time, was trying to run an art gallery, organise the honeymoon and finalise the purchase of their new home.

Penny, too, was still feeling the pressure. Besides her own wishes for a really special wedding, there were the challenges of keeping her mother and Viktor apart and also a new job running a department at work – now under the scrutiny of the new Managing Director, Jonathan Northgate. Northgate had already upset a number of Sotheby's senior staff and his attitude was making Penny's decision on her future career all the easier. Once the wedding was over, she would certainly be reviewing all of her options.

When Ian and Emma arrived back in the UK, Emma set about the task of identifying the full provenance of the painting of Lord Rye. She had already told Ian that she wanted to investigate the history of the painting all by herself. Ian was happy for her to do so and encouraged her in the admirable quest. As a result, Emma was now spending a significant amount of her time on the internet and had very quickly established some interesting facts about Lord Rye, including a connection with Sir Edgar. Both men had apparently worked in South Africa and Rhodesia at about the same time.

Lord Rye, she discovered, was originally a mining expert and made his fortune investing in the diamond industry. However, he subsequently sold all his shares when he had to return to Britain for medical reasons. One of the purchasers of Lord Rye's shares was none other than Sir Edgar!

Whilst in South Africa, Lord Rye was simply known as Gordon Carter from Seaford in East Sussex. However, when he returned to the UK, the British government recognised his contribution to the development of the diamond industry and awarded him with a life peerage of the realm and the title of 'Lord'. It was Gordon's wish that he should be known as 'Lord Rye and Rother', as Rye was where his mother was born.

Emma's investigations unearthed some other interesting facts too. Sir Edgar and Lord Rye's paths crossed several times whilst they were in Africa and, gradually, they became close colleagues. When Lord Rye had to return to England, he and Sir Edgar still kept in touch. Indeed, when Sir Edgar returned to the UK on his infrequent visits, they sometimes met up at Lord Rye's club in Pall Mall. Lord Rye was always keen to hear what was happening back in South Africa. Unfortunately, two days after their last meeting Lord Rye died. Sir Edgar was one of the pall-bearers at his friend's funeral.

The Gamble

Okay, thought Emma, that establishes who Lord Rye was and his loose connection with Sir Edgar, but it doesn't take me any closer to the painting's early history. I think this is going to be a time-consuming exercise.

Ian, meanwhile, had taken the original painting of 'Lord Rye' to the Courtauld Institute of Art for forensic investigation. He was promised the results would be ready in approximately ten days' time.

School had restarted for Robert after the holiday break and Emma had taken the opportunity to make an appointment to speak with Miss Wardley before she collected Robert that afternoon. When she met with the headmistress, Emma explained Ian's recent findings, namely that the supposed Sir Edgar Brookfield picture was, in fact, a portrait of Lord Rye.

Miss Wardley was flabbergasted and looked up at the copy now hanging above her desk. "This was supposed to be a copy painting of the original Sir Edgar Brookfield portrait that was donated to the school nearly a hundred years ago. So where's the correct Sir Edgar Brookfield portrait now?" asked Miss Wardley, somewhat dispirited and confused.

"We don't really know right now," replied Emma. "We don't even know if a painting of Sir Edgar actually exists. That's partly why I'm here today. I'm hoping you may have some old original records from the time the painting was donated to the school. I'm trying to unravel the mystery as to why the original painting of Lord Rye somehow, over time, became Sir Edgar Brookfield."

Miss Wardley sat back in her chair. "We do have some old papers in the basement, but I really cannot tell you if any directly relate to Sir Edgar… sorry, Lord Rye… or whatever the name of the painting is. The best I can offer is for you and Mrs. Bailey to have a look."

"Thank you," responded Emma. However, she did have

an idea. "I wonder if I could have a look tomorrow after I've dropped Robert here at school?"

"That should be fine. I'll speak to Mrs. Bailey after this meeting. Should we say 9.15?"

Emma rose from her seat. "Thank you again. I'll be here then."

At 9.20am, the following morning, Mrs. Bailey escorted Emma along a long corridor, through an old side door and down some worn and uneven wooden stairs. They eventually entered the dark and gloomy basement. The air was cold and musty, but not as damp as Emma was expecting. Cobwebs were hanging against a small dirty window. This was the only window in the basement so its light only lit up a small portion of the room.

Standing in the doorway, Emma could see it was a large, drab room and even when Mrs. Bailey pressed the wall light switch, the light level hardly improved as there was only one low-wattage light bulb that was illuminated.

"I think the files you're looking for are over there in that metal box," suggested Mrs. Bailey pointing to a black metal box. It was lying on a shelf about two metres away from them. "Be careful. Some of these boxes have been here for ages. Touch them and they might fall over."

"I should have brought a torch," said Emma, peering through the gloom and brushing a cobweb away from her face.

Mrs. Bailey picked up the box and walked towards an old dusty table. Emma gave her a hand. "Let's put the box on here, under the light." She blew a cloud of dust from the box's lid. "As you can see, none of us come down here very often. I hope you're not frightened of spiders. There's a big black one over there." Mrs. Bailey pointed to a cobweb on the far wall.

The Gamble

"Fortunately, no," responded Emma with a wary smile. "But they aren't one of my favourite creatures either."

Mrs. Bailey smiled and lifted the box's lid. Inside there were some old folders, small cardboard boxes and a number of envelopes. Mrs. Bailey lifted some of the contents and handed them to Emma. Emma flicked through each item looking for any clue that would lead her to either Lord Rye or Sir Edgar Brookfield.

"Ah, ha!" announced Emma. She was looking at a large brown envelope with writing on the front. She angled the envelope so there was slightly more light shining on the faded writing.

Sir Edgar Brookfield.
Donated paintings, documents and associated paperwork

"I think this might be what you're looking for," said Mrs. Bailey

Emma placed the large brown envelope on the table and helped Mrs. Bailey to put all the other files and papers back into the metal box. After the lid was closed, they both lifted the box back into its original position on the shelf.

"Pick up that envelope and we'll go back to my room," said Mrs. Bailey. "The papers will be easier to read there… and it'll be a bit cleaner and warmer too." She was also eager to get out of this cold, dusty and uninviting room.

"That's fine with me," replied Emma, keen to leave this 'dungeon' as well. She grabbed the brown envelope and followed Mrs. Bailey back towards the door.

Five minutes later they were both back in the headmistress's outer office. They sat at Mrs. Bailey's desk and looked through the contents of the envelope. After about ten minutes Emma asked if she could take the papers home as Ian would have a better idea of what was relevant to their search.

Mrs. Bailey said that was fine and Emma promised to bring the envelope and its contents back to the school the following morning.

Later that afternoon, Ian and Emma sat in their home office and were reading through every item and document found in the envelope. One notebook, Emma was reading, contained a listing of all the pictures donated by Sir Edgar to the school. Each picture's entry recorded its title, artist's name and a brief description of its composition. The so-called Sir Edgar Brookfield portrait was listed as being painted by William Arthur Breakspeare.

After about another 30 minutes, a disappointed Emma was returning the papers back into the envelope, however, a handwritten note suddenly caught Ian's eye. He picked it up and slowly read the note's contents. His face began to develop a knowing smile.

"Something interesting?" asked Emma, hopefully.

"It could be," said Ian. He stood up and went over to their printer, which also included a photocopying function. He placed the handwritten note onto the glass screen and made two photocopies. He handed the original back to Emma to put in the envelope and also one of the copies for her to read for herself.

"What have you found?" asked Emma, looking down at her photocopy. She was curious to find out what she'd missed.

Ian explained what he was thinking.

"Of course!" exclaimed Emma. Suddenly she'd regained all her original enthusiasm. "I'll follow that up straight away."

Chapter 20

Oscar had returned from his early morning swim. He switched on the kettle for his breakfast coffee and read the news headlines on his computer.

Not surprisingly, the news programme was still dedicating coverage time to Clancy Hobbie and the late Jack Binder. The main news this morning, however, was that Clancy was no longer on bail. All potential charges against Clancy had been dropped late yesterday afternoon. The police announced they were no longer pursuing their enquiries into Millie's death, the inference being that the late Mr. Binder was the killer of Millie Hobbie and there was no other provable connection with Clancy.

The news report then switched to yesterday's television coverage outside the St John's police station. There, standing side by side, were Sheldon and Clancy facing the television cameras and a number of newspaper reporters. This time Sheldon was dressed in a light blue $2,000 suit. He'd previously insisted that Clancy should be similarly smartly attired. Clancy had also been told by Sheldon that under <u>no</u> circumstances should he say <u>anything</u>. Not one word, no matter what questions were thrown at him. He should just smile at the television cameras and leave all the talking to him.

Sheldon raised his right hand to try to stop the barrage of questions. Once there was relative quiet, Sheldon gave his usual big smile and said his piece. "This is a great day for justice, my friends. As you know, my client has consistently protested his innocence. Now, I'm pleased to announce, the police have dropped all possible charges. My client has also been released from all his bail conditions. I'm sure you'll all agree with me that this is indeed a very special day. Thank you."

After Sheldon's speech, and, despite the usual bombardment of more questions from the reporters, Sheldon said no more and both he and Clancy climbed into the rear seats of a waiting large Mercedes car. They were driven away at speed.

"Thank you, man," said Clancy, relaxing back into the leather seating. "You were brilliant."

"You, my friend," replied Sheldon, with a stern face and more serious tone to his voice, "is one very, very lucky bastard!"

When the news report changed to discussing Antigua's next cricket match, Oscar shook his head and switched off his computer. He now poured the hot water into his mug and finally made his coffee. Picking up his mug, he walked outside onto his patio and sat down on his lounger. He couldn't help but think that there were two very fortunate men living in the Caribbean. One now back in his large mansion in Antigua and one who had recently moved to a new home in Montego Bay, Jamaica.

To everyone's delight, Penny and Viktor's wedding day was a complete success. The weather had been warm and sunny, the church service first rate and the reception's food and service excellent. Lots of hard work had been justly rewarded.

The Gamble

Ian, especially, felt very special to be Penny's temporary father for the day. Even Penny's mother was able to find time for a tear and a smile, particularly when she saw Penny walking down the aisle on Ian's arm. She wished it could have been her late husband, George. He would have been so proud to see what a beautiful woman his daughter had grown up to be.

Viktor's parents found some of the proceedings a little different from the Russian Orthodox Church ceremonies they'd been used to before. However, even they did admit later that they'd both thoroughly enjoyed the day. They were very proud of their son and agreed Penny would be an excellent wife.

Penny and Viktor left the reception party at 6.45pm to start their honeymoon. Penny was still unaware of what Viktor had arranged but, as she was so happy, she didn't really mind what he had planned. The only clue that Viktor did give her was that she should pack clothes suitable for a tropical beach holiday… and plenty of bikinis!

Bob and Zoe Taylor had been invited to the wedding and Ian and Emma had insisted they stayed with them in Esher for a few days. Just after the happy couple had left the party, Emma and Zoe suggested they leave as well, especially as Bob and Zoe's flight back to Nice was leaving Gatwick at 11.02am the next morning.

Emma was driving her car away from the party and the four of them discussed the wedding and a special mention was made of Ian's performance. Bob teasingly said it was good practice for Ian's own daughter. Emma quickly reminded him that Robert was a boy, but Zoe then laughed and said, "Surely you're not going to stop at just one!"

Once the ladies had gone to bed, Ian poured two glasses of his 25-year-old malt whisky for Bob and himself to enjoy.

They sat down and began to talk about the former partnership and the world of art in general. This reminded Ian that he still had the Watts publications Bob had lent him.

"Those books about Watts were excellent," said Ian. "Do you want to take them back with you?"

"No. Keep them for as long as you like. My father-in-law has no real use for them now," replied Bob. "Have they helped to solve your problem?"

Ian relayed to Bob the whole story and where he and Emma currently were with their investigations.

"So, you may have a million-pound painting. Well done you."

"I've still got the problem of establishing the early provenance, before 1912, and I'm hoping for positive news from the Courtauld Institute in the next couple of days," replied Ian.

Ten minutes later, they'd both finished their whiskies and decided it was time for bed. Ian reminded Bob that he would take him and Zoe to the airport. Breakfast would be about 6.30am.

Whilst Ian was in the bathroom, he thought about the handwritten note he had photocopied. He had deliberately excluded this bit of information from the story he'd told Bob. He wanted Emma to explore the extra details that the note had revealed before sharing them with a much wider audience.

Chapter 21

Whilst Ian drove Bob and Zoe to Gatwick airport, Emma had dropped Robert off at his friend Arthur's house. Robert and Arthur had formed a good friendship at Brookfield School and gradually established they had a number of similar interests outside of school as well. About every three weeks, one of them would be invited to the other's house for the day. Today it was Robert's turn to visit Arthur's home. He lived about 30 miles away, so Emma had to make an early start, straight after breakfast, to make Robert's day worthwhile.

When Emma arrived home, she immediately went into the home office and collected the photocopy of the handwritten note from her desk drawer. She sat at her desk and started to make some notes:

Check the address and names on the note

Trace the painting back to Watts

Try to identify and follow the family tree

Make further checks that the painting is really of Lord Rye / Gordon Carter

Try and find any paintings / pictures of Sir Edgar Brookfield.

From the photocopy she had an address, two names and a date. The address was in South London and the names were Julian Stockholm and Victoria Watson. The date was the 2nd February 1912. Tomorrow, she planned to visit the address in South London. She had to start somewhere.

With the aid of her London A-Z street map and the car's satnav, Emma pulled up outside a large, white-painted Georgian House at 11.30am. She double checked the address. Yes, it was the correct property. She parked her car in the street and entered the long gravel driveway. Looking around her she saw more of the front of the house. Mmm, she thought, this has obviously seen better days. She carried on walking towards the front door and noticed the front garden was very spacious and contained many different rose trees and large shrubs. Many were currently in flower. Very nice, she thought.

"Hello. Can I help you?"

Emma jumped at the sound of the voice and looked all around her. She eventually spotted an elderly gentleman, probably in his late 70s, emerging from behind a large hydrangea bush. He was obviously dressed for gardening and had a pair of secateurs in his hand. She walked towards him.

"Hello," she said, still trying to recover from the surprise. "I'm sorry to bother you, but I'm trying to find out any information about the people who lived in this house in 1912. Sorry, my name is Emma Caxton."

"Hello, Emma Caxton. My name's John Watson," responded the elderly gentleman. "Now, you'd better explain why you want to know that information."

Emma explained that she was trying to find out about the history of a painting which had been donated by a Julian Stockholm to a school in 1912. She understood he lived in this house at that time.

"Indeed. Well, young lady, you are speaking to the right person. Julian was my grandmother's brother-in-law."

"Oh!" said Emma, somewhat surprised.

The Gamble

John Watson smiled. "Fancy a cup of tea? My wife should have brewed one by now."

"Thank you. That would be very nice," responded Emma, who then followed Mr. Watson as he walked around the side of the house and into a large conservatory. There she was introduced to an elderly lady putting a tray containing two cups of tea on a small table.

"Georgie, this is Emma Caxton. She wants to know about my grandmother's sister and husband."

"Oh," said Georgie, looking suspiciously at Emma. "Would you like a cup of tea?"

"If it's no trouble, yes please," replied Emma, a little nervously. She thought Georgie must be about the same age as John.

"You take those two cups and I'll fetch a separate cup and saucer for me," said Georgie, turning and wandering back towards what Emma assumed was the kitchen.

"Do sit down, Emma. Can I call you Emma? Surnames are so formal."

"Emma is fine... John," she replied, sitting down on a large, colonial-style wicker chair.

John passed her a cup and saucer and sat down himself. At this point Georgie reappeared carrying another cup and saucer. She sat down next to her husband on a similar, but much larger, wicker chair. It certainly had room for two people, if not three, thought Emma.

Emma was hoping John would start the conversation.

"So how did you find us? Is it Mrs. Caxton?" asked Georgie, before John had a chance to speak.

Emma said, "Yes, it is Mrs. Caxton." She then summarised how she, and her husband, had bought a painting that had previously been donated by Julian Stockholm, and possibly a Victoria Watson, to Brookfield School in 1912. She explained that the school had some papers that stated

Mr. Stockholm was living at this address and that she was trying to trace the painting's history before 1912. "The records say it's a portrait of Sir Edgar Brookfield but we think it could be a portrait of Lord Rye."

"Confusing, but interesting," said John, who then looked at his wife.

"Is this painting valuable?" asked Georgie.

Emma was taking an opportunity to sip her tea. When she put her cup back on its saucer she said, "It could be. But without the full history of the painting, we don't really know."

John was still looking at his wife but, when she didn't say any more, he began to speak. "Our family tree is a little complicated. Sir Edgar had two daughters, Victoria, my grandmother, and Margaret. Victoria married Henry Watson and Margaret married Julian Stockholm. What I do know is that when my great-grandfather died, neither Victoria, nor Margaret, were interested in great-grandfather's painting collection. They sold a few of his more valuable paintings and, as per Sir Edgar's instructions, the rest were donated to Brookfield School. Apparently, Sir Edgar had specifically listed which paintings should go to the school. He was responsible for establishing the school, you know, hence its name."

"I see," said Emma, trying desperately to remember these details. She wished now that she'd brought note paper and a pen. "Do you happen to know if there are any old records dating back to the time when Sir Edgar purchased his paintings?"

John considered the question and then said, "My sister, Julie, may know. She has a lot of the history relating to our family tree. She may have something."

"Do you think I could speak with her?" asked Emma, more in hope than expectation.

"She lives in Worthing. I can give you her telephone number. I'll tell her to expect a call from you."

The Gamble

"You are very kind, Mr. Watson. That would be so helpful."

John stood up and walked out of the room. Emma and Georgie looked at each other, but then Emma broke the silence by saying, "You have a beautiful house and garden."

"It's too big, and far too much hard work now, but John…"

"Here we are," interrupted John. "I've written Julie's number on this piece of paper." He handed it to Emma. "Her surname is Williams. Married a Welsh chap."

Emma knew she had taken up too much of their time and so, after sipping a little more of her tea, she stood up. "Thank you, both, for the tea and the information. You have been extremely kind. I must go now. I've taken up far too much of your time already."

"I'll show you out, Emma," said John, leading her out of the conservatory and into the back garden.

Emma smiled at Georgie, but did not receive a similar response. She followed John back around the side of the house and onto the driveway. When John stopped, Emma once again smiled and said thank you.

"Have you travelled here by car?" asked John, who could see there was no vehicle in the driveway.

"Yes," replied Emma. "I left it parked at the side of the road."

John nodded and smiled at Emma but then glanced up at the house before turning back to face her. "You've made my day, young lady. It's not very often nowadays that I get the chance to talk to such an attractive woman."

Emma smiled and slightly blushed. "You are a lovely man, John. Goodbye… and thank you." Emma shook his hand, turned and started to walk along the driveway.

John watched her walk away with a sad smile on his face, but then whispered quietly to himself, "Goodbye, Emma."

Chapter 22

When Emma got back into her car, she remembered there were three sheets of old photocopied maps in the glove compartment. She removed one of the sheets and then found a ballpoint pen from her handbag. She turned the sheet over to the blank side and quickly wrote down as many of the facts she could remember from the meeting. She also drew a sketch of a family tree and noted the names from Sir Edgar down to John Watson. Because of the confusing changes in surnames since Brookfield, she kept having to swap people's places on some of the branches. Eventually she was satisfied that all the relevant facts had been written down. At least she hoped so.

Emma folded the sheet of paper and placed it, and the pen, into her handbag. She sat back and pondered on what she thought she'd achieved. Although she felt she'd not really progressed any further with Lord Rye, she did now feel she was getting closer to Sir Edgar. Maybe after talking to Julie Williams, she might find out a closer connection to Lord Rye.

As she started the car's engine, she made a mental note to make sure, in the future, that she carried a notebook in her handbag.

Later that evening, Emma explained to Ian what she'd

The Gamble

found out. Ian laughed when Emma mentioned John's compliment just before she left their premises.

"The man certainly has good taste. Cheeky, but good taste," replied Ian. He already knew his wife was very attractive. "So, what are your plans now?"

"I'm going to telephone John's sister tomorrow morning. I hope she'll let me visit her and discuss the family's history," replied Emma. That seemed to her to be the most logical next step.

"Sometimes these things involve a lot of leg work. Mind you, I've always found the detective work quite interesting. You never know what you're going to uncover."

Next morning, after dropping Robert off at school, Emma sat in her car and used her mobile phone to telephone Julie Williams. Unfortunately, there was no answer. She therefore decided to do the shopping she'd planned instead. She would ring Mrs. Williams again later.

It was just after 2.30pm when Emma redialled Julie Williams' telephone number. This time she did get an answer. Emma started to explain who she was but Mrs. Williams interrupted and said, "Yes, hello, Mrs. Caxton. My brother telephoned me to say you would be ringing. I gather you're looking for information about our family."

"Yes, that's right. Mainly about Sir Edgar Brookfield, and any connection he had with Lord Rye and Rother. I was also wondering if you had any information about Sir Edgar's painting collection?" asked Emma, hopefully.

"Oh, yes. Lots," she replied. "Are you interested in any particular painting?"

"Yes. Two actually," she said, excitedly. "A portrait of Lord Rye, painted by George Watts, and a portrait of Sir Edgar Brookfield."

"Do you want to visit me and I can then show you what details I have?"

"That would be wonderful… if you don't mind," replied Emma. This was going much better than she dared to hope.

"Thursday morning at about eleven o'clock would be best for me," suggested Mrs. Williams.

"That's fine with me too. Could you give me your address please?"

Mrs. Williams gave Emma her full address and said she looked forward to meeting her on Thursday.

Emma put down the telephone and shouted out, "Yes!"

Later that afternoon, Ian returned home from collecting his Lord Rye painting from the Courtauld Institute of Art. The Institute had completed their forensic work and, in summary, they said that the picture could well have been painted by George Watts. It was his style and the palette of paint colours matched the paints Watts had used on other similar paintings towards the end of the 19th century.

Ian was pleased, but not surprised, with the Institute's findings, but it was still excellent news to get such professional support. Mind, he still didn't really understand why the latest catalogue raisonné of Watts' work didn't include the Lord Rye painting, especially when the older publications did. What had happened that made the experts drop the painting… and why?

Emma arrived outside the Worthing address of Mrs. Julie Williams. She looked at her watch. It said 10.46. As she had a few minutes to spare, she checked she had her new notebook, pens and that her mobile phone was fully charged – just in case there were any useful documents she could photograph. Satisfied all these items were in her handbag, she then checked her hair and makeup in the rear view mirror.

Pushing open the driver's door, she stepped out of her car and onto the pavement. Immediately she noticed the

The Gamble

cooling sea breeze, which was taking the edge off an otherwise warm and sunny day.

Emma glanced along the quiet avenue and looked up at the surrounding properties. Most were substantial, probably Georgian, detached properties. It was obviously one of the better areas of Worthing, thought Emma. At 10.55, she pressed the front doorbell.

Mrs. Williams opened the door almost immediately. She was obviously a much younger sister to John, and greeted Emma with a welcoming smile. After exchanging introductions and greetings, Emma was invited into the lounge and Mrs. Williams pointed to the sofa for Emma to sit on.

"First things first," said Mrs. Williams, still standing. "Would you like a cup of tea? The kettle's just boiled."

"That would be lovely, thank you," replied Emma.

Mrs. Williams smiled and left the room. Emma looked all around her. It was a very large room and the decor and furniture were slightly old fashioned. Still, she thought, it was all very tidy and felt warm and cosy.

Mrs. Williams returned with a tray containing two cups of tea and a small selection of biscuits. She put one of the cups on a small oak table next to Emma.

"We'll have our tea first and then I'll show you what I've found."

Emma smiled and nodded. "Thank you."

Whilst their teas cooled to a drinking temperature, the two ladies chatted, firstly about general matters and then Emma explained why she was looking for information about the two pictures.

"Have you finished your tea, my dear?"

"Yes, thank you," replied Emma. She put the cup and saucer back on the oak table.

"In that case we'll go through to the dining room. My papers are spread out on the table."

Emma followed Mrs. Williams into the hallway and then into the dining room. It was another large room. Again, slightly old fashioned, but once more, there was the cosy feel. A nice setting for a relaxed and convivial dinner party, she thought.

On the table there were many folders, files and photo albums. Emma just stared and wondered where Mrs. Williams was going to start.

"Now then, this is the main folder relating to Sir Edgar." Mrs. Williams opened the lid of a blue box folder. Inside there were various papers, three files and two notebooks. "I think this book may give us a good start." She passed an old, red notebook towards Emma.

Emma opened it carefully. Gently turning the old pages, she immediately realised that it was a comprehensive inventory relating to Sir Edgar's art collection. Oh, wow, she thought. This could be the jackpot!

"As you can see, Sir Edgar was quite meticulous."

Emma nodded enthusiastically and gently turned more pages. Each entry was in date order according to when the painting was purchased. It then listed the name of the painting, the artist, who the painting was purchased from and the price paid. Some entries were crossed through in red ink, indicating that the painting had been sold, and a red sale price was written above the original purchase price. Sometimes the sale price was for substantially more than the purchase price, but others showed a loss. It was a fascinating historical record. Emma carried on turning the pages. Suddenly she stopped at the entry which stated:

28/2/1898 'Lord Rye and Rother', portrait, unsigned, G. Watts. Jackson and Son. £16 5s 6d.

It was not crossed through with red ink.

"Mrs. Williams, would it be alright if I took some photographs, please?" asked Emma.

The Gamble

"Of course, my dear. There's nothing confidential here."

Emma removed her mobile phone from her handbag and took two photographs of the entry.

She carried on gently turning the pages but, by the time she got to the last entry, she hadn't found any reference to Sir Edgar Brookfield.

Mrs. Williams lifted out another file and handed it towards Emma. "These papers in here are some of the purchase receipts."

Emma looked carefully at each receipt, but there was nothing relating to the Lord Rye painting nor was there anything relating to Sir Edgar Brookfield's portrait either.

"Is there anything else relating to the painting collection?" asked Emma, a little more desperate this time.

Mrs. Williams passed Emma the other notebook. "This is an inventory of the items that were donated to Brookfield School by my grandmother, Victoria Watson and Margaret's husband, Julian Stockholm."

Once again, the record was meticulous. Emma turned to the section titled 'Paintings'.

Running down the two pages, she immediately spotted *'Lord Rye and Rother', a portrait.* Then on the second page, the last but one item, *'Sir Edgar Brookfield', a portrait.*

Emma took a photograph of these two pages and stood back. "This doesn't really make sense," said Emma, standing back up to her full height. She looked across to Mrs. Williams with a confused look on her face. "Sir Edgar's name appears on the inventory of paintings donated to the school, but not on his painting collection inventory."

"I'm sorry, my dear, but that's all I have concerning Sir Edgar's paintings."

Chapter 23

When Emma arrived home, Ian had already collected Robert from school. Robert was now in his room doing his school homework and Ian was in the home office looking at his computer screen. He heard Emma's car arrive in the driveway so got up to greet her when she entered the hallway.

"How did it go?" asked Ian, who then gave Emma a gentle welcome home kiss.

"I'm not sure. I've got some interesting news, but also some extra queries," replied Emma, taking off her jacket and changing her shoes.

"I've just made a cafetiere of coffee. Let's go into the kitchen and you can tell me all the details."

Over the next 15 minutes, Ian made Emma a mug of coffee and Emma explained all her findings.

"Well, that's great news about Lord Rye. We need to check up on the Jackson and Son connection. They could be the agents Watts used to sell his paintings. I think we're nearly there!"

"But what about Sir Edgar?" asked Emma, after finishing the last of her coffee.

"To be honest, I'm not that bothered," replied Ian. "There's obviously been a mix up somewhere in the past."

The Gamble

"But the school, they've got a copy painting of Lord Rye on display, thinking it's Sir Edgar. I did tell Miss Wardley that, so the school does already know, but I don't think we can just wash our hands of that situation, Ian," replied Emma firmly. "According to the information I found out today, a portrait of Sir Edgar was definitely donated to the school, but it was not part of Sir Edgar's collection. So, where did it come from and where is it now?"

"If you want to carry on your detective work on Sir Edgar, then fine. In the meantime, I'll check out Jackson and Son," replied Ian. He'd decided the priority was to complete the provenance for 'Lord Rye and Rother'. After all, that was where the money was going to be.

Emma said she was still determined to get to the bottom of the Sir Edgar mystery.

The next morning Emma parked her car in the school's visitors car park and followed Robert towards the main school building. She wanted to speak to Mrs. Bailey and was carrying a copy of Ian's valuation.

She followed Robert as he pushed open the entrance door and went upstairs to the headmistress's outer office. She knocked on the door and walked in. Mrs. Bailey was sitting at her desk, but immediately stood up when she saw Emma enter the room.

"Hello, Mrs. Caxton. Can I help you?"

"Hello," replied Emma. "I would like to talk to you about the school's painting collection."

"Indeed. In that case you'd better sit down."

Emma sat opposite Mrs. Bailey, who had now returned to sitting on her own chair. Emma explained that she'd found out some more information about Sir Edgar Brookfield and had an idea where his original portrait painting might be.

"I see," replied Mrs. Bailey, now very intrigued.

"As you're probably aware, my husband has now

established that the original painting hanging previously in Miss Wardley's office was not that of Sir Edgar Brookfield. That got me thinking. Has that painting been hanging there since 1912?"

"As far as I know, that's right," replied Mrs. Bailey.

Emma continued. "So, in that time people have just assumed, because it had been hanging on the wall all those years, then it must be Sir Edgar."

Mrs. Bailey nodded. "I guess so."

"Well, I now know for certain that a painting of Sir Edgar was donated to the school, but the real question is, which portrait painting in the school's collection is actually the one of Sir Edgar?"

"Oh, I see. So, you think one of the other paintings could be the correct portrait of Sir Edgar."

"That's my thinking," replied Emma. "I've got here a copy of the valuation Ian completed for the school, so what I would like to do is check this list off against all the other portraits donated in 1912. My guess is that there is one extra painting in the building somewhere."

"But shouldn't the valuation have identified that one?"

"My husband said that when you and he toured the building, he called out the painting's name and you showed him which one it was."

"That's right."

"So, in fact, you did not necessarily show him every painting, just those that he asked about."

Mrs. Bailey thought for a moment. "Yes, that's probably true. Oh, how stupid of me."

"No, no," replied Emma. "You did exactly what my husband asked. Nothing stupid about that. What my husband didn't ask, however, was were there any other paintings <u>not</u> included on the valuation. So, my question now is… are there?"

The Gamble

"To be honest, Mrs. Caxton, I'm not sure. I don't really know. What I do know is I showed Mr. Caxton every painting I knew about."

"I was wondering if we could have another look and check?" asked Emma, hopefully.

Viktor and Penny had just begun their second week of married life. After flying out of Heathrow airport, following the wedding reception, they had initially enjoyed a brief three-day stopover in Dubai. Then they flew on to, and were now properly honeymooning in, the wonderful archipelago of the Maldives. Their hotel, a small, all-inclusive island resort, was the only hotel on the tiny, sun-drenched atoll. The island boasted powder-sand beaches, lush coconut trees and was fringed by 40 charming water-sited bungalows. Their 'room' was one of the lovely water bungalows, located about 30 metres out into the Indian Ocean and sitting on several pairs of stilts. All the water bungalows were linked to the island by a single elevated wooden walkway. Not the easiest passage to navigate after too many cocktails!

Directly from their balcony they could step down immediately into the warm and crystal-clear water. This they did almost every morning to snorkel and swim out to the nearby coral reef. There, they found the reef teeming with multi-coloured fish of all shapes and sizes. Snorkelling around the reef was their usual morning activity, the rest of the day being spent sunbathing and reading, only interrupted by mealtimes and Penny taking full advantage of the excellent Balinese-style spa facilities.

It was 9.30pm and they were just returning to their bungalow from a meticulously prepared barbeque on the beach served with true Maldivian hospitality. There was the usual wide selection of delicious food to choose from and all complemented by traditional Maldivian Boduberu music.

They'd been dancing with two other honeymooning couples under a wonderful, clear, starlit sky. Now they'd soon be getting ready to go to bed and prepare for another early morning start tomorrow… and to begin their usual daily leisure activities all over again.

When they entered their property, Penny went to the bathroom, whilst Viktor walked through the main room and out onto the balcony located at the rear of the water bungalow. He stood and looked out across the Indian Ocean. He watched as the moonlit waves gently caressed the coral reef some 20 metres away. The sea breeze had slightly increased and Viktor was enjoying the cooling effect on his face.

Suddenly Viktor felt Penny's presence. She'd walked up from behind him and stood at his side. She gently grasped Viktor's left hand and stared out at the same view.

"This is a seriously wonderful place, Vic," whispered Penny, who then rested her head on Viktor's shoulder.

"Yes, it is," sighed Viktor. "A true paradise."

They both stood in silence and were mesmerised by the sound of the rhythmic waves gently hitting the wooden stilts under the bungalow.

Penny eventually spoke in a hushed tone. "Are you happy?"

Viktor suddenly stood away and looked at Penny a little stunned. "What sort of question is that? Of course, I'm happy. I can't believe how lucky I am. I'm on my honeymoon with the loveliest woman in the world and we're sharing this wonderful experience together, in paradise."

Penny smiled, leaned over and gave Viktor a sensuous kiss. After a few seconds, she slowly pulled away and looked deeply into her husband's green eyes. "I hope you're not too tired, because I think we ought to go to bed!"

Chapter 24

Ian was searching the internet for any information about a company called 'Jackson and son', operating around the time of the 28th February 1898. That was the date written in Sir Edgar's inventory when he'd purchased the 'Lord Rye and Rother' painting. Ian had also expanded his search to include the last 20 years of the 19th century. He was guessing the company would have probably been based somewhere in London.

After having to eliminate several results listing 'Jackson Brothers' and 'Jackson and Co.', he was left with three possible 'Jackson and Son' companies to investigate further. The first turned out to be a firm of cobblers, situated in Walthamstow. This firm he quickly dismissed. The second proved to be a firm of fishmongers located in the Billingsgate fish market. He decided to turn his nose up at that one! But the last offering was more promising. They were a firm described as 'fine art, design and antique dealers' and were based in Leadenhall Market.

Okay, Ian pondered, so how is or was this firm involved with George Watts? Maybe they don't have a direct connection. Could it be that the painting had been just part of their normal stock. A lot more digging was still to be done.

Ian now decided to check for the firm's exact street address in Leadenhall Market. Once he'd been able to establish that then, maybe, a visit to the famous old market would be required. He wondered if Jackson and Son were still in existence and still residing at that same address.

Then, of course, there's always Henry Gillard, he pondered, but then decided it might be better to leave him until he was absolutely certain.

About an hour later, Emma arrived home with a huge smile on her face.

"Hello," said Ian, seeing the big grin on Emma's face. "Have you won the lottery?"

"I've found Sir Edgar Brookfield!" announced Emma, with much pride.

"Wow, well done you. Is he still alive then?" teased Ian. "Tell me more."

Emma ignored Ian's joke and went on to explain her meeting with Mrs. Bailey and their subsequent search of every portrait painting in the school.

"Well, I did all that searching with Mrs. Bailey," said Ian, now curious as to what he'd possibly missed.

"No, you didn't. What you did was to follow the existing valuation listing. Bizarrely, there are two additional paintings not on the listing. One was an insignificant landscape, some battle scene, and the other... I'm fairly sure, is the missing oil painting portrait of Sir Edgar Brookfield!"

"You're kidding!"

"No. There were two paintings in an old store cupboard. I don't think anyone's been in that cupboard for 50 years!"

"Okay, so how do you know it's Sir Edgar?" asked Ian. He was impressed with his wife's revelation.

"Well, Ian Caxton, you're just going to have to wait for the answer to that question, because, tomorrow morning,

I've got another meeting with Julie Williams, in Worthing. After that, I'll reveal everything."

"Promises, promises," joked Ian, smiling. "I can't wait."

Emma blushed and walked away. However, when she reached the doorway, she turned and replied. "This will be something you've not seen before!"

The next morning, Emma drove herself down to Worthing for her second meeting with Julie Williams. This meeting was going to be much shorter than the first. Mrs. Williams had, amongst all the family's records, a black and white, grainy photograph of Sir Edgar. It was obviously taken in London as Nelson's column was in the background. Emma picked up her mobile phone and took a photograph of the grainy picture. She then selected 'photos' from the phone's menu, and flicked through her archive until she came to the photograph she'd taken of the 'new' portrait she'd found yesterday at Brookfield School. She and Mrs. Williams compared it to the black and white, grainy photograph of Sir Edgar. They looked away from both pictures and smiled at each other. Yes, it was a match! There was an obvious time gap between when the two pictures had been produced, but Emma was convinced that there were enough similar facial features to conclude they were definitely two pictures of the same man. Mrs. Williams enthusiastically agreed.

A few days later Emma produced all her evidence in a meeting with Miss Wardley and Mrs. Bailey. They were overjoyed with Emma's investigations and her sheer doggedness, all on the school's behalf. Miss Wardley promised that the 'new' portrait, the correct Sir Edgar portrait, would be professionally cleaned, reframed and definitely be replacing the copy painting of Lord Rye, still temporarily hanging on the headmistress's office wall. They were all disappointed that this new Sir Edgar painting didn't have George Watts's signature on it, but that was probably too much to ask. In fact, Emma was not really sure whose signature it was on the painting. It was a bit of a scribble. It looked possibly like R.S. Bateman, but that meant nothing to her.

"It seems, Mrs. Caxton," said Miss Wardley, with a droll smile on her face, "that, after over 100 years, Sir Edgar Brookfield is finally coming out of the cupboard!" They all laughed at Miss Wardley's joke. "He's going to be displayed in his rightful and proper place."

Emma and Mrs. Bailey smiled back with satisfaction.

Miss Wardley continued, "Everyone appears to be a winner now. Thank you, Mrs. Caxton. Thank you very much."

Ian arrived at Leadenhall Market just after 11am. He guessed it was probably 12 years since he'd last visited this historical part of the old City of London. He could remember it well. A potential client, who was an insurance broker at nearby Lloyds of London, had suggested they meet there, 'over a pint', to discuss the possible purchase of a painting that Sotheby's had been commissioned to sell. The potential client had previously seen the painting at Sotheby's premises, but had told Ian he wanted time to think about it. He'd now thought about it and after two pints of beer and a bit of negotiating, he'd agreed to Ian's revised price. The two men had shaken hands and celebrated with more alcohol. Ian had awoken the next morning with a good sale, but also a very serious hangover.

Ian stood at one of the entrances to the market and gazed at the view down the avenue. He marvelled at the ornate metal roof structures, painted green, maroon and cream and the old cobbled 'road' surface. He wondered what modern day 'Health and Safety' made of these walkways. Ian knew there'd been a market here for over 600 years.

The Gamble

Located in the heart of the old, original City of London, the early vendors sold mainly meat, game and poultry, but now, whilst some butchers still traded here, Ian noted the present occupants were mainly restaurants, public houses, florists, cheesemongers and various other small retailers.

He walked along the avenue directly in front of him until he came to a junction. As the market is built roughly in a 'cross' layout Ian was now standing in the centre. He looked along the four separate avenues and then walked slowly in the direction of the Lime Street exit. He kept looking at the addresses and then stopped outside what was now a man's clothes shop. The name of 'Banks and Son' was proudly displayed on a large wooden sign above the entrance doorway. Ian checked his notes on his mobile phone. Yes, this is the right address. He took a deep breath, pushed on the door and walked in.

"Good morning, sir," announced an elderly, but well-dressed, gentleman from behind the counter. "How may I help you?"

Ian walked over towards the counter. "A bit of a shot in the dark really," he said. "I believe that back in 1912 these premises were occupied by an antiques dealer, by the name of Jackson and Son. I was wondering if you knew anything about this firm or the premises' history?"

"Well, sir, my family has been here for over 80 years," replied the man. He was thinking whilst he spoke. "My father established this firm. I do believe there was some sort of art dealer here before him, or, was it an antiques dealer? However, I don't recall their name."

"Oh well, as I said, a shot in the dark," replied Ian, somewhat disappointed. "Thank you." He was just about to turn around to leave the shop, when the old gentleman spoke up.

"Just a minute!" he exclaimed. "Just a jolly old minute!" he repeated. "Give me a few seconds would you. There are some old rent books in the back. Dad found a lot of old rent books in a cupboard when he first moved in. He used to keep all sorts of old files and papers. He was frightened that someone would chase him up for the previous tenant's debts. Would you mind the shop while I find them?"

"Of course," replied Ian. "I'll have a browse at the same time."

"You do that, sir," responded the man before disappearing through the door at the rear of the shop.

Ian wandered around the shop and looked at the various clothes. Lots of suits and cotton shirts that he didn't need to wear too often anymore, but when he came to the tie section, he was more interested. He had always been gullible when it came to silk ties and had quite a collection in his wardrobe at home. Most of them were purchased when he worked in Hong Kong. One blue and white patterned tie now caught his eye. He picked it up and walked over to the mirror. He held it under his chin so it dropped down the front of his chest.

"Here we are, sir," said the old gentleman. He had returned with three old, blue-covered invoice books. "Might be something in these. They are the earliest copies Father kept."

Ian held on to the tie and wandered back to look at the books. He placed the tie down on the counter and quickly glanced at each book. He selected the earliest dated one, 1897–1904. He opened it at the first page and there at the top was printed 'Jackson and Son, Rent payments'. The first entry was dated 5th March 1897.

"Do you mind if I take a photograph of this page?" asked Ian. His enthusiasm had now returned. Jackson and Son were in existence in 1897.

"No, no problem. Actually, you can take the whole book. I probably should have thrown them out years ago. Take all three if you want."

The Gamble

"Are you sure? By the way, I do apologise, my name's Ian Caxton."

The old gentleman nodded. "As you probably saw on the sign over the door, I'm the son in the 'Banks and Son'. George."

"Then thank you, George. I'll take all three books… oh, and this tie as well."

"Very good, Mr. Caxton. That will be £95, please."

Chapter 25

On the train journey home from London, Ian pondered on his findings from the trip to Leadenhall Market. He was convinced he'd now obtained authenticated provenance dating back to the 28th February 1898. He also remembered that one of Bob Taylor's old publications stated that the Lord Rye picture was painted in 1889, so he still had the gap of the first nine years. What he needed to know now was, where had the painting resided between its completion by Watts and the eventual possession by Sir Edgar?

As his train began to slow for its stop at Esher station, Ian stood up and began to walk along the corridor. He'd decided it was now time to speak to Henry Gillard.

When Ian arrived home, he immediately noticed how quiet it was. Emma had obviously not yet returned from collecting Robert from school.

Ian went straight into the home office, placed the three rent books on his desk and sat down. From the top right-hand drawer, he removed his old contacts book and opened it at the letter 'G' He then checked through the list of names until he found Henry Gillard's entry and his telephone number. Henry Gillard is one of the trustees of the charity, 'Watts Gallery and Artists' Village', situated in the Surrey Hills. First opened in 1904, it is an art gallery that was created to display a number of the works of George Watts. Currently there are over 100 of his paintings on display, which span the whole period of the man's 70-year career.

Ian dialled Henry's number.

"Hello, Henry Gillard speaking," answered the voice at the other end of the line.

"Henry, Ian Caxton."

"Well, well, well. A name from the past. How are you doing, Ian?"

"Very well, thank you, Henry. And you?"

"Very well too. Been very busy at the gallery this last week, finalising a nice grant from the National Lottery. That should keep us afloat for a while. So, how's the world of Sotheby's? I gather Michael's finally retired."

"Lots of changes have been going on there, Henry. I resigned nearly 12 months ago."

"Really! Resigned? So, what are you doing now?" Henry was intrigued. He thought Ian was heading for the top job.

"I decided it was time to move on. With Michael retiring, I could see a lot of changes happening which I knew I wouldn't approve of. So now I'm working with Emma. We're in the world of buying and selling paintings."

"How intriguing. How's it all working out?"

"Early days, but we're doing okay. Which is one of the reasons I thought I'd give you a ring."

Ian explained the background to his purchase of the Lord Rye portrait and the results of his subsequent investigations. He asked Henry if he knew anything about the painting, particularly relating to the late 19th century.

"It's not a painting that I readily recognise, Ian. 'Lord Rye and Rother', you say. I'll have to look at our records. You'd better give me your telephone number."

Ian gave Henry both his landline and mobile telephone numbers and then said, "By the way, Henry, my Lord Rye painting was included in some of the earlier George Watts' catalogues raisonné, but now seems to be missing from the later ones. Have you any idea why?"

"Let me guess, Ian. The painting's not signed."

"That's right, but I'm totally convinced it's a George Watts piece and so were the previous authors of Watts' catalogues raisonné."

"About 1953, I think it was, there was a decision taken to downgrade some of the paintings previously attributed to Watts because they were not signed. As you can imagine, it caused quite a stink at the time. Eventually some of those paintings were reinstated on appeal. My guess is yours was one that was missed… or nobody appealed."

"It was owned by a school. They thought it was a portrait of a completely different person. They wouldn't have known anything about this controversy."

"Let me find out about the early provenance, Ian. Bring the painting over and I'll give it a 'once over' for you."

"I'll do that, Henry. Many thanks."

"Nice chatting again, Ian. Look forward to meeting you again."

They both said their goodbyes.

Oscar had spent the last few weeks doing nothing. He still got up early each morning, walked the short distance to his local beach and had his usual swim in the Caribbean, but the rest of the day just seemed to drift by. He went to bed each evening just after 9pm and slept through until the sun woke him up again the next morning. He hadn't even opened his computer for over two weeks. His good neighbour, Garfield, had tried to gee him up with invitations to the local cricket matches and friends' barbeques, but Oscar decided, for various reasons, to give them all a miss. Wesley Fredericks, the owner of the 'Shell Gallery', was also concerned. Oscar had arrived in Antigua with lots of enthusiasm, drive and ambition and Wesley had given Oscar his first big opportunity, his first connection on the island, but now Oscar was, seemingly, just not interested anymore.

Ian had emailed Oscar three times and telephoned him twice, only to get his answerphone… and he never responded to any of Ian's messages. Ian knew his old pal very well and he also knew Oscar could sometimes 'disappear' for weeks without contact, but even Ian thought that this time it was definitely different. He was aware that his former business colleague and drinking partner, Gladstone, had recently moved to another island and that Oscar was very unhappy with the dissolution of 'the partnership'. But what else could Ian do? Oscar was 4000 miles away but that didn't stop Ian being very worried.

After another no reply to his last telephone message, Ian decided to try and be a little more proactive. He knew Oscar had a business relationship with the 'Shell Gallery' in St John's, so he looked the gallery up on Google and, from there, accessed their website. He wrote down their telephone number, email address and sent an email to Wesley Fredericks.

A day later, Wesley had replied. He told Ian that he, too, was concerned. He stated that he hadn't seen or heard from Oscar for several weeks, but he had planned to visit Oscar's villa that evening and he promised to report back on the situation.

Well, that's something, thought Ian, but I shan't hold my breath.

The next email from Wesley was not very encouraging. Oscar had told Wesley he was seriously thinking of moving on. Wesley said he'd asked Oscar where to, and why was he thinking this way? Oscar told Wesley that he still loved

Antigua, but needed a change and, maybe, a new challenge. He admitted he was lonely and felt a little lost. Wesley told Ian that Oscar was thinking maybe a long holiday might help, but acknowledged he would still be on his own. Wesley then went on to say that Oscar had mentioned you, Ian. He envied your life and your family, Emma and Robert. He missed his fishing trips with his buddies in Hong Kong, but didn't want to go back to Hong Kong with all the Chinese issues. He felt tired, a little angry, but mostly sad.

Ian felt Oscar's pain and frustration. He partly blamed himself because it was largely in response to his own suggestion that the partnership had been discontinued. He knew all the other partners had decided that the partnership had run its course and it was only Oscar who had wanted the partnership to carry on.

Ian was very concerned and afraid about his old chum and what he might do next.

Chapter 26

Mary Turnbull was quite content and happy to be running the 'Taylor Fine Arts Gallery' whilst her employer was away and enjoying his honeymoon. Viktor had emailed her twice, both times whilst Penny was being pampered in the luxurious spa facilities. He'd asked Mary for an update on what had been happening. Mary had responded, in general terms, to say that all was well and that Viktor should just concentrate on enjoying his honeymoon with his lovely new wife.

In fact, Mary had been doing a lot more than 'all was well'. She had managed to sell two watercolours for a nice profit and had completely tidied up the storeroom. The pictures and contents previously stored there were now organised and labelled properly. There had also been several enquiries requesting a visit from Viktor, so she had updated his diary in readiness for his return to work.

Viktor was due back next Monday, but, on the previous Thursday, a well-dressed man had called into the gallery and asked for Viktor, by his full name.

Mary explained to the man, "I'm sorry, but Viktor's not in the gallery today. He'll be back on Monday. Can I help?"

The man put his hand into his jacket pocket and pulled out a business card. He handed it across to Mary. "Tell Mr. Kuznetsov I called."

Mary took the card, briefly glanced at it, and said, "Can I tell Viktor why you've called…" Mary glanced again at the card. "Mr. Crawshaw?"

"Just tell him I have a client who's interested in doing business with him," responded Mr. Crawshaw. He then turned around and walked out of the gallery.

Mary put on her reading glasses and read the full details on the card. Well, she thought, now there's a surprise for when Viktor returns!

It had been two weeks since Ian's telephone conversation with Henry Gillard. Henry had telephoned Ian back and told him he had some information, but he was still investigating. If he wanted to bring the painting over to the 'Watts Gallery' he would have a look at it and they could also discuss Henry's findings so far.

Ian was now driving his car through the countryside and heading towards the Surrey Hills. He tried to recall how long it had been since he'd last visited the gallery. He'd heard there had been a number of refurbishments carried out over recent years, so now he was keen to see all the changes and meet up with his old colleague, Henry, once again.

He parked in the main gallery car park and retrieved his painting from the boot. It was secured in the usual trusty canvas bag. Locking the car, he then headed towards the main reception. It was just beginning to spit with rain so Ian dashed the last few yards. At reception he announced his name and said he had an appointment with Henry Gillard.

Ten minutes later, after greetings and big smiles, Henry and Ian sat down in Henry's office. Ian stood his canvas bag at the side of his chair.

"It's so good to see you again, Ian. I took the opportunity to arrange coffee for us. How do you like it?"

The Gamble

"White, no sugar, please."

Henry poured two cups of coffee and pushed one across his desk towards Ian. "My, you haven't changed at all. What is it, eight years?"

Ian sipped his coffee and said, "I was thinking about that when I was driving over. It must be nearer ten, at least, Henry. Could be more. Time flies. I must say there's been quite a few improvements here."

"We've been very lucky with some grants. Do you approve?"

"From what I've seen so far, it's wonderful. Been restored really well."

"Good. We've had lots of compliments. Now then, your painting. I presume it's in that bag." Ian nodded. "Good, I'll take a look at it shortly."

"Thank you," responded Ian. He was anxious to hear what Henry had discovered.

"I've been able to find out a bit about your painting's history, but only up to 1898."

Ian gave a big smile. That's exactly what he wanted to hear.

"You probably know," continued Henry, "Watts painted the portrait in 1889." Ian nodded again. "It was in his studio collection until 1894 and was then purchased by a firm called Jackson and Son. They were fine art, design and antiques dealers, located in Leadenhall Market, London. They had it on sale until 1898, when it was purchased by a Mrs. Baker, who gave it to Sir Edgar Brookfield as a 60th birthday present. Apparently, there was some South African link between Lord Rye and Sir Edgar Brookfield. Maybe they worked there at the same time? After that our records end, I'm afraid."

"Henry, that's fabulous!" exclaimed Ian. "I've got the rest of the painting's provenance. Sir Edgar Brookfield's children donated a number of Sir Edgar's paintings and other items to Brookfield School in 1912, just after Sir Edgar died. This portrait of Lord Rye was part of the donation." Ian tapped his canvas bag. "Sir Edgar was instrumental in establishing the school and it was named after him. Since 1912, there's been some confusion at the school as to who the portrait was actually of. The school, somehow, thought it was of Sir Edgar himself and it's been hanging on the headmistress's wall for over 100 years – as Sir Edgar! That is, of course, until I bought it a few weeks ago."

"Quite a story… and quite a shock for the school, I guess. Let's have a look at this painting then. Bring it over to the table," said Henry, standing up and walking around his desk.

Ian picked up the canvas bag and carried it over to the table at the rear of the room. There he unbuckled the three straps, gently eased the painting out of the bag and finally removed the thin fleece-like inner covering. He then laid the painting face upwards and stood back, giving Henry more room to view the picture properly.

Henry removed a magnifying glass from his pocket and bent down to inspect the picture more closely. There was complete silence in the room, bar for the ticking of a nearby wall clock. After about two minutes, Henry lifted the painting and examined the back and the frame. He then said, "I've certainly not seen this painting before. Interesting that it's not been signed," said Henry. "But I've seen one other portrait that wasn't signed. I'm not sure why Watts didn't sign all his work. You say Courtauld's have had a good look at it?"

Ian nodded. "Yes, about a month ago. They confirmed the paint used matched the same chemical compositions of the paints Watts was using at the end of the 19th century."

"It looks to me, Ian, that you've unearthed a good find.

It has all the hallmarks of being a George Watts portrait. Not many of those about. As you know, Mr. Watts mainly painted biblical scenes."

Ian was smiling. "Thanks again, Henry."

"Yes, I think I'd be prepared to include it in our collection." Henry returned to his seat behind the desk. "So, what are you going to do now?"

Ian repacked the painting into the inner cover and then the canvas bag. He sat down again and finished his coffee. "I've got all the evidence I need, so my next step is to convince the catalogue raisonné experts… and get it reinstated as a genuine George Watts painting."

Henry nodded. "I can't see you having any problems with that. It would get my vote and recommendation."

After their meeting, Henry offered to show Ian around the gallery to see the restoration changes and the latest paintings on display. There was a small group of more contemporary works, but Ian was more focused on the much larger collection of George Watts paintings.

Ian and Henry viewed each painting together. They discussed and critically assessed each composition. Ian was particularly interested in the two George Watts portraits that were on display. He inspected each one very closely. They compared very well with his painting of Lord Rye.

At the end of the tour Ian said he'd enjoyed his visit and thanked Henry for his time and especially the invaluable extra information he'd provided. He promised him that it wouldn't be another ten years before he revisited the gallery.

During his journey home, Ian considered all the information he'd now accumulated. He was especially pleased that all the pieces making up the painting's provenance now seemed to be in place.

It was now time to get the Lord Rye portrait back where it really deserved to be. To be included in the next official copy of the George Frederic Watts' catalogue raisonné. Without this final achievement, both his and Emma's hard work would, regrettably, have all been in vain.

Ian was determined this wasn't going to happen.

Chapter 27

On Monday morning, Viktor arrived back at work completely refreshed, excited and with a deep golden suntan. When he walked into the gallery, it was about five minutes after Mary had arrived.

"Welcome back, Viktor," announced Mary, as Viktor closed the door behind him. "Did you have a great time?"

Viktor walked over to the front desk where Mary was sitting and sat down on the chair facing her. "Mary, it was just wonderful. Lots of swimming, snorkelling, eating and drinking. What else does a person need?"

"Did Penny, your new wife, did she enjoy herself?"

"She did the same as me, plus she took full advantage of the excellent Balinese-style spa facilities. She says she's never felt so toned."

Mary smiled.

"So, what's been going on here? You wouldn't give me any details in your emails." Viktor was keen to know what had been happening during his absence.

"It's all ticked over fine. I told you there was nothing to worry about." Viktor nodded and gave her a smile. "I've sold two of the four watercolours you wanted to get rid of and… oh, yes, I've also tidied up the store area. I can finally find things now!"

"That probably means I won't be able to find anything," replied Viktor, and they both laughed.

"I've otherwise put all your messages and personal post in your in-tray. Just one other thing. Last Thursday, a Mr. Crawshaw came into the gallery. Well-dressed, middle-aged, quite well spoken. He asked for you by name. When I said you wouldn't be back in the gallery until today, he just gave me his business card and left."

"Did he say he'd call back or ask me to telephone him?"

"No, nothing more." Mary opened her right-hand desk drawer and removed the business card. She checked it was the correct one and passed it to Viktor.

Viktor leaned forward to take the card. He read the details and particularly noted the occupation of Mr. Crawshaw. "Well, well, well," said Viktor, "I wonder what this is all about?"

"That's what I thought at the time, but he wouldn't tell me. All he would say was that he had a client who was interested in doing business with you. Then he left the building."

On this same Monday morning, Penny was approaching the main building of Sotheby's in Bond Street. She was apprehensive and certainly not looking forward to this moment. After a wonderful, relaxing and magical honeymoon, there was no pleasure in walking back through the main entrance to Sotheby's. She had been discussing with Viktor her feelings about her new role, the absence of Ian and the presence of Jonathan Northgate, the new MD. She really didn't want to go back. Ideally, she wanted to resign and find a new and different challenge, well away from Sotheby's. But not, she emphasised, away from the art world, which she still thoroughly enjoyed.

Viktor's reaction and subsequent suggestion was that she should give it another month before making any rash, or sudden, decisions. He had continued by saying that things might have already improved whilst she'd been away. Plus, she owed it to both herself and Ian to try and make her new job work. After all, Ian had such confidence in her ability. If, in a month's time, she still felt the same way, well okay, they could talk about it again and she could say what she'd like to do instead.

In Antigua, Oscar was making plans to go back to Hong Kong. Not a permanent move, but just to have a holiday. Since he'd arrived in Antigua, he'd still kept in touch, mostly by email, with some of his old pals and colleagues in Hong Kong and Macau. Now, as part of much wider proposed holiday plans, he was going to join up with some of them again, on their annual 'boys' holiday fishing trip in the tropical waters around Fiji. It was three years since Oscar last had a proper holiday, and he now hoped this change would reinvigorate his outlook on life. Who knows? he pondered, I might even find a new direction to consider, or maybe surprise myself by discovering a new and exciting challenge to take on.

When Oscar informed both Wesley and Ian, separately, of his decision, they both agreed that a change of scenery and meeting up with old friends was a good idea. Ian went further and said that continually feeling sad and down was obviously no life at all and it was good that he was trying to change his outlook for the better. They both wished Oscar well and wanted him to keep in touch.

Five days later Oscar climbed aboard the aeroplane that was taking him to Las Vegas, where he planned to stay for just two days before flying on to Honolulu. There, plans were for a three-week stay, which included a cruise tour of a number of the other Hawaiian Islands. From Hawaii, it was then on to Hong Kong to meet up with his old pals.

The group's plans were then to fly to the island of Viti Levu, part of the volcanic Fijian islands. Two days later they would board their chartered sport fishing yacht, the 'White Shark' and set sail for the warm, blue waters of the South Pacific Ocean. Their aim was to drink lots of alcohol, reminisce about the old days, catch lots of Black or Blue Marlin, plus, maybe, some Sailfish, Wahoo, Giant Trevally, Dogtooth Tuna and… generally have a great time! The usual US$10,000 cash prize would be awarded, at the end of the charter, to the angler who had caught the largest fish. Each member paid US$2,000 and the winner took all!

Oscar had never won this prize, yet. That was his ambition this time.

Emma was in the home office when the telephone rang. "Hello?" she answered.

"Is that Emma? Michael Hopkins here, Ian's former boss at Sotheby's."

"Oh, hello, Michael. I thought I recognised the voice. So how are you enjoying retirement?" replied Emma.

"I'm still getting used to it. It's not easy to go from a full-time job straight into retirement."

"Yes, I know. At least when I stopped working full time, I had a baby to deal with."

"So, how is young Robert? I'm right with the name, aren't I?"

"Very good, Michael. Yes, it is Robert. He's fine and in his second year at school."

"My, my. How time flies. I wanted to speak to Ian. Is he about?"

"I'm sorry, Michael, but he's at a meeting in London. Can I get him to give you a call?"

"That would be very kind of you, Emma. You both

should come over for dinner one evening. No doubt we'll all have lots to talk about."

"That would be really nice, Michael. I'll tell Ian you called. Pass on my regards to Jean, please."

"Of course. Goodbye for now, Emma. Lovely chatting with you."

"Goodbye, Michael."

Well, thought Emma, that was a surprise.

Chapter 28

Ian's meeting in London was a complete success. Both the author and publisher of the George Frederic Watts' portrait paintings' catalogue raisonné, had agreed that it was very likely that Ian's picture had been painted by George Watts. Their decision was based on all the provenance evidence Ian had provided and the fact that the painting had been previously included in much earlier catalogue raisonné publications of George Watts' work. In their final statement, they said, *'there is no reason to reject the painting any longer. The "Lord Rye and Rother" portrait will be reinstated immediately and be included in our next catalogue raisonné publication'*. They also promised Ian a letter, confirming this decision.

On his train journey home Ian reflected on a positive and successful day. He now intended to sell the painting, either via one of the three gallery connections he knew would be interested in George Watts' work, or by auction. He then pondered on the conundrum as to whether, if he did decide on the auction route, he would use Sotheby's, or not. Times had changed at his former employer since both he and Michael Hopkins had both worked there. He certainly hated the idea of supporting Jonathan Northgate.

As his train pulled into Esher station, Ian picked up his briefcase and the canvas bag containing his painting.

The Gamble

He left the carriage and walked along the relatively quiet platform. The station clock said 4.12pm. Ian smiled at the thought of him missing the heaving throng of homebound commuters who would start to walk this route in just over an hour's time. He was so pleased not to be part of that soulless rat race any more.

Ian exited the station and began his usual walk home. En route, he thought about all the people who had helped him to get this far with his painting. Miss Wardley and the governors of Brookfield School; Bob Taylor and his father-in-law, in Monaco; the Courtauld Institute's forensic science department; John Watson and his sister, Julie Williams, for the helpful information they gave Emma about Sir Edgar Brookfield's family; George Banks at 'Banks and Son' in Leadenhall Market and Henry Gillard, at the 'Watts Gallery and Artists' Village'. Ian thought it was always important to remember such people, and the help they had given him. After all, proving a painting's provenance was often challenging and rarely something one person could achieve on their own. He had earlier mentioned these points to Emma and they'd both agreed, if all went well with the catalogue raisonné people, and after the painting was sold, they would express their gratitude... in a much more tangible way.

Just as he entered the house and switched off the burglar alarm, Ian heard Emma's car arrive behind him in the driveway. He placed his briefcase and canvas bag on his desk and wandered out to join her.

Robert was first out of the car. Dressed in his school uniform, Ian thought how much older he now looked. Robert walked over and gave his father a hug. Ian hugged him back.

"Have you had a good day at school?" asked Ian, as they broke away from each other's squeeze.

"Yes, it's been okay," responded Robert, not very enthusiastically. He then ran off, through the front door and upstairs to his room. He wanted to get changed out of his school uniform as quickly as possible.

Emma closed and locked the car door. She walked over to join Ian and gave him a kiss. "Well, how did the meeting go?"

"It went really well. We, officially, own a George Watts painting!"

"Well done, you. Let's get inside and you can tell me more. By the way, Michael Hopkins telephoned this morning. I told him you'd ring him back."

"Okay," replied Ian, following Emma into the house. However, he now wondered what Michael had said to her. He'd telephoned Michael some weeks ago with regards to the letter Michael had given to him at his retirement, but he only got the answerphone.

Ian joined Emma in the kitchen. She had already switched on the kettle to make them a cup of tea.

"Did Michael say anything about why he wanted to speak to me?" asked Ian. He assumed it was Michael returning his own earlier call.

"No. We just had a general chat and Michael suggested we go to their house for dinner sometime. Nothing else. Why? Were you expecting something?"

"I don't know. Michael gave me a note at his retirement function which said he'd contact me."

"Well, I suppose he has now. Give him a call. Dinner will be ready in an hour. Take your tea through to the office," replied Emma, passing him his mug.

Ian clasped the mug in his right hand and walked through into the home office. He put the mug down on the desk and searched through his in-tray for Michael's note. After a few seconds he found it and read it again. Still no clue, but Michael had put his address and telephone number at the top of the note. He dialled the number again.

The Gamble

After four rings a female voice answered. "Hello," she announced.

"Jean? It's Ian Caxton."

"Oh, hello, Ian. Are you well?" replied Jean.

Ian thought it was an odd phrase to start a telephone conversation with. "Yes, we're all fine, thank you. How are you coping with Michael being around all the time?"

"He's a bit of a lost soul. Gets under my feet."

Ian laughed. He couldn't imagine Michael having so much free time on his hands. "Michael telephoned me earlier. I'm returning his call."

"Just a minute, Ian."

Ian heard the telephone receiver being put down, and a few seconds later he heard Jean call Michael's name.

"He's in the garden, Ian. Just coming. Goodbye, and say hello to Emma."

"Goodbye, Jean," replied Ian, again smiling at Jean's choice of words.

"Hello, Ian?"

Ian immediately recognised his former boss's voice. "Hello, Michael. How are you keeping?"

"Physically fine, mentally unstimulated. How's things with you? I had a lovely chat with Emma this morning. She sounds very happy."

"I'm fine, Michael, thank you. And a lot happier than I would have been at Sotheby's under Northgate."

"Well, you know the job was yours before he was appointed."

Ian didn't want to go over all this old ground once again. "So, Michael, you gave me a note and telephoned me this morning. What can I do for you?"

"Not over the telephone. What about lunch, just the two of us?" replied Michael, keen for Jean not to overhear any details of their conversation.

"That's fine with me. When and where?"

The two men discussed dates and possible pubs, or restaurants, approximately halfway between their two houses. Eventually the date, time and venue were agreed.

Ian put down his mobile phone and entered the appointment into his diary. He then tidied up the contents of his briefcase and put his painting, still in the canvas bag, temporarily at the side of his filing cabinet out of harm's way. Finally, he drank the rest of his tea and returned the mug to the kitchen.

"Can you pop upstairs and speak to Robert?" said Emma, peeling some potatoes. "He seems to be stuck on a bit of his homework. We can talk about your day over dinner."

"Okay." Ian turned around and headed towards the stairs.

He was still none the wiser as to what Michael wanted to talk to him about.

Chapter 29

At the 'Taylor Fine Arts Gallery', Viktor was slowly catching up on messages and emails. The business card left by Mr. Crawshaw still sat on his desk, facing him. Because it was constantly in view, Viktor felt it was prompting, or reminding, him to do something. But what? He wasn't sure whether to telephone him or just wait and see if the man got in touch again. Eventually, he picked up the card and put it into the top drawer of his desk. Out of sight, out of mind, he hoped. He decided to just wait and see what happened next.

In anticipation of Mary joining the gallery, Viktor had made some changes to the layout of the premises. Mary, as her primary role was to be 'front of house', had taken over Viktor's desk in the main picture display area. This meant that for Viktor, when he was on the premises, he had to use part of the large store area at the back, behind the picture displays. This, however, was already being used for storing paintings not currently on display, a packing area, a small kitchen facility and also some filing cabinets. Now, with the addition of an extra desk, the room had become noticeably cosy. However, as Viktor's aim was to be out of the gallery a lot more, visiting existing and potential clients, he had to accept this situation for the time being. Mind, he had to agree that Mary's reorganisation, whilst he'd been away, had created a little more space.

The main problem now, Mary had suggested, was that the premises were not as customer friendly as she would have liked. There was nowhere suitable for private conversations or for personal presentations, especially when there was more than one customer in the gallery. Mary had also suggested that the rear part of the left-hand display area could be converted. She pointed out that it was quite a dark area and not used for display purposes. A bit of a dead area in fact. Viktor had to agree and was in the process of obtaining quotations to install internal walls and an up-to-date lighting system. One quotation had arrived whilst he was on holiday and he was totally shocked to see that it was double the price he'd hoped for. He was also beginning to realise that whilst the size of the gallery had been fine when he'd been on his own, extra space for improvements both now and in the future were going to be a serious problem. There were two alternatives: reduce the display area even more… or move premises. He would need to speak to Bob Taylor.

Penny's first four days back at work were typical for someone returning from a lovely holiday. Lots of catching up with her team, emails to respond to and a few telephone calls to make. All being dealt with whilst her mind was still wandering back to a lovely honeymoon. To be fair, though, she thought her team had carried on very competently during her absence and Angie, her PA, had covered well for her in management meetings. However, she still felt unsure of herself, being relatively new to the role. She assumed it would all come to a head, very soon, with Jonathan Northgate. It was just a matter of time.

However, that time might now have come a little quicker

The Gamble

than she'd anticipated. Later that morning she received a telephone call from the MD's PA, telling her that Mr. Northgate wanted a meeting, next Tuesday morning, at 9.30am. He wanted to discuss the future of her department!

Welcome back, she thought, welcome back to the real world!

Emma had been staying with her parents in the Cotswolds for two days. It was the start of the school holidays and Emma's parents had asked if Robert might like to join them for a brief stay. Robert loved his grandparents and jumped at the opportunity. Emma knew, only too well, that Robert would be totally indulged.

As she was leaving, she told Robert to be on his best behaviour, but quietly knew he wouldn't be a problem. She kissed and hugged him goodbye and then all four waved as she drove out onto the lane and headed towards home. It was 10.30am and she decided to stop at the small market town of Burford. Although now quite touristy, she remembered visiting Burford many times in the past. She always enjoyed browsing through the eclectic mix of independent shops.

Emma parked her car in a public car park next to the River Windrush. She would then cross the bridge and cut through to 'The Hill', where many of the shops were located. She wandered up and down both sides of the main road and called in to browse in some of her favourite establishments. She then had a late ploughman's lunch at the 'King's Arms'. In the hallway, on her way out, she spotted some local pamphlets and advertisements. She collected two pamphlets and then noticed a card advertising 'Wendy's Antiques', in Duck Lane. It was not a name she recognised, so decided to give it a try.

Although Duck Lane was only a five-minute walk away

from the 'King's Arms', 'Wendy's Antiques' was situated halfway down the street. She had to walk some distance along Duck Lane from the busy main road, before she eventually saw the old establishment coming into view. Emma guessed that the building was two, maybe three, hundred years old. Most of the properties in Duck Lane were constructed of the typical golden Cotswold stone. She assumed they were all built about the same time. When Emma arrived at the front of the shop, she briefly glanced through the windows before pushing at the front door. The doorbell above her head immediately rang. She closed the door and looked all around her. Stacked on numerous shelves was an extensive and varied collection of ornaments, bric-a-brac and curios. As she walked through the shop, it all reminded her of 'The Old Curiosity Shop' in Charles Dickens' book.

Emma appeared to be the only customer. A large wall clock ticked in the background, but otherwise, there was not another sound to be heard.

The shop was much deeper than it appeared from the street, so Emma followed the route of a narrow aisle towards the rear. There was every type of antique anyone could imagine. As she got towards the end of the aisle, she spotted a group of pictures. She eased her way along to see the display more closely. There were seven pictures in all. Three nondescript watercolours, three prints and one unusual oil painting on canvas. It was of a young woman, sitting down, with most of her bare back facing the artist. She was half dressed, in a bedroom setting and was looking into a mirror. The artist had captured the woman's reflected face with a rather forlorn profile. Emma was intrigued. Her main fascination was with how the picture had been painted. It had been created by applying many thousands of tiny, joined up coloured dots! When Emma stood very close to the picture, the seated woman seemed to disappear into

The Gamble

an abstract collection of multi-coloured dots. She picked up the painting and stood it on an old chest of drawers. She was then able to walk slowly backwards down the aisle to look at the picture properly from different distances and angles. At each step backwards she stopped. The abstract appearance gradually disappeared and the woman and her surroundings came fully back into focus.

Emma was captivated by how her eyes kept having to adjust slightly each time she moved closer, or further away, from the picture. She found the painting's construction quite mesmerising. She walked up to the painting again and looked at its title, written on the sales label, 'Mademoiselle Chad'. However, when she looked for the artist's signature, she noticed that the painting had not been signed. She turned it over to see what was on the painting's rear side. In the top right-hand corner, was an old, yellowed label. On the label was the painting's name, 'Mademoiselle Chad', a brief description of the picture in French, the artist's name, Georges Seurat and the date it had been painted, 1889. She turned it back over and looked again at the sales label. £65.

"Fascinating isn't it," said a female voice close behind her. Emma jumped in surprise. "Sorry," apologised the lady.

Emma turned around and smiled. "I didn't hear you," she said, taking a deep breath. "Yes, it is quite mesmerising."

"Hello, I'm June Connolly. Did you want to buy this picture?"

Emma was still holding the painting. She looked down and rechecked it for any damage. It certainly looked original or, if not, a very good copy, she thought. "What's your best price?"

"What about £50?"

"Yes, I'll buy it then," said Emma.

"Good decision. I like it too. Should we go over to the counter?"

Emma passed the painting to June and followed her back along the aisle.

When they arrived at the counter, June continued speaking whilst she wrapped the picture up in brown paper. "This shop was my aunt's. She's the Wendy above the door. She died six months ago and left the premises and business to me in her will. I've been offered a good price for the whole business, so I'll only be here for a couple more weeks." Emma nodded. June continued. "It's sad, but really too much for me. I've got a husband and three children to look after, you see. The shop… well, it was my aunt's life."

"I'm sorry to hear that," replied Emma, sympathetically. She removed two £20 notes and one £10 note from her purse.

"There we are, my dear. I'll just pop it in a bag for you as well."

"Thank you," replied Emma. She handed over the money and collected the wrapped picture. "I don't suppose you know when your aunt bought this painting?"

"My aunt was 87 when she died, so she didn't have computers, or anything like that. She kept everything written down in books and journals. They're in the back, but they go back over 50 years."

"Okay, never mind, just a thought," said Emma.

"It's been very quiet lately so I could have a look for you."

Emma put her hand in her handbag and pulled out her business card. She offered it across to June. "Please, don't spend a lot of your time looking, but if you do find something, I really would appreciate it if you could ring me or, better still, drop me an email with the details."

"I'll do that, certainly, my dear," replied June.

Emma put her hand back into her handbag and pulled out another £20 note. "Hopefully, this will cover your time."

"Well, that's very kind of you, my dear. Thank you very much," replied June.

"Thank you," replied Emma. "Goodbye."

"Goodbye to you as well, my dear," said June, slipping the £20 note into her trouser pocket.

Chapter 30

Ian and Michael Hopkins had agreed to meet at the 'Five Bells' restaurant, close to the historic market town of Godalming, just south of Guildford. The restaurant is located next to the River Wey and Michael and Ian were now sitting in the main dining area admiring the excellent view through the window along about 50 metres of the river.

It was 1.35pm and whilst there were other diners in the room, it was a relatively quiet day.

Michael and Ian had just ordered their food and were enjoying a cold glass of chardonnay. They were talking about 'old times' at Sotheby's and both were sceptical about its future under the stewardship of Jonathan Northgate.

"I'll say this once only, Ian, and never again, I promise. You were by far the best candidate. I wanted you. The board wanted you. But I accepted your reservations. Northgate was the chairman's choice, not mine."

"Michael, those words are all very flattering, but you said, yourself, the job is a huge challenge and responsibility. I could never put my relationship with Emma and Robert at risk, and for what? The glory, the prestige, some extra money and benefits. No, what Emma and I now have is worth much more to me and my family than the MD's role."

The Gamble

"So, Ian, what are you doing now? You were very evasive when we were both still at Sotheby's."

"I'm having serious fun, Michael. My income is much higher than Sotheby's would ever pay me and I work with Emma. I see Robert nearly every day, before and after school, and finally, I do not have the horror of commuting anymore. I don't live by the sound of the alarm clock and I can have holidays whenever I want and for however long I want. My job now, Michael, is so simple. I buy and sell paintings."

Michael leaned back in his chair, raised his eyebrows and laughed. He then picked up his glass and made a toast, "To having serious fun!"

Ian laughed, lifted his own glass and said, "I'll drink to that!"

"You don't know this Ian, but from the earliest days in Bond Street, when you were fresh out of university, I said to my boss at the time that you were going to go places. You had a special talent, drive and ambition. We sent you out to New York and you excelled. That is, until you had your squabbles with Jonathan Northgate. We then got you promoted to Hong Kong. You did well there too, but I began to wonder if I was right. Let's just say you seemed to be enjoying yourself... just a little too much! But then you met and married Emma. What an excellent choice. You then came back to London. I know you weren't keen and tried to find ways to avoid commuting, but you still ran a successful department and developed young Penny to be your natural successor. Sotheby's are missing you, Ian. You would have taken them onto another level."

"Again, Michael, flattering words. Yes, I loved Hong Kong. It was so vibrant, exciting and challenging, but Emma would have nothing to do with it. It broke my heart, Michael... seriously. But life goes on and now... well, I wouldn't swap anything," replied Ian. He now had a small amount of emotion in the tone of his voice. "As for Penny, yes, she's talented, not ambitious, but certainly quality. And very soon, my guess is, she'll be jumping ship too."

"Why do you say that?" asked Michael, somewhat surprised. Although he didn't work at Sotheby's anymore, he maintained a keen interest in what was going on there.

"Two words. Jonathan Northgate. He will bully her until she resigns. Any previous contacts and connections with me he'll want to get rid of. It's his way of getting his own back for New York."

"What happened in New York? I heard about a few incidents, but it was obviously a lot deeper with you two."

"I think I'd prefer to keep that issue just between Northgate and myself. It was very serious at the time."

"Okay, so we didn't get to know about everything," replied Michael, with a sneaky smile on his face.

They were interrupted when their main courses arrived. Both declined top-ups of wine as they were both driving, but Michael did order a bottle of mineral water. They both started to eat.

It was Michael who reopened the conversation. "You're probably wondering why I gave you that note and wanted us to meet in private."

Ian nodded. He'd wondered when Michael was going to explain his proposal.

Michael continued, "Well, my youngest son, Alexander, runs his own business and has three employees. His company concentrates on house clearances, mainly in London and around the home counties. However, they don't just do any old house clearances. They operate and specialise in large homes and estates. It's a quiet, but growing, market particularly with the current economic situation and the inheritance tax laws being as penal as they are. Inheriting

The Gamble

children cannot afford the inheritance tax, or the upkeep of their parents' large homes, so they employ Alexander and his team. Alexander is, let's say, 'cute' and makes sure everyone is a winner except, maybe, the inland revenue."

Ian smiled. "Okay, so where do I come in?"

"Ian, I know about Andrei Petrov and Monaco!"

Ian sat back in his chair and stared at Michael. His eyes opened wider in surprise. He was astonished and his heart began thumping against his chest. He stopped eating and placed the cutlery down on his plate. He'd lost all his appetite.

"I never said anything to you at the time," continued Michael. He'd now placed his own cutlery down on his plate, "because, well, it wasn't, or appeared not to be, impacting on your work at Sotheby's. But I was concerned for you and your future... and for Sotheby's future too. Nevertheless, you seemed to be able to 'juggle both roles'. Penny and young Viktor protected you well."

Ian still couldn't believe what he was hearing. He'd always admired Michael and had the greatest respect for his former boss. After all, Michael was one of the most talented men he'd ever known. But this! This was all such a bombshell... and landing fairly and squarely on top of his head!

"So, having said that," Michael continued, "I recognised your added abilities to be able to work successfully, let's just say, outside the rules of Sotheby's. Digressing for a minute. Did you know, I met Andrei Petrov, once, in Paris, I think it was? Maybe about 15 years ago, possibly a little more. He was good company, interesting, but certainly someone who Sotheby's would never do business with. I never really trusted the Russians."

Ian was struggling to breath. He took a long draught from his glass of water. He could feel his forehead perspiring. His heart was still thumping hard against his chest.

"Alexander is looking for an expert, Ian. An expert who knows about paintings. Their quality and their value. Someone with an instinct, a feeling, whether they are genuine, good fakes or copies. He wants someone who knows the art market, the big buyers… and sometimes, with few questions asked. In short, Ian, he needs someone like you."

Ian was still in shock. What a revelation. What should he say? What could he say?

Michael was conscious his food was getting cold, so picked up his cutlery and started to eat again. He'd said his piece. The ball was now firmly in Ian's court.

It was about an hour later when Ian and Michael said their goodbyes. Ian climbed into his BMW car and headed along the B3000 to join the A3 main road. His head was still buzzing and he decided to pull into the convenient lay-by he'd spotted just ahead. He parked, switched off the engine and stared out through the windscreen. He saw a bench which seemed to have a view looking out over the surrounding countryside. He wandered over and sat down, taking in deep breaths of the warm, summer air.

Well, he thought, Michael has really come up with a couple of whammies there. But, at the moment, he was more concerned about the past than the future. He wondered how Michael had been able 'to follow him'. How much did he really know? Moscow, Hong Kong, the partnership? He never gave me a clue, not one hint, that he was following me… watching me! Was this because the company saw me as Michael's natural successor and wanted to make sure I was the right person? Who'd been following me? Or was it insider information? But nobody knew it all, not even Vic. Besides, he and Penny would never have said anything to Michael. Or would they? No, no, that was just not possible. Nobody knew… not everything! Not Andrei, not Oscar, nor Sergei… not even Emma!

The Gamble

Ian gazed across the countryside, but his eyes failed to focus on the green hedgerows and trees, nor the early blooming yellow rapeseed fields. Neither did he hear the chattering and songs of nearby birds.

Eventually, he concluded that he couldn't do anything about the past, except learn from it. But, what about the future and the possibility of working with Michael's son, Alexander? Was that really an option he wanted to take? He'd promised Michael an answer after he'd had more time to think about the matter properly. He wouldn't make any snap decisions, and certainly not until he'd met up and spoken with Alexander. Michael and Ian had agreed that was probably the next step.

But privately, Ian felt a little trapped. Did he really have any choice?

Chapter 31

Viktor returned to the gallery from visiting a client in North London. It was 2.32pm. Mary was sitting at the gallery's main desk looking at her computer. When she saw Viktor walk through the doorway, she looked at the clock on the wall and was pleased to see he had returned before 3pm.

"Hello, Vic," said Mary. "Did you have a successful morning?"

Viktor walked over and sat on the chair located immediately in front of Mary's desk. He placed his briefcase down at the side of the chair. "I've given Mr. Hitchins an initial valuation, but told him I would firm up once I'd done some research. He seemed to be pleased, so hopefully we'll obtain his agreement to sell the painting."

"That's good. I'm pleased you're back," said Mary. "We had another visit from Mr. Crawshaw this morning. I told him you'd be back in the gallery this afternoon, so he's returning at three o'clock."

"Oh, right," replied Viktor. He was still unsure about the visit. "Okay, so then we'll find out what he's got to say."

"I think you ought to have the meeting in your office. I've tidied the room up a bit and put in an extra chair. It's more private than out here," said Mary, standing up. "Come and

The Gamble

see what I've done. If you don't like it, we still have time to change it around."

Mary walked towards the rear of the gallery and Viktor followed saying, "I'm sure you've done a great job."

They both walked into the room that was primarily used for all the 'behind the scenes' functions, plus Viktor's desk and filing cabinet.

Viktor stood just inside the doorway and looked around the room. The desk and cabinet had been moved slightly, creating more space for a second chair. The kitchen, packing and storage sections had all been tidied up, but as they were fixed units, nothing more could be done there. The collection of paintings not currently on display and packing materials had all been moved out of the room. They were now temporarily stored at the rear of the display area, hidden from view by four paintings being displayed on easels.

"That's excellent, Mary. Well done. There seems to be a lot more room. I think I'll have a cup of coffee before he arrives. Do you want one as well?"

"No thanks. I just finished one before you returned. Is there anything else you want me to do?"

"Not at the moment. Just show Mr. Crawshaw in when he arrives, please. In the meantime, I'll sort myself out from my meeting this morning."

As Mary left, Viktor put his briefcase on the desk and made himself a mug of coffee.

At exactly 3pm, the front doorbell pinged and Mr. Crawshaw walked into the gallery. Mary stood up and walked towards him. "Mr. Kuznetsov is waiting for you in his office. Would you walk this way."

Mary led Mr. Crawshaw to the rear of the gallery, knocked on Viktor's door and announced the visitor's name.

Viktor stood up and walked to the side of his desk. Mr.

Crawshaw entered the room, looked all around him and walked towards Viktor. They both shook hands.

"Please, sit down," announced Viktor, pointing to the additional chair at the front of his desk. Mr. Crawshaw sat down and Viktor returned to his own seat. "I gather you wanted to speak to me."

Mary walked away and left the two men to their conversation.

When Viktor arrived home that evening, he told Penny all about his meeting with Mr. Crawshaw. Penny listened and was quite surprised at what she was hearing.

"What are you going to do?" asked Penny, wondering what Vic had planned to do next.

"I don't know. I've been thinking about that all the time since Mr. Crawshaw left my office. Ideally, I'd like to have a chat with Ian and get his thoughts on the matter. What do you think?"

They were both standing in the kitchen in their apartment. Penny decided to sit down on one of the high stools located next to the breakfast bar. Viktor sat down next to her.

Penny was pondering Viktor's question. "I think that might be a good idea. Probably the best option at this stage, before informing Bob Taylor. Give Ian a ring now whilst I finish preparing dinner."

Viktor walked over to a large bookcase on which he'd placed his mobile phone. He dialled Ian's home number.

Ian had just arrived home from his luncheon meeting with Michael. He was on his own in the house as Emma had telephoned Ian's mobile phone earlier and told him she would be home later than planned. That is, she explained, because she'd bought a painting in Burford. So, when the landline telephone rang, Ian assumed it was Emma with an update on her journey time.

The Gamble

To Ian's surprise, he found it was Viktor. Immediately he started to ask lots of questions about the honeymoon, the new apartment, Penny, and how she was coping being back at Sotheby's… with Northgate.

Eventually, Viktor was able to explain his situation. Ian agreed that they should meet up and discuss the matter in more detail. Viktor offered to travel out to Esher as he wanted to meet with Ian as soon as possible. They agreed to meet in two days' time. Ian said he would collect Viktor at Esher railway station, just before 1pm.

It was just after 7.30 that evening when Emma arrived home. Ian had prepared the evening meal and over two glasses of Chablis, Emma described her brief stay with Robert at her parents' house. She concluded by saying that Robert seemed to be very pleased to be staying there. He was happy and smiling when she left.

Ian dished up their pasta meal and he then explained briefly about his conversation with Viktor and his lunch meeting with Michael. He deliberately excluded Michael's bombshell about Andrei and made the possible meeting with Michael's son, Alexander, a little vague, saying he'd probably meet him sometime soon to find out exactly what he was looking for.

"Anyway," said Ian, anxious to change the subject. "What's this painting you've bought?"

"It's still in my car with my suitcase. After we've finished dinner, can you give me a hand and we'll bring them both in?"

Chapter 32

After dinner, Emma and Ian went outside to Emma's car. Ian volunteered to take the suitcase into the house whilst Emma followed closely behind carrying the wrapped picture.

Whilst Ian carried the case upstairs, leaving it in their bedroom for Emma to unpack later, Emma had taken her parcel into the home office where she placed it on her desk.

When Ian entered the room, he saw that Emma had already started to remove the brown paper wrapping. He stood at her side and watched with eager anticipation.

"So," said Emma, finally revealing the painting, "what do you think?"

Ian stepped forward and picked up the picture. After his initial examination he placed it on a nearby table so that it would lean back against the wall. He crouched down and inspected it more closely.

"Well?" asked Emma, impatiently.

Ian stood back up to his full height, turned and looked at Emma. "This looks like the work of Georges Seurat."

"I know that much, myself. That's what the label says on the back. The label also says the painting is called 'Mademoiselle Chad'," responded Emma. She was getting a little frustrated with her husband.

Ian turned back to look at the painting again. "Where did you get it?"

"In an antiques shop, in Burford. It cost me £50."

Ian suddenly laughed and turned back to face Emma. "Do you know, if this IS genuine… and I think it probably is, it could well be worth between two and three million? Not a bad return on £50!"

"Ian!" exclaimed Emma out loud. Her eyes suddenly opened fully in surprise. "Seriously?"

"What's the provenance?"

"Ah… well that's a bit trickier. There isn't any… well, none at the moment." Emma explained how she'd come across the painting, the discussions with June Connolly and her decision to buy it.

"So, you're hoping that June will come back with more information?"

"Yes."

"Well, it's definitely worth the gamble and it certainly looks like Seurat's work. However, because the picture's made up of all these coloured dots, it does make his style reasonably easy to copy."

"I've never heard of Georges Seurat before. I assume he's French."

"Look, it's getting late, so my suggestion is we start to do our own investigations in the morning, and, at the same time, I'll tell you more about the artist."

Next morning, while eating their breakfast, Ian started to tell Emma about Georges Seurat and his work.

"Seurat," he said, "was born in France, sometime in the 1850s. He had quite a privileged childhood as his father was extremely wealthy. I think he was a lawyer. Anyway, he was successful enough to retire in his early 40s and was then able to pay for young Georges's education. Georges showed some interest and promise in art, and in 1878 enlisted at the famous 'École des Beaux-Arts'. There, for just one year, he studied the old masters' paintings and much of his time was spent copying their work. However, he was easily bored with this more traditional art education and spent more and more of his time in the school's library. There he discovered a number of books dealing with the subject of colour. He was particularly fascinated by how colour could be used and how different colours worked side by side. He was also intrigued by how the human eye reacts to colour, especially when a person looks at a group of colours from different positions."

"That's what I found so fascinating about my painting when I first saw it," interrupted Emma. "It looked quite different depending on how far away you stood and from different positions."

Ian nodded and continued, "Seurat became very interested in the work of a French chemist, Michel-Eugene Chevreul. Chevreul was also fascinated by colours, especially with different coloured dots and their scientific relationship with each other. At the same time Seurat was also curious and inquisitive about the current trend towards 'impressionist' art. These impressionists were slowly moving art into a new and modern direction. Seurat decided he wanted to be part of this new and exciting movement. Unlike most Parisian artists of his day, Seurat didn't have any money worries because of his father's wealth. As a result, he left the 'École des Beaux-Arts' and started to paint and experiment on his own."

"He was a lucky man having 'Bank of Daddy' to back him up," said Emma.

"Surprisingly, Seurat started his new career by using crayons to create the coloured dots. However, he soon changed, and following Chevreul's influence, he moved over to using paints."

The Gamble

"Quite a rebel for his time."

Ian nodded. "But, of course, this period was a special time, a revolution in art was happening and wealthy Parisians were looking for something different to buy and display on their walls in their homes. Hence the creation of more abstract pictures and artists deciding to paint wealthy Parisians enjoying themselves, especially close to the River Seine. Think of some of Manet's work."

Emma nodded and sipped the last of her breakfast cup of tea.

"Where our man, Seurat, began to stray from the usual impressionist paintings, was on the subjects he painted. He didn't need to follow the now popular impressionist type of work exactly, like just painting the wealthy, because living in Paris there was also a large community of poor people. Most artists of the day ignored these people's plight because their income came from painting the wealthy, not the poor."

"So was Seurat something of a social reformer?" asked Emma, wondering where this direction was taking her.

"Maybe. Seurat liked to paint sad faces, the poor and the working class. He was not so bothered about the happy and wealthy. He liked to record the darker side of life and often went much deeper with his paintings. He particularly wanted to highlight the differences between the 'haves' and the 'have nots' in Parisian society. Later, we'll have a look at some of Seurat's more famous paintings, particularly 'The Bathers of Anjou' and 'A Sunday Afternoon on the Island of La Grande Jatte'. In these two paintings Seurat tries to highlight the huge differences between the rich and the poor people living in Paris."

Emma nodded.

Ian continued, "Seurat was, as you'll soon see, an unusual painter. His paintings often wanted to convey messages, hidden meanings, puzzles and mystery. He saw many of the poorer women being used by the wealthy as tokens, playthings or far worse. The more attractive women became mistresses and were 'paraded', as Seurat emphasised in some of his paintings. 'A Sunday Afternoon on the Island of La Grande Jatte' was a good example. After all, these women needed to make a living too."

"So do you think my painting was deliberately highlighting the plight of Mademoiselle Chad and the other similar working women?"

"Let's go into the office, I've got a book about Seurat's work. I'll show you some of his paintings."

Emma stood up and carried the breakfast plates and bowls over to the sink as Ian walked through to the home office. Emma then joined him.

Ian picked a book off his bookcase and laid it on his desk. "Look at the front cover here. This is part of the painting of 'A Sunday Afternoon on the Island of La Grande Jatte'."

Emma looked at the quiet relaxing scene of smiling men parading with well-dressed ladies on their arms. They were walking beside a river. It all looked calm and peaceful. Happy people enjoying a quiet Sunday afternoon stroll.

Ian then opened the book and flicked through the pages until he found the colour photograph of another painting, 'The Bathers of Anjou'. "Now look at this picture. The people are dressed differently. The whole atmosphere says working class, the poorer people of Paris. If you relate this painting to that other one you'll see the river is between the two groups. The 'haves' on one side and the 'have nots' on the other. Notice too that many of the 'have nots' are looking across the river. Watching, probably enviously, the happy and contented wealthy Sunday afternoon strollers."

Emma smiled. "Yes, he's even given them much sadder faces and… look." Emma pointed to the distant background in the picture. "There's a more industrial and bleak background to this painting."

"Well spotted. So now you can begin to understand Seurat's approach to his subject matter. He saw Paris in a different light to other Parisian artists. He wanted to emphasise the hypocrisy and deceitfulness. The real Paris as he saw it."

Emma nodded. "Yes, I see."

"Okay, let me find another painting," said Ian, turning more of the pages. He flicked past more colour pictures until he found what he was looking for. It was a photograph of a painting simply called, 'The Models'. In the picture there were three naked women in different poses. They appeared to be in a women's dressing room. Two were sitting down, one on a stool and one on the floor. Neither of these women were facing the artist. The third woman was standing in the middle of the group and facing directly towards the artist. She was completely naked and had a sad and forlorn expression on her face. The other two models simply had despondent body postures. In the background, on part of the room's rear wall, there was a section of the painting, 'A Sunday Afternoon on the Island of La Grande Jatte'.

"These women look so sad, Ian. I can see a similar dejected expression in my 'Mademoiselle Chad' painting."

"Do you notice anything else in common with your own picture?"

Emma picked up Ian's book and walked over to the small table where her own painting was still leaning against the wall. She looked backwards and forwards between the book and her painting. "Yes!" she suddenly shouted. "My 'Mademoiselle Chad' looks identical to the woman sitting on the right. She has a few more clothes on and is probably looking into a mirror, which is out of sight in your picture. But look!" Ian walked over to join her. Emma pointed to the watercolour painting hanging on the wall behind and above the head of 'Mademoiselle Chad'. "That looks like the same watercolour painting, in the same position on the wall, as your picture."

Ian waited for Emma to find any more comparisons.

A few seconds later she exclaimed, "Oh, Ian. Wow! Do you think my painting is connected?"

"Well done, you," said Ian, with genuine praise. "However, do you now want to hear the bad news?"

"No, not really," said Emma, suddenly feeling a little deflated. "But you'd better tell me anyway."

"Last night, whilst you were getting ready for bed, I looked for an entry for 'Mademoiselle Chad' in this book. It's not included."

Chapter 33

Ian parked his car in the ten-minute waiting area next to Esher railway station and checked his watch. He got out of his car, walked into the station and looked up at the 'Arrivals' board. After he'd established that Viktor's train was due in two minutes' time, he walked back outside and stood in the sunshine. Three minutes later, Viktor joined him. The two men shook hands and Ian pointed to his car.

"You've still got quite a tan, Vic," quipped Ian, as they walked towards his parked car. "You obviously had a great time in the Maldives."

The two men got into the car. Ian started the engine and they drove away.

Viktor gave Ian a summary of his and Penny's honeymoon.

"So, how's married life, Vic? I hope you're treating Penny especially well."

"It's really good, Ian. Penny hasn't thrown me out... well, not yet, anyway."

Ian laughed. "I've booked a table at the 'Anglers Rest'. It's a lovely old pub, situated next to the river."

"Sounds good. So, how's things with you, Emma and Robert?"

Ian turned his car off the main road and headed along a country lane with fields on both sides. "We're fine. Emma's really taken an interest in the art world and Robert's thoroughly enjoying school. Ah, here's the pub."

Viktor looked through the windscreen and saw part of an old, grey stone building coming into view. It was partially hidden by some thick bushes and a large overhanging oak tree. Just before a stone bridge ahead, Ian signalled to turn right and entered a newly tarmacked car park. Viktor guessed the car park was probably about half full. He could glimpse views of the river and more fields in the distance.

After Ian parked the car the two men got out. The sunshine was still warm and Ian suggested they might want to sit and chat outside on the patio after they'd finished their meal. They walked across the lane towards the pub and Ian pushed open the old, oak entrance door.

They were shown to a table which was located next to a picture window giving views of both the river and patio. Three enthusiasts sailed by in their canoes.

A few minutes later two pints of beer were delivered to their table.

"Well, Vic, cheers to you, Penny and married life." Ian raised his glass and Viktor did likewise.

"Cheers to you too, Ian. This is a nice pub. Quite olde-worlde."

"Yes, Emma and I, we like it. The food's usually good too. So, you wanted to have a chat. You sounded very mysterious on the phone."

Viktor took a sip of his beer and leaned back in his chair. "There are a few things coming to a head at the gallery and I'm not totally sure what to do next. If you don't mind, Ian, I'd be really interested in your thoughts and advice before I go back and talk to Bob in Monaco."

"Okay, I'll try my best," replied Ian. He also took a sip of his beer.

"A few months ago," commenced Viktor, "business was

very busy and I was finding it difficult to divide my time between seeing clients at their homes and being at the gallery. Bob agreed to my suggestion to employ an assistant manager to help run the gallery. I've taken on a lady called Mary Turnbull. She's really experienced and has been excellent at running the gallery… far better than I was, or ever could be. She's rearranged the displays, website, back office… and me, too!"

Ian smiled.

"Anyway, she's also suggested some internal changes which I agree need to be done. I asked two builders to give us a quotation. These I've now received and they're at least double the amount I was expecting. So, that got me thinking. We probably need to transfer to larger premises. Also, whilst I was away on our honeymoon, I began to think about my future and did I really want to be involved with the gallery long term. I'm much keener on the idea of building up my client numbers without the extra headache, constraints and costs of the gallery. Then, when I returned to the gallery, Mary said a Mr. Crawshaw had been asking for me. He'd left his business card, which stated he was a 'Property Consultant'."

At this point a waitress arrived at their table and asked if they were ready to order their food. Neither had even looked at the menu so Ian recommended the 'Beer-battered Fish and Chips' and Viktor agreed.

After the waitress had left them, Viktor continued. "I saw Mr. Crawshaw the other day and, in summary, he said he had a client who was interested in buying our gallery's lease."

"Interesting coincidence."

"That's what I thought. I told him that I had a partner and would need to discuss the matter with him before any decision could be made. I asked Mr. Crawshaw how much his client was willing to pay for the lease and he just responded by saying that at the moment he was just sounding me out to see whether there was a possibility of a sale. So, that's the current position."

"I see," replied Ian. "Have you mentioned any of this to Penny?"

"Oh, yes. She says she'll support whatever decision I come up with... and she also thought it was a good idea for me to talk to you before I went back to Bob."

"So, what do you really want to do in the future?"

"It's as I've said. I really enjoy face-to-face contact with clients but less so the day-to-day running of the gallery... it's all too restrictive. My thoughts at the moment are to tell Bob of the enquiry for the gallery and get Mary to investigate the availability of larger premises... which really, needs to be in the same area. I know Bob likes our current location. If this all happens, I'll try to negotiate the best deal possible with Mr. Crawshaw and then suggest to Bob he buy my share of the business."

"What does Mary think about this change?"

"She knows about Mr. Crawshaw's inquiry, but not my present thinking. I decided not to raise the matter directly with her until I'd formulated all the plans in my own head. Mary would be very capable of running the gallery on her own or maybe with the help of a part-time assistant."

"I think you need to sound her out. Despite all her qualities, she might not want to go along with your plans. She may not want to move offices or even be pleased with the idea of running the gallery without you. Also, with Bob, he might not be so keen to buy you out."

"They're all good points. I'll start by speaking to Mary tomorrow morning."

"The only extra advice I would give you, Vic, is to take your time and make sure you're going to have a suitable

The Gamble

number of clients first. I presume you're intending to work from home?"

"Yes, I don't need an office away from the apartment. Otherwise, I might as well stay in the gallery."

"Talking of extra clients, there's another idea I've got that you might want to consider. At Michael Hopkins's retirement send off, he gave me a note. The note just said that he'd be in touch again soon. Well, a little while ago, we met for lunch. He told me that his youngest son, Alexander, has a small, but growing business. It focuses on house clearances, mainly in London and around the home counties. However, they specialise with big houses and, sometimes, large estates. The top end of the market. Properties often worth millions!"

Viktor raised his eyebrows and leaned forward. He wanted to know more.

"Michael suggested my name to Alexander. What he wants me to do is to provide valuations and possible sales of all the valuable paintings they come across. I've not given Michael my answer so far, and haven't even met Alexander, but what I'm now thinking, Vic, is, and if you're determined to give up the gallery, then maybe the two of us could meet up with Alexander and listen to what he's got to say. What do you think?"

"It sounds really interesting and promising, Ian. If you're in, then count me in too. It'd be great to work with you again."

"Okay, I'll get in touch with Michael and ask him to fix an appointment with Alexander. I'll let you know what transpires."

"Excellent," said Viktor, with a broad smile on his face. This is the art world he really wanted to be part of!

"Now then, look at these," said Ian, as the waitress placed two large plates of fish and chips on their table. Ian also ordered two more pints of beer.

Chapter 34

Oscar was enjoying his stay on the Hawaiian Islands. This was the first real holiday he'd experienced since moving to Antigua. He'd never been to Hawaii before so he had to read up about what there was to do and see. However, it wasn't until he'd arrived at his hotel on Oahu that he realised Pearl Harbour was not too far away from where he was staying. He'd always thought that this famous US naval base, bombed by the Japanese in 1941, was actually located on the west coast of America, somewhere close to San Diego.

The hotel's concierge had recommended a visit to this historic site. He told Oscar that, although it still remained a naval base for the US Pacific Fleet, the area around where the original bombing took place was now a museum and a solemn reminder of the tragic events that happened on that fateful day, the 7th of December. He also warned Oscar that most visitors find the visit a moving and emotional experience.

Oscar followed the concierge's recommendation and, a day later, he took a taxi ride to the naval base. His driver told Oscar that he'd visited the site about ten times with different members of his family and friends. Nearly all of them came away with a mixture of sadness and deep thoughts.

The Gamble

Oscar stayed at the museum for about four hours and came away feeling emotionally drained. The memorial listing all the hundreds of servicemen killed and the sunken USS Arizona ship, part of which is still just protruding above the sea level, was, to Oscar, a very strong and sobering scene. A serious reflection on man's stupidity and just one example of the many atrocities that result from wars. That evening he decided to dine on his own in his room, making use of the hotel's room service facility. He was certainly not in any mood for people or potential conversation.

The next morning Oscar was feeling much happier, even more so when he opened up his email inbox on his mobile phone. He quickly spotted a message from May Ling. She had written:

Hi Oscar,

I've just met Peter Wong and he told me you are going to join their group this year on the annual fishing trip to Fiji. When you get back to Hong Kong, call me, or send me an email. It would be great to meet up for a chat and a meal. I hope you have a lovely holiday with the boys. Don't get too drunk!

Best wishes,

May x

Suddenly a large smile appeared on Oscar's face. It would be wonderful to meet up with May 'face to face' once again. It had been such a long time. Seeing her on Ian's former partnership video conferences and exchanging business emails were one thing, he thought, but this was… well, personal… and she'd put an x after her name!

He quickly switched to the calendar app on his phone. He reminded himself which dates he'd booked to stay in Hong Kong. He found the copy of his itinerary and wrote down the dates of the four days he'd planned to be staying at the 'The Peninsula Hong Kong' grand hotel in Kowloon.

Flicking back to his emails he composed the following reply message:

Hi May,

What a wonderful surprise your email was this morning! It would be brilliant if we could meet up in Hong Kong. I'm booked into the 'Peninsula' on Kowloon, from the 26th. My flight out of Hong Kong is on the 30th. I really hope you can fit in with at least one of those dates.

Really looking forward to seeing you again.

Oscar x

Oscar double checked his draft and wondered about the 'x' after his name, but then smiled to himself and pressed the 'send' button. He quickly forgot the events of the last 24 hours and decided life had suddenly become much, much better!

In the UK, Emma had started researching her painting, 'Mademoiselle Chad'. It was a bit of a blow when Ian had mentioned that the title didn't appear in his catalogue. Ian had tried to comfort her by saying that it was not unusual for this situation to occur. After all, it was well over 100 years since the picture was painted and it could quite easily have changed hands many times during that period without being recorded. Now Emma was hoping June Connolly would be able to provide the spark of information that would get her started.

Fortunately, Emma didn't have to wait too long. It was two days later when she received an email from June, which said:

Dear Mrs. Caxton,

I'm sorry for not coming back to you sooner, but the buyer of the shop has been in and out and checking on stock and things.

I've been through my aunt's records and am pleased to tell you that I found what you were asking about. In 1967 my aunt bought your painting for £2 7s 6d from Mrs. Lucy Charlton. Mrs. Charlton's address is entered as 'River View', River Close, Burford.

I hope that information is useful.

By the way, my shop will be sold in two days' time, but I can still be contacted at this email address if you think I can help any further.

Best wishes,

June Connolly.

Emma read the email for a second time and wrote down in her notepad:

1967: Mrs. Lucy Charlton, River View, River Close, Burford, sold to 'Wendy's Antiques' for £2 7s 6d.

Emma then wrote a reply email to June, thanking her for all her help and assistance. She also hoped the sale of the shop would go well and she gave June her best wishes for the future.

"Right, at least we've got started," Emma said to herself, whilst rubbing her hands. "So, 1967, that's what? Well over 50 years ago. The probability, of course, is that Mrs. Charlton is no longer residing at 'River View'… but you never know. No harm in sending a letter and see what happens."

Emma switched her computer from emails to its word processing facility and started to draft the following letter:

Dear Sirs,

*I am trying to trace the whereabouts of **Mrs. Lucy Charlton**, who I understand was living at the 'River View' property in 1967.*

I have enclosed a stamped addressed envelope and would be obliged if you could tell me any information you may know about this lady.

Yours faithfully,
Mrs. Emma Caxton.

Emma addressed the envelope to 'The Occupier', 'River View', River Close, Burford and put it on the side of her desk. She intended to post it first thing in the morning.

Chapter 35

Viktor had finally made his decision. He'd written a long email to Bob Taylor explaining the issues with the gallery and the approach made by Mr. Crawshaw. However, he deliberately didn't mention his own possible plans and ideas.

Bob replied two days later suggesting he and Mary might want to start looking for a potential larger gallery site, preferably in the same local area. If they found something suitable, then he wanted to know what the new lease costs would be and how much work would be needed, timescales, etc.

Viktor decided it was now time to speak to Mary. It was a quiet time in the gallery when he walked from his office area to join her. She was sitting at her desk at the front of the gallery. "Can we have a chat, please, Mary?" Viktor pulled up a chair and sat down.

"About Mr. Crawshaw, is it? I was wondering when you were going to speak to me."

"Yes, it's partly to talk about his visit, but there's more."

"Okay," said Mary. She shut down her computer and waited for Viktor to speak.

"Mr. Crawshaw was inquiring whether I would consider selling the lease on this property. He said he's got a client who's very keen to move into this area and the size of this property is probably ideal. I told him I have a partner and can't make any decision until I've discussed it with him. I also emphasised that it will also depend on what his client is prepared to pay."

"Are you thinking of closing down this business then?"

"No, nothing like that. You've made the gallery far more profitable than when I was trying to juggle both my jobs. No, you and I have been discussing the possibility of making changes at the back of the gallery, haven't we?" Mary nodded. "Well, the two quotations I received to complete the work were more than double what I'd hoped for. So that started me thinking about the possibility of moving to larger premises.

"Are you thinking locally, or further afield?"

"That's the tricky bit. I don't know what premises are available and if they are, would they be a better size... and how much would they cost? This is a great location so I don't want to move very far."

"I'm really happy here, Vic. It's so convenient for me on the Underground. I don't have to change lines at all to get home."

Viktor scratched his head. This was all becoming more difficult by the minute. "Well, why don't you start by trying to find out if there are any other premises currently available in this area? We can then go and look together at any you think might be about the right size for our needs. We'll then take it from there."

"Okay," said Mary, unenthusiastically. She started to wonder if this move would work out for her. She didn't want to look for another job, but...

When Viktor returned to his office, Mary pondered on her options. Gradually she concluded that the best answer would be to find larger more suitable premises even closer

The Gamble

to her usual Underground station. Now that would be a challenge… and a real bonus.

Ian was still thinking about his George Watts painting, 'Lord Rye and Rother'. He'd already sent emails to a select few galleries who he thought might be interested in the picture. However, nobody had yet returned with a positive, or even an inquisitive, inquiry. He was beginning to think that maybe an auction would be the only option. But if so, would he consider using Sotheby's? He'd really like Penny to get the full benefit of the sale, but he definitely didn't want to give Northgate the opportunity to steal Penny's thunder. Ian just knew the sort of barbed comments Northgate would make – 'how he'd personally helped Caxton with a "problem" painting!' No, I'm not going to give Northgate that sort of pleasure, I'm not that desperate… well, not yet!

It was two days later when Ian answered the telephone call. "Ian Caxton," he announced.

"Ian, hi. Toby Williams, Cameron Gallery."

"Toby, hello. Good to hear from you. How's things?"

"Yes, good thanks, Ian. Look, the reason I'm ringing is that I gather you have a George Watts painting for sale."

"That's right, but I thought your company wasn't interested."

"I've been on holiday and only just been informed. I have a client who's an avid collector of Watts paintings. He might be interested. Can you give me some of the details?"

Ian told Toby the picture's details and gave him a summary of its provenance. Finally, he mentioned that he'd obtained a letter from the catalogue raisonné people confirming the painting was to be reinstated in their next publication.

"All sounds interesting, Ian. What sort of price are you looking for?"

"Ideally, I think it is worth about 1.3 million pounds, but if you pushed me, I might accept 1.2."

"That's not bad for a Watts portrait. Leave it with me. I'll have a chat with my client."

"Thanks, Toby. Speak to you soon."

"Bye, Ian."

The line went dead.

Well, that's more like it, thought Ian. He liked Toby and also knew that when Toby made an inquiry, it was usually a serious one.

Emma walked into the office after Ian had finished his telephone call and asked who had been on the phone.

"Toby Williams. He was enquiring about my George Watts painting."

"He's with one of the galleries you emailed, isn't he? I thought they'd all turned you down."

"Apparently Toby's only just become aware. He wanted the full details to chat with one of his clients."

"Do you think he's serious?"

"Toby's not the sort of person who wastes his and other people's time. He's interested alright."

"So, the auction route's now dead is it?"

"Not necessarily. I've offered Toby a good deal, but I'd probably still get more from an auction."

Chapter 36

The following Sunday, Ian was in his car with both Emma and Robert. They were on their way to Ian's parents' as they'd been invited to enjoy a Sunday roast lunch.

Whilst Ian was driving, his mind was still occupied by his father's comments earlier in the week, when they'd spoken on the telephone. He was particularly worried about what his father **hadn't** said during the call. He'd mentioned these concerns to Emma, but she'd just asked, "What did he say to get you so worried?" Ian explained that it was not what he'd said, it was the way his father had spoken to him. Sort of hesitantly, not his usual authoritative way of talking at all.

"You're quiet," said Emma, from the front passenger seat. "Are you still thinking about your father?"

"Yes. I'm just wondering if we're going to be walking into a bombshell moment!"

"I don't think so, Ian. If I was going to do that, I wouldn't invite us all over for lunch to do it."

"No, you're probably right. At least I hope you're right."

Forty minutes later Ian drove his car into his parents' driveway, passing the old wooden house sign, 'The Willows'. He parked in front of the double garage and climbed out of his car. He looked across the large front lawn and then sideways towards the house. The house he'd grown up in. The only property he'd ever lived in until he'd left for university. It was no longer his home, but it still felt like he was coming home. He took a deep breath of the cool, fresh air.

Emma and Robert got out of the car and Robert immediately spotted his grandmother standing outside the front door. He ran over to give her a hug. Emma joined them and she followed her mother-in-law and Robert into the house. After Ian had locked the car, he stood and looked around the garden once more. As usual, it was immaculate. Now mainly laid to lawn and flowering shrubs, it was slightly different to how he remembered it. The large willow tree had been removed after a storm, but the place still 'felt' the same.

"Penny for your thoughts." It was Ian's father, Richard, who was walking across the pathway from the house to greet him. Although now in his late 60s, Richard was tall like his son and still had an authoritative stride in his step.

"Hi, Dad. Just admiring the front garden, it's immaculate as usual." Ian shook his dad's hand. Still the firm grip as ever, he thought.

"Maybe not for much longer though, Ian. Your mother and I have been thinking about whether we should move somewhere smaller. Somewhere that requires less work and maintenance."

"Oh!" said a very surprised Ian. Was that the bombshell, he wondered?

"I know we have a gardener and your mother organised a part-time cleaner for the house about six months ago, but there's a lot for us still to do… and, unfortunately, we're not getting any younger. Your mother still wants a garden and a nice house but everything now needs to be much smaller… with a lot less need for maintenance."

"Yes, I can see your logic, Dad. I guess it comes to us all, sooner or later."

"We've been lucky, Ian. Some of our friends, or people we've known for just a little time, they've recently died or had to have major surgery. We're still okay, but we don't want the worry of the upkeep any more. The property deserves a new, energetic, young family to look after it. It's a big house, Ian… a family home."

Ian nodded and looked across from the lawn to the front of the house. He spotted his old bedroom and smiled.

"You're not angry are you, Ian?"

"Angry?" Ian looked directly at his father. "Why on earth should I be angry?"

"Because this is your home too. At least it was. It's where you grew up."

"Dad, honestly, I'm not angry. I want what's best for you and Mum. I'll be sad when you finally move, naturally, but I'm sure you and Mum will be too. You've both lived here for more years than I've been alive! No, honestly, Dad, and I repeat, I want whatever's best for you two."

Ian and his father looked at each other and both gave an emotional smile.

"Come on, son," said Richard, patting Ian on the shoulder, "the ladies will be wondering where we've got to."

Oscar finished his Hawaiian holiday with a seven-day cruise around some of the major volcanic islands. He was reminded of the impenetrable jungle-like mountain scenery from the *Jurassic Park* films. Although he wanted to see some of the jungle areas on foot, he was told there were no short excursions into the interior.

For Oscar, the holiday was all about relaxation, new views and sea life. From the cruise ship he'd spotted a number of Green Sea Turtles, Spinner Dolphins and, unusually for this time of year, one Humpback Whale, which to Oscar seemed too close to their ship for comfort.

The next day was Oscar's final day in Hawaii. He was packed and ready for his next adventure, meeting up with his fishing buddies. He sat in the reception area of the hotel until he was informed that a taxi was now waiting outside. Oscar stood up, collected his bags and walked towards the taxi. Next stop, the airport… and then Hong Kong.

As Oscar entered the aeroplane he felt an air of excitement, but this was tempered by equal amounts of apprehension. This would be the first time he'd returned to Hong Kong since he'd packed his bags and headed for a new life in Antigua. Lots had changed in his own life and he now wondered what changes he would find in Hong Kong. He was particularly concerned following the news reports he'd read and seen about the increasing influence and control the Chinese authorities in Beijing were having on the people in Hong Kong. He seriously wondered if returning to Hong Kong was a good idea!

Chapter 37

Emma heard the postman delivering their mail, so she picked up the postbox key and went outside to collect their post. She opened the metal black box to find three letters. Glancing at each one in turn, she found what she was hoping for. One of the envelopes was addressed to her and had been written by her own fair hand. She relocked the box, closed the front door and walked back into the kitchen. There she opened the self-addressed envelope and read the contents:

Riverside Cottage
River Close
Burford

Dear Mrs. Caxton,
You recently wrote to my neighbour's address, 'River View' asking about the whereabouts of my great aunt, Mrs. Lucy Charlton. Unfortunately, Aunt Lucy died in 1972. My father, Aunt Lucy's nephew, is the only surviving member of our family that remembers anything about her living at 'River View'. Could you let me know what information you are looking for, and why, please? I can then ask my father.
Yours sincerely,
Clare Bellamy (Mrs.)

Okay, thought Emma, we might be getting somewhere, but I'm not too sure where at the moment. Five minutes later she decided to write her reply to Mrs. Bellamy at Riverside Cottage:

Dear Mrs. Bellamy,

Thank you kindly for spending the time to answer my letter about your great aunt, Mrs. Lucy Charlton. I recently purchased a painting from 'Wendy's Antiques' in Duck Lane, Burford and the proprietor told me their old records state that this painting was purchased from Mrs. Charlton in 1967.

I'm now trying to follow the ownership of the painting all the way back to when it was probably painted, in about 1885. If your father can remember the painting in Mrs. Charlton's home (its composition is a series of painted coloured dots), I would be extremely interested.

Please find enclosed a stamped addressed envelope for your reply,

Yours sincerely,
Emma Caxton.

As it was a lovely warm day, Emma decided she would walk to the local mailbox and post her letter immediately. It would then be picked up with the afternoon collection.

Three days later Emma received a reply from Mrs. Bellamy. She quickly opened the letter and read the following:

Riverside Cottage
River Close
Burford
Dear Emma,

Lovely to hear from you. What a strange painting you seem to have purchased.

As you requested, I have spoken to my father. He's rather frail nowadays and some days his memory is better than others.

However, I seem to have caught him on one of his better days yesterday. He told me he does remember the funny picture hanging on Aunt Lucy's wall. He cannot remember when exactly, but it was certainly when he was a boy. So that puts it probably in the early 1940s.

I do hope this information is of some use to you.
Best wishes,
Clare.

Emma walked into the office and picked up her notebook. She now entered:

Mrs. Lucy Charlton, River View, Burford, owned the painting, possibly in the 1940s.

After she'd finished writing, Emma placed the pen back on her desk and pondered on what she was going to do next.

When Oscar arrived at Hong Kong International airport, on the island of Chek Lap Kok, he was met by his old pal, Peter Wong.

Both men greeted each other like long-lost brothers. Oscar had known Peter from when he was about 11 years of age. They'd both been to the same school but their friendship had drifted apart when Peter went off to university and they hadn't seen each other again until ten years ago when the boy's annual fishing trips began.

It was the leader of the fishing trips, Lee Cheung, who had come up with the idea. He worked in HSBC's head office with Peter. When Lee suggested the scheme to Peter, he thought it would be a fun idea and was excited by the prospect. They decided they really needed at least six people on board to make the trip worthwhile… and cost effective. That way they could rent a much larger, and a more specialist, fishing craft.

Peter had asked Oscar if he was interested, and he was. Oscar then suggested the trip to Ian and he joined the group on their maiden ten-day fishing trip. Ian knew that this would probably be his only chance because he was marrying Emma shortly afterwards and there were already discussions at Sotheby's about him moving back to London.

The two final members of the group were friends of Lee, Oliver Lam and David Leung.

Over the next nine years, the ten-day fishing trip for 'the boys' became an annual event. Lee, David and Peter took part in every one of the sailings. Oliver missed two and Oscar had been absent for the last three. Each year, where they were short on the regular six, other colleagues were invited and took the opportunity to experience the fun and games the others had told them about.

This time, however, there were only five of the regular group making the trip. They were all much older now and each had various new responsibilities. Some were married and raising children and two had moved abroad with their work. It was also becoming much harder to agree on the same holiday dates. Lee had already suggested that this trip might be their last gathering. Nobody appeared to raise any strong objections.

So, it was with mixed emotions when Lee, Peter, Oliver, David and Oscar all climbed aboard *'The White Shark'* for probably their very last time. There was still the usual air of excitement, banter and laughter, but this time it was intermixed with some heavy-heartedness as well.

Chapter 38

After six days fishing in the south Pacific Ocean, 'the boys' were having one of their better years, catch-wise. The US$10,000 prize for the largest fish caught was still very much in the balance. Lee and Peter were well out in front of the other three with regards to total numbers of fish caught but, to everyone's surprise, Oscar, who had never won the prize money before, was currently leading with the heaviest fish of 87 lbs! This was for a medium size 'Dogtooth Tuna'. Nevertheless, the rest of the group were still confident that at least one of them would pass Oscar's target. Experience reminded them that in most of the previous years, the winning fish had usually been over 100 lbs in weight.

It had always been the boys' policy to fish for fun and not for food, so every serious catch was weighed and then released back into the ocean. Before the better catches were released there were always a few selective photographs taken of the angler and his catch and of course of the year's US$10,000 winner, smiling with his prize fish. That particular picture was always framed, brought back on board the following year and placed on the wall of the main cabin. It was the inspiration for the next trip. This year, it was a colour photograph of a grinning David Leung with his 102 lb 'Blue Marlin', that was on display.

The total number of hours spent fishing each day was largely determined by two main constraints and considerations. One was the weather and the other was how much alcohol the boys had consumed the previous evening! If the sun was strong and the sky clear of clouds, then fishing would start at about 7am and finish for the morning at about 10.30am. That would signal a break for some food, alcohol and a long siesta. Fishing would then recommence about four o'clock and carry on until nightfall. If the weather was wet and windy then the fishing may only last for a few hours before they'd all decide to shelter, eat some food, drink alcohol and play poker.

This was the fifth year running that *'The White Shark'* had been hired for ten days. It was designed to sleep a maximum of eight adults, so only having five or six adults on board meant there was plenty of room for everyone to spread out. Late on this particular afternoon, Oscar was in need of a rest and some time to himself. He was one of the lucky three that had drawn one of the four double cabins for himself only. He lay on his bed and was reading a magazine article about the Fijian islands. However, he was struggling to stay awake and decided to look at his mobile phone instead. The boat came equipped with modern technology, which included a reasonable satellite wifi link. He accessed his emails and was pleased to see May Ling's response to his earlier email, which he now read:

Hello Oscar,

I'm assuming that when you receive this email, you will be somewhere on the Pacific enjoying fishing and the company of your good friends. I really hope you're all having a great time.

At the moment the dates you have given me are a slight problem as I'm supposed to be in Beijing on all those days. However, I think I can make a few changes, but I won't be able to tell you the exact dates for a few more days. But, I promise you, I will see you during your Hong Kong stay.

Say hello to Peter from me.

Have a great time and enjoy the rest of your holiday,

May x

Typical of May, thought Oscar to himself. Business always comes first! Still, at least she's made a promise, but I guess I'll just have to wait and see if she can still keep to it.

The final three days of fishing were tense and exciting. Oscar was still in the lead, but had to hold his breath when 'the expert', David Leung, landed a large 'Blue Marlin' weighing in at 81 lbs! Until Lee and Peter were able to weigh it, David was convinced he had managed to sneak past Oscar's still leading catch. When the result was announced, David shook his head in frustration and Oscar stood staring at him with a huge grin on his face.

On the final morning, all five anglers were up early and fishing by seven o'clock. The cut off time was twelve noon. They all knew that by 1pm they needed to be heading back to port to guarantee mooring before dark. Breakfast was largely ignored, although, at given opportunities, each of them popped into the galley to snack on the last remaining supplies of food. The alcohol had been completely consumed by 6pm the previous evening so there was no chance of hangovers today.

By eleven o'clock Oscar began to relax. He'd decided there was little chance of anyone beating him now. Depending on the size of any fish potentially bigger than his, it would likely take until after midday to land it. The rules strictly said that only catches landed before midday qualified.

Oscar, Peter and Oliver started to pack up their equipment. The extremely competitive David and Lee, however, were still trying up to the very last minute.

Suddenly, Lee snapped at his rod and shouted that he'd hooked a biggie! Oscar, Peter and Oliver stopped what they were doing and watched Lee heave at the rod and wind the line onto the reel. They all agreed it was a big one. Shit, though Oscar. He looked at his watch. 11.40.

Lee continued to battle but the fish was fighting back. Even David had now given up the challenge and watched Lee fighting with his rod.

Oscar looked at his watch again. 11.44. God, he thought, there's still a chance I could lose this. The final trip and the last opportunity to collect the US$10,000!

Lee heaved and wound in the line. He was now sweating, his arms ached and his legs were sore from being jammed against the rail at the side of the ship. Despite being strapped into his seat, he still felt the full force of the pull of the large fish. The leather retaining strap was now seriously uncomfortable, causing a tight grip on his stomach. Nevertheless, he still heaved again and wound in a few more precious centimetres of fishing line.

Suddenly, after one last heave, Lee's line finally snapped and he fell backwards, exhausted, into his chair.

"That would have been a real biggie," said Oliver.

"Must have been well over a hundred pounds," replied Peter, giving Lee a consoling pat on his back.

David shook his head. He felt for Lee and his disappointment.

Oscar, meanwhile, had an even bigger grin on his face!

Chapter 39

Ian sat in his home office staring at the computer screen. He was looking at Christie's website and was particularly interested in the way they were advertising their forthcoming auction. He looked at all the paintings listed, but wasn't overly excited as most were by modern artists. Only a couple of the paintings, he eventually decided, were of marginal interest. Some of the collection, by two young artists, did show a degree of promise but he wasn't in the market for gambling on this level of raw talent.

He left Christie's website a little dismayed and decided to look at his emails instead. There he spotted Toby Williams's reply and read the following message:

Hi Ian,

Sorry for not getting back to you earlier, but my client has been abroad. I've now had an opportunity to chat with him and I am pleased to say, he's very interested in your George Watts portrait painting of Lord Rye.

I hope it's still for sale and at your quoted price of £1.2 million.

I await your reply,
Regards,
Toby.

Ian sat back and pondered on both Toby's email and the forthcoming Christie's auction. He'd noticed that the auction's reserve prices had slowly been creeping up over recent months and he now wondered if he should decline Toby's option and take a chance of getting an even higher price at auction.

Later that same day Ian and Emma were in their lounge sitting together on the settee. They were finishing off a nice bottle of chardonnay. Dinner had been eaten, pots and plates were in the dishwasher and Robert was fast asleep in bed.

Ian was thinking about his parents and, particularly his father's comments about selling 'The Willows', the family home. He'd told his father that they should go ahead as he no longer had an emotional attachment to the property. But, as Ian thought more and more about it, he realised he did still have an emotional attachment. He'd lived in the house, full time, for the first 18 years of his life and then part time for the next six. It was only when he moved to New York that he'd finally cut the last ties and shipped all his possessions out to the USA. Yes, he still went back 'home' for holidays, but when he then moved on to Hong Kong, all his possessions moved with him from New York. After Hong Kong it was back to the UK, but by then he had married Emma and they'd purchased their first property together. That was their current house in Esher. This was now Ian's 'home', his and Emma's family home, so why all of a sudden was he emotionally returning back to 'The Willows'? The answer, he eventually concluded, was because it had always been there. His parents had always been there too. It was the safe and solid bolthole that he could always depend upon... whatever, or wherever he was. If the worst came to the worst, he could always return back home. Now

The Gamble

this 'security' was about to change… and he'd now realised he was definitely concerned!

"What are you thinking about?" asked Emma. She was conscious that Ian was spending an unusual amount of time being very quiet, and, apparently, thinking.

"Sorry, Emma," replied Ian, "I've been thinking about what Dad said."

"What? About them selling their house?"

"That's just it. It is their house, but it's also the 'family home'. Dad asked me if I was emotionally concerned or attached. I just said no, not any longer, but the more I think about it, the more emotional I still feel. It's as though my final safety net is being taken away. Weird, isn't it? I almost feel as though I ought to buy it."

Emma raised her eyebrows in surprise. "Even if you did buy 'The Willows', then what? You cannot recreate the past. Your parents won't be living there and there's also Robert and me to consider. I like the house, but here" – Emma waved her hands in the air – "this is OUR family home. Let's say you bought your parents' house and rented it out, it would be strangers who'd be living there. It still wouldn't be the old family home."

"Emotions and common sense are not compatible bedfellows," said Ian, gently shaking his head. "I've just got to accept that this is the best option for my parents, at their time of life."

"I agree. They'll psychologically be removing a big millstone from around their necks and probably a serious worry. They'll replace it with a new, easier to maintain, house and garden… and a happier life. Plus, the option of being able to spend more time away from the UK in the winter. All that has got to put a smile on their faces."

"You're right, Emma. Thank you."

"Now then, Mr. Caxton, talking about British winters, we need to make some plans to return to Monaco."

For Oscar, the good news from May Ling was that she would be in Hong Kong for the final two days that he would be staying there. They both agreed to meet at one of May's favourite restaurants, the 'Yung Kee', on Hong Kong Island. She knew it was one of Oscar's favourite restaurants as well. Also, it was only a short walk from her apartment.

Oscar, when planning this holiday, had decided to treat himself to a four-night mini-break staying at the famous five-star 'Peninsula Hong Kong' grand hotel, in Kowloon. When living in Hong Kong, he'd promised himself an indulgent stay there one day. He had previously visited 'The Bar' with colleagues when they'd been celebrating special occasions. And he'd also eaten with business clients, in both the 'Spring Moon' and 'Felix' restaurants. Therefore, it was with a mixture of nervous anticipation and excitement, that he was specially welcomed at reception and then escorted up to his luxurious suite.

On the evening of his planned meal with May, he decided to catch the famous Star Ferry across Victoria Harbour to Hong Kong Island. It had been a long time since he'd used the famous ferry and, when he'd purchased his return ticket, he immediately noticed the cost was still unbelievably cheap. Mind, he also noticed the crossing time and distance was now much reduced following the large amount of land reclamation that had been carried out over the last few decades.

It was a hot and sultry evening and Oscar was enjoying the cooling breeze blowing onto his face. He sat on a green wooden bench seat and gazed at the approaching Central skyline. It too had changed in recent years and he wondered if, like most other things he'd seen so far in Hong Kong, the 'Yung Kee' had also changed as well. Or, he hoped, the food and atmosphere would still be as good as the last time he'd dined there.

The Gamble

As the ferry slowed down in readiness to dock, Oscar stood up and joined the queue of people waiting to disembark. His mind turned to thinking about May Ling and then to the excellent Cantonese food that he'd missed since he'd moved to Antigua. He just hoped, in lots of ways, that this was going to be another excellent evening. Maybe, a very special evening!

After stepping off the ferry, Oscar walked the short distance to the restaurant. He was early, so decided to wander around the area and look at some of the changes to the local district. After a few minutes, he spotted the familiar figure of May walking from the opposite direction. He waved and May smiled and waved back. They greeted each other with a big hug, huge smiles and two kisses on each other's cheeks.

"It's wonderful to see you again, May, you look fabulous," said Oscar, still with a huge smile on his face.

"Thank you, Oscar. You're looking pretty good yourself. How was your fishing trip? You'll have to tell me all about it."

They walked together towards the restaurant. May put her arm through Oscar's. He was surprised, but enjoyed the intimacy. Two minutes later, they entered through the large, shop-front-like doorway of the 'Yung Kee' restaurant. May announced her name and she and Oscar followed the maître d' towards their reserved table. As they walked through the restaurant, Oscar looked around the room and sniffed at the familiar aromas. Yes, he thought, it still 'feels' as I remember. The warm and enticing atmosphere was making him hungry. He hoped the food would live up to the previous high standards.

They both sat down and Oscar suggested a bottle of champagne. May smiled and nodded her agreement. The maître d' said he would get a bottle to be delivered immediately.

"It really has been a long time since we were last in here," said Oscar, still looking around the room. "I hope the food is still as good as it smells."

"I ate a meal in here with a client about a month ago and yes, the food was still fabulous. That's why I suggested it. I knew you'd missed it."

"There are many pluses about Antigua, May, but top Chinese restaurants are not one of them." said Oscar, smiling, but with feeling. "I've not found one that comes even close to this place."

"Are you still enjoying your life living in the Caribbean?"

"The first year was tricky and then when the partnership ended I became quite depressed. But in between, I've had a great time."

May was surprised and a little anxious about what Oscar had just said. "You don't seem depressed now. What happened?"

"Several things came to a head. I really wanted the partnership to continue. Gladstone, remember him?" May nodded. "Well, he decided to move to Jamaica to be closer to his son, daughter-in-law and their new baby. Not only was he a business colleague, but he was my main beer-drinking pal as well. Also, the art market had become very quiet and, to be honest, I was, for the very first time in my life, feeling lonely."

"I'm sorry," said May. She reached out her hand and touched his arm. "I didn't realise. Did you want to come back to Hong Kong?"

"Oh, no. I wasn't missing Hong Kong at all. It was the people I was missing… my friends, colleagues and my fishing pals. I've made some friends in Antigua, but the culture is so different. It was very frustrating in the early days."

Their bottle of champagne arrived. The waiter popped the cork and slowly poured the champagne into two glasses. He then put the bottle into a metal wine cooler next to their table.

The Gamble

"Well, Oscar," said May, picking up her glass, "here's to you and a happier future."

Oscar picked up his own glass, gently chinked May's and said, "Thank you, and here's to happiness for the both of us!"

They both sipped their champagne and then Oscar said, "It's so good to meet up with you again, May. I've really missed you."

They ordered their food and Oscar went for his favourite, Yung Kee's version of Authentic Cantonese Roast Duck. May decided to join him with the same order.

The meal was just as delicious as Oscar remembered. He savoured every morsel. At least something in Hong Kong had not changed, he thought. Very little had been said whilst they enjoyed their meal but, once their chopsticks were laid down, they returned to their conversation.

"When was the last time you had a holiday, May?" asked Oscar. He couldn't remember ever hearing May mention any holidays she'd had.

"I cannot remember," she replied, after thinking about Oscar's question. "I've been so busy with work, especially in Beijing. And now I've got four new clients in Shanghai. So it's all been so very busy. Holidays haven't come into my thoughts."

"Why don't you come out to Antigua? I'll show you a new world. My villa's next to the beach and the Caribbean Sea. I go swimming almost every day. The sea temperature, it's so warm."

"It sounds lovely… and tempting, Oscar, but over the next few weeks, I've got so much on."

"Okay, so what about in one or two months' time? Let's fix a date now," said Oscar, his voice a little excited and forceful.

May Ling sat back in her seat and looked directly at Oscar.

She pondered on his suggestion. Suddenly, she removed her mobile phone from her handbag and accessed the calendar app. She flicked through the dates. Oscar sat quietly with his fingers crossed under the table.

"What about the 18th of November? I could come out for about three weeks then."

"Excellent!" said Oscar, "It's a date." He didn't have a clue if he had any arrangements already booked for this period, but if he had, then they would just have to be changed… and quick!

Chapter 40

Emma was still researching the 'Mademoiselle Chad' portrait, but was struggling. Despite the benefit of using the internet to try and find any provenance connection in the period prior to the 1940s, her efforts were not producing any useful results. She finally decided that the next option must be to revisit Burford and, if necessary, knock on some doors. She was not sure what this would achieve but, at the moment, all other avenues seemed to be taking her nowhere.

Ian brought Emma a mug of coffee into the office and placed it on her desk.

"Ian?" asked Emma, looking away from her computer.

Ian stopped in the doorway as he was about to leave.

"I've come to a full stop with finding any provenance earlier than the 1940s for 'Mademoiselle Chad'. I think I'm going to have to visit Burford and knock on some doors. I'll also take the opportunity to call on Mum and Dad if that's all okay with you?"

"Yes, fine. When are you thinking of going?"

"Maybe early next week, but I'll need to speak to my parents first."

"Okay. I need to speak to Miss Wardley, so I can take and collect Robert from school whilst you're away."

"Have you made up your mind about the George Watts painting? Are you going to sell it privately?"

"Yes. That's my thinking now. As I've always advocated, we don't need to be greedy. I'm going to arrange to see Toby's client before you go to Burford. Let's hope he'll be happy with the painting when he sees it."

Ian had earlier telephoned Toby and they'd agreed to visit the client together in four days' time. Toby had insisted he would collect Ian from his home and drive them both to the client's property. He also explained that the client lived in a remote part of Surrey, on a large estate, and it was not the easiest of properties to find.

When Ian told Emma about the arrangements she had been intrigued when he mentioned that the client lived on a large estate in rural Surrey. She, like Ian, was interested to discover who this client was and, just as importantly, how he could afford to live on an estate in Surrey.

"Probably a pop star… or a footballer," joked Ian.

"More like a Lord or, maybe, somebody wealthy working in the city," replied Emma. "One way or another, they can obviously afford the £1.2 million for your picture."

"The £1.2 million is what Toby's company will be paying me. Unless Toby says anything during our journey, the price the client will be paying is a private arrangement between Toby and the buyer. After all, Toby needs to make his profit too."

"Of course," responded Emma. "What do you think Toby will be charging his client?"

"I doubt the final price will be discussed at our meeting but, with the gallery's usual markup, my guess is it would probably be in the region of £1.5–1.6 million."

"Must be a pop star, then," responded Emma.

Chapter 41

Much to Penny's surprise, she was beginning to build a good working relationship with her new boss at Sotheby's, Jonathan Northgate. His style was quite a contrast to Michael Hopkins, the former MD. He was certainly making his presence felt, ruffling a few feathers. This had resulted in some resignations and also a number of the older members of staff putting their names forward for early retirement. Penny, however, felt less intimidated than she thought she would, mainly, she decided, because their age difference was not as great as it was with Michael Hopkins. Northgate was only a few years older than Ian.

After the difficult start when she'd first replaced Ian, Penny was enjoying her work once again. This in turn seemed to give her a boost in confidence which meant she felt much stronger when contributing to the senior management meetings... in front of Jonathan Northgate.

Now she realised why Ian had been so confident in her ability and his positivity that she would have little problem stepping into his shoes.

Indeed, even at home, Viktor was noticing this new side of Penny. Gone was the quiet, lacking in confidence and questioning her own ability Penny. Viktor could see how much stronger, more positive and ambitious she'd become.

She'd even told him recently that she was certainly determined to prove to any doubters that not only could she do her new job, but she could do it very well.

Penny strode into her third senior management meeting full of confidence. She sat at her usual place at the conference room table and looked around her, nodding and smiling to the other five people present. She saw some worried expressions. Two of the group had recently been promoted. Both were quiet and apprehensive young female managers, whilst another two were older and more traditionalist men. The final member was a noisy, know it all, over-promoted young man. Penny thought he was all bluster and totally lacking in substance. The quality of her colleagues, she'd concluded, was not really that much competition at all. No wonder Jonathan Northgate was determined to make yet more changes.

The door opened and the MD entered the room to join the group. Penny watched the same faces around the table wince or sigh. Yes, she decided, with a slight smile, she had very little competition!

Chapter 42

On the planned day of the 'showing' of his painting to Toby's client, Ian was standing in his driveway. The painting was secured in his trusty padded canvas bag. It was 9.28am. Toby said he would collect Ian at 9.30.

Ian heard a car turn into the driveway, but it was Emma, arriving home after dropping Robert off at school. Her car was immediately followed by a dark blue Audi. Emma parked and walked over towards Ian. The Audi turned around in the driveway, making it easier to exit.

"Is that Toby?" asked Emma.

"Yes, and bang on time. Come and say hello."

Toby got out of his driver's side and Ian and Emma walked over to join him.

"Good morning, Toby. Meet my wife, Emma."

Toby and Emma briefly shook hands and Toby said, "Hello, Emma, nice to meet you at last."

All three chattered for a few moments and then Toby suggested it was time to go.

Emma kissed Ian and whispered, "Good luck."

Ian smiled, put his canvas bag into the car's boot and got into the car. They then headed off towards the M25.

"I assume you've been to your client's house before," said

Ian, desperately wanting to know all about who it was that lived on this estate in Surrey.

"Oh, yes. Probably about ten times. Sir Edward Ferguson, he's an avid art collector. His current passion is George Watts, but next week it could be somebody completely different. Then he'll want to sell some of his existing collection. However, he always tries to make a profit so, if he owns paintings by an artist that suddenly comes back into vogue, then he'll ring and expect me to get a good return on his investment. It doesn't always work, but he wins more than he loses."

"So, he's more of a dealer than a collector?" queried Ian.

"No, not really. He only wants to buy what he likes so he can show his collection off to friends and relatives. But, as I say, he's also in the business of making a profit."

Toby indicated to turn left and they accessed the M25 slip road at junction 10. They then joined the motorway properly. "It should be about 45 minutes from here."

"Okay," said Ian. He watched the heavy volume of traffic that was heading in their direction. He was so pleased he didn't have to travel on this road very often.

It was not long before Toby turned off the motorway and headed south on the A24.

"Is there anything I shouldn't talk about with Sir Edward?" asked Ian.

"No, not really. We've both seen the photos of the painting you sent to us. Sir Edward seems happy with that. Obviously leave the price of the picture to me, but otherwise Edward is fine on most subjects. Oh, maybe don't bring up his work. He can be a little cagey. All I know is that he's made a lot of money as a 'name' at Lloyds of London, the insurers. He also has fingers in some hedge funds and several directorships. His father, Sir Audley, was also a 'name' at Lloyds."

The Gamble

"So, is this a family home we're going to?"

"Yes, it goes back to the 19th century, I believe. Edward once told me that 'Ferguson Hall', that's the property's name, was once only used as a weekend retreat. The family's main home was originally somewhere in London."

Toby turned left off the A24 and joined a 'B' road, which they travelled along for about five miles. Other than the odd cottage, both sides of the road were now lined with a variety of mature trees in full leaf. The strong sunshine made driving a little tricky, going from shade, to brief sunlight and back to shade again. Toby stopped at a 'T' junction, turned right and drove at a slower pace along a narrow country lane. This lane was also largely in shadow due to the high hedges and tall trees.

"This is serious rural Surrey," said Ian. "I hadn't realised that these sort of quiet rural roads and properties still survive today… in Surrey. Such discreet privacy."

After about another mile Toby announced, "Here we are." He slowed down and suddenly a large gatehouse appeared on the right-hand side. Toby turned off the lane and drove under the red brick archway, passing a pair of ornate metal gates. When the car joined the long gravel driveway Ian could see nothing but open fields and an old specimen tree. It reminded him of the Baltoun Castle grounds in Scotland… but this was rural Surrey!

The driveway slowly curved to the right. Either side were two rows of old London plane trees. Gradually Ian started to see part of a very large red brick house emerging from behind the trees. "Wow," he said out loud and leaned forward to get a better view through the windscreen.

"Impressive, isn't it?" responded Toby. "It never ceases to amaze me every time I arrive at this point."

Chapter 43

Toby parked at the end of the driveway and both men got out of the car. Ian looked up at the large red brick house and then at the surrounding countryside. The house and grounds reminded Ian of an old National Trust property.

"It's magnificent!" announced Ian.

"Blows me away every time I come here," replied Toby, who then spotted Sir Edward walking towards them.

Both men watched as a tall man, thin in build and in his late 50s, joined them. He greeted Toby like a long-lost friend and welcomed Ian into his home. Ian collected his painting from the car's boot and they set off towards the house.

Sir Edward led them through an old side doorway and along a corridor. At the end he opened the last door on the right and they all entered what Ian thought was the largest hall he'd ever seen outside of palaces or university colleges. Everywhere he looked, all four walls were covered in paintings. The only exception was the two windows. It was truly an enormous collection of pictures.

"This is really exceptional, Sir Edward," said Ian, as he gazed from wall to wall and painting to painting. "Unbelievable."

"You're very kind, Ian. But please, just call me Edward."

Toby kept quiet as he wanted Ian to take in the full magnificence of all the pictures. He'd been in the room before but was still staggered by the sheer volume of Edward's private collection.

"This hall is a perfect setting for the paintings, especially when you're entertaining. But the sunlight through the windows, isn't that a problem?" asked Ian.

"My great-great-grandfather, Sir Andrew Ferguson, had the building designed with his own painting collection in mind. The largest window, over there." Edward pointed. "That's facing due north, so we never get any direct sunlight through there. The other smaller window to the side is west facing. If you look through that window, there's a large oak tree which, when it's in full leaf, gives good protection. If we do get any low, winter sunshine, then there's a blind we can pull down." Ian nodded. "Unfortunately, about 60% of the paintings in the house aren't mine. They're held in a special family trust. That was set up by my grandfather after a number of Sir Andrew's collection of Scottish landscape paintings had been sold."

"The house looks rather special too. Did Sir Andrew have a personal input into the design as well?"

"Well, the true answer to that question is yes, and no!" Ian smiled.

"The old medieval hall dates back to at least the 14th century but was burnt down in 1843. Sir Andrew and his family moved down from Edinburgh to London in 1852. They lived in Mayfair but wanted to get away at the weekends from the London smells and pollution. Sir Andrew employed an agent to find him the perfect site for the family's weekend retreat. After a number of attempts, the agent finally persuaded Sir Andrew to visit this site. This he did and both he and his wife fell in love with the peace and quiet and the pleasing views. The clincher was when the agent produced some old drawings of what the former hall once looked like. Sir Andrew was particularly impressed with the huge multi-functional hall located in the centre of the ground floor. He worked with the architect to create something similar. The house was completed some seven years later. It was about half the size of the house you see today. Several extensions have been sympathetically added since that time."

"I see," said Ian. The property was unbelievable.

"So, in the true spirit of Sir Andrew's intentions, this room is our own modern day multi-functional hall. We use it for entertaining, large dinner parties mainly and the occasional film show. Our children, when they were younger, used it for table tennis, carpet bowls and soft ball cricket, especially when the weather was wet."

Both Ian and Toby smiled at the thought of soft ball cricket being played with all these valuable pictures around!

Toby decided it was now time to deal with the main purpose of the meeting. "Edward, Ian has brought the painting we discussed earlier. Should we have a look at it now?"

"Yes, fine. Looking forward to seeing it," replied Sir Edward, and then, looking directly at Ian, he said, "I've developed a penchant for George Watts paintings, you know."

Ian smiled and put his bag on the large table next to where they were all standing. He then unbuckled the three straps and slid out the painting. It was packed in bubble-wrap. He slowly unfolded all the packing and passed the painting over to Sir Edward to inspect.

Sir Edward held the painting and then took it over towards the large window. He wanted to see all its details in a better light. He inspected the picture very closely, then the frame and finally its rear side. Next, he placed it on a nearby chair and removed a magnifying glass from his

The Gamble

jacket side pocket. Bending down he examined the painting once again, this time looking through the magnifying glass.

Ian and Toby watched his every move without saying a word.

After a couple of minutes, Sir Edward straightened up, carried the painting back to the table and placed it on the plastic wrapping. "You say you have proven provenance and confirmation that the painting will be included in the next catalogue raisonné?"

"I have all the paperwork here in my bag, Sir Edward, including the letter confirming the inclusion in the next catalogue raisonné," advised Ian. He then looked across towards Toby.

Toby, directly coming in on cue, said, "I've checked all Ian's paperwork and can confirm it's all authentic and properly authorised."

"Lord Rye and Rother, you say." Sir Edward was rubbing his chin and still staring at the picture.

"Yes," said Toby, "that's the painting's full title. Painted by Watts in the late 1890s."

"Still the same price we agreed?" asked Sir Edward, looking directly at Toby.

"Yes, sir... as we agreed," replied Toby. He was beginning to perspire a little.

"You have a deal, my boy. I like it. It will go well with my four other paintings by Watts... over there." Sir Edward pointed to a far wall. "Mind, I'll have to move something first."

Both Ian and Toby breathed a sigh of relief and smiled at Sir Edward's comment.

"Are you going to leave the painting with me?" asked Sir Edward, again looking at Toby.

Without a blink, or a glance at Ian, Toby immediately responded, "Yes, of course, Edward. If that's your preference."

Ian was sure Sir Edward's credit with Toby's company was good, but his own contract was with Toby and his company, so he expected to be paid within the week.

It was the following Monday morning when Ian took Robert to school and Emma left the house in her car. She was heading towards the Cotswolds to stay with her parents and to carry out more detective work in Burford.

When Ian and Robert arrived at the school, they both got out of the car and walked towards the main building. Robert saw one of his friends, Arthur, and asked his father if he could catch up with him. Ian let Robert run ahead, whilst he strolled more sedately towards the main entrance.

The previous Friday, Ian had telephoned Miss Wardley and asked if he could see her this morning. They'd discussed Ian's painting and Robert's school fees for the next six years.

Ian arrived at the main entrance where Mrs. Bailey, the headmistress's secretary, was on duty. They chatted briefly before she told Ian to go straight up the stairs as Miss Wardley was expecting him.

Ian wandered into the headmistress's outer office, where he found Miss Wardley looking at a file on Mrs. Bailey's desk.

"Good morning, Mr. Caxton. Please, come through to my office," said Miss Wardley, who immediately picked up the file and walked towards her own office. Ian also said good morning and followed directly behind her.

"Please sit down. I gather you have some interesting news."

Ian sat down opposite Miss Wardley and told her briefly about the sale of the Lord Rye painting. The same painting that had been hanging on the wall directly behind where Miss Wardley was now sitting. The portrait, for the last 100 years, had been erroneously attributed to the school's founder, Sir Edgar Brookfield.

The Gamble

Although Ian mentioned Toby's company by name, he was deliberately vague about the buyer's name and the sale price that had been achieved.

"I can see I've missed my vocation," joked Miss Wardley.

"I think your role here is much safer and more secure than it would be in the risky art world," replied Ian.

"You may be right."

"Anyway, as promised, I've got a cheque here for Robert's school fees for the next six years." Ian put his hand inside his jacket and removed the cheque. He passed it over to Miss Wardley. "As you can see, it's made payable to the trust fund, as you suggested. The amount is net of the discount we agreed."

Miss Wardley leaned forward, picked up the cheque and read its details. "Yes, that's all fine, Mr. Caxton. We always suggest any advance payments should be dealt with this way… it 'ring-fences' and protects your money. I will make sure a receipt is posted to you shortly."

"Excellent," said Ian standing up. "I must be off now, but thank you for your time."

Miss Wardley also stood up and walked around to the front of her desk. She stood opposite Ian and held out her hand. Ian shook it. They held eye contact for a few seconds. "Thank you, Mr. Caxton, it has all been a thoroughly interesting experience. Good luck for the future… in your risky art world!"

They both laughed.

Chapter 44

When Emma arrived at her parent's house it was mid-afternoon. Although it had only been three weeks since she and Ian had last visited, her father, Bob, greeted her as if he hadn't seen her for some time.

They chatted and walked through to the kitchen where Emma's mother, Diana, was peeling some potatoes. She quickly wiped her hands and gave her daughter a warm embrace. The ladies sat down at the kitchen table, whilst Bob switched the kettle on. Questions were asked about Robert and school and then Emma told them about the painting she was investigating and mentioned that Ian's parents were now looking to downsize and move house.

With this information, Diana said, "Well, we've no intentions of moving, not yet anyway. We're far too involved with the local community. Besides, our cottage and garden are nowhere near as large as Richard and Elizabeth's. We can maintain and manage ours quite easily."

Emma glanced at her father and wondered what he was thinking. He just casually smiled back.

Over dinner Emma's father asked her for more details of the painting she was investigating. Emma explained about the French artist, Georges Seurat, and his use of coloured dots to create his paintings. She also told him how the

The Gamble

eye can be fooled into seeing the same picture differently, depending on how close or far away one stands. She then described the possible link with three of Seurat's more famous pictures, which were painted about the same time.

Although her father seemed fascinated, Emma's mother had a different point of view. "Have you given up on accountancy?" she queried. "These hobbies are fine, but accountancy's your profession."

This was not what Emma wanted to hear. She knew her mother was not happy when the accountancy firm, in which she was a partner, was sold, and unhappy yet again to hear that Emma had reduced her commitment further to just handling one client after Robert was born. She had hinted before that she thought it must all be to do with Ian's demands.

Emma took a deep breath. "No, Mother, I haven't necessarily finished with accountancy. I decided, when Robert was born, to take the opportunity to have a career break. Ian supported my decision. We are financially secure and, at this moment, I'm thoroughly enjoying my life working with Ian. I also have lots more time for Robert too. As a family we're all so much closer together, certainly a lot better than when we were both working full time."

Emma's father knew he would be 'between a rock and a hard place' if he intervened, so decided to just keep quiet. He just nodded and smiled in Emma's direction.

Emma's mother stood up and said, "I'll bring in the dessert." She disappeared into the kitchen.

"That woman!" whispered Emma to her father.

Her father smiled and whispered back to Emma. "Don't get annoyed, Emma. Remember you're talking about your mother. She's only thinking of you."

"She has a funny way of showing it."

Next morning Emma was up early, before her parents

had arrived downstairs. She was determined to have a full day of investigating in Burford. Her planned first port of call was to visit Mrs. Clare Bellamy, at Riverside Cottage.

She helped herself to a mug of tea and a slice of toast. After unlocking the back door, she quietly walked to where she'd parked her car in the driveway. Fifteen minutes later she'd joined the A361 and was heading in a southerly direction towards Burford. It had rained during the night and the car in front of her was throwing up a light spray and dirtying the windscreen. She slowed down and created a larger gap between the two cars. After all, she thought, I'm not in a great hurry.

Just under half an hour later Emma had parked in the same car park she'd used before. She checked the street map of Burford on her mobile phone and headed for the bridge back across the river. After walking down two streets she arrived in Duck Lane. She spotted 'Wendy's Antiques', which was only about 30 metres up the road. She decided to divert briefly to see if there had been any changes. Outside the shop she noticed the 'closed' sign in the entrance door's window. There was also a message written and glued underneath. The message explained that the premises were temporarily closed due to a change of ownership and would be re-opening shortly. Emma then peered in through the main window, but couldn't see much difference. It still reminded her of the 'Old Curiosity Shop'.

Rechecking her street map, Emma turned around and headed back down the hill. At the end of Duck Lane she'd arrived by the river. Across the water and through the trees she could see her car in the car park.

To her left there was a narrow lane called 'River Close', which ran parallel with the river. She looked down the lane and saw six small cottages tucked well back from the waterside. Each one had a frontal view of the river. Emma walked along the grit and stone pathway located between the cottage fences and the river. She immediately noticed all the cottage gates had similar names containing the word 'River'. How cute, she thought. The first cottage was called 'River Scene', then it was 'River View'. Ah, thought Emma, so this is where Mrs. Lucy Charlton had lived. Next was 'Riverbank' and then 'Riverside Cottage'. So, here we are. Emma gazed at the cottage. It looked very similar to the neighbours' cottages. Old Cotswold stone and a thick slate tile roof. The front garden was not large, but packed with colourful cottage garden flowers, plants and shrubs. Emma pushed open the creaking wooden wicket gate, walked up to the front door and pressed the doorbell.

"Hello," said Emma when the door was opened. A portly, middle-aged lady, with bright blue eyes and a cheerful moon face, had opened the door. "I'm looking for Mrs. Clare Bellamy."

"That's me, my dear," said the lady. "I presume you've come to tell me I've won the premium bonds?"

Emma was initially surprised and confused, but then with a smile on her face, said, "No, I'm sorry. Not this time."

"Well, it would have been a big surprise, as I don't own any!" said the lady laughing.

Emma laughed too. "I'm Emma Caxton, Mrs. Bellamy. We've been corresponding by post."

"Oh, that's right, my dear. How lovely. Come in. I wondered what you looked like."

Emma smiled again as she followed Mrs. Bellamy into her home. Emma decided this was a fun lady.

Mrs. Bellamy led Emma through to the back parlour.

Small, but it had a really cosy and inviting atmosphere, thought Emma. "This is a lovely cottage, Mrs. Bellamy. Such character."

"Please, Emma, I'm Clare. The last person to call me

Mrs. Bellamy was my barrister. Sorry, only joking," replied Clare.

Emma laughed again. This lady is a riot. Emma had now forgotten what she was going to say! She laughed again and then remembered. "I've called to see you, partly to say thank you for the particulars you sent me and, secondly, in the hope you might be able to give me some more information."

"Well, my dear, that's going to be challenging. How about we have a cup of tea to enliven my brain?"

"That sounds like a really nice idea. Thank you," said Emma, giggling again. She needed the break to concentrate her mind on what she wanted to ask.

Clare got up from her seat and went into the kitchen.

Suddenly Emma heard Clare shout, "Milk and sugar? Or are you sweet enough already, my dear?"

Emma laughed again. "Yes, I'm sweet enough already, but a dash of milk would be good. Thank you."

Two minutes later Clare returned with a tray containing a pot of tea, two cups and saucers, a small jug of milk and a few biscuits. She gave the pot a stir and then poured the tea into the cups. "There we are, my dear, help yourself."

"You're very kind."

"Right, let me get my brain lubricated and you can then give me the starter for ten!"

Emma laughed again. This is ridiculous, she thought. Now the lady is talking about the television programme, *University Challenge*.

Emma helped herself to some milk and a chocolate biscuit.

"Right then, my dear, my brain's active," said Clare, after sipping her own tea.

"You're so funny," said Emma. "You should be on the stage."

"What, sweeping up you mean?"

Emma started laughing again and had to quickly put her cup back down on the saucer before spilling it. Eventually, after wiping her eyes, Emma looked across to Clare. She was just sitting quietly, all innocent and calmly sipping her tea.

"Well," said Emma, attempting to get back to the point of the visit, "what I'm trying to find out is more of the history of the painting your great aunt owned. Your letter said she owned it when your father, her nephew, was a boy. I'm guessing that would take us back to about the 1940s. I'm trying to go back, as far as possible, to when the picture was painted in 1889. Have you any idea when your great aunt bought, or first acquired, the picture?"

"No, I'm sorry on that one. My father's the only person left who saw the painting at her cottage," replied Clare, now with a surprisingly serious frown on her forehead. "Although... now then, let me think." Clare picked up her cup and sipped some more tea. Emma smiled. Clare continued. "Now, Tom and Dorothy Wilberforce, they lived at Riverbank, next door to Aunt Lucy. It must have been just after the war. I think they moved in about then. They were very friendly with Aunt Lucy."

"Do you know if either of the Wilberforces are still alive?"

"I doubt it, my dear. But their daughter still lives in Burford. Laker Street. Alice Jarrett, that's her married name. She's the treasurer of our local WI. Lives at number 20, or thereabouts. You could try there and ask."

Emma smiled. "Yes, I'll do that. Thank you very much. You've been very helpful... and so entertaining."

Chapter 45

Emma left Riverside Cottage still smiling and followed Mrs. Bellamy's directions. Laker Street was on the other side of 'The Hill', which was the main road through Burford. It only took her about ten minutes before she arrived outside number 21. She pondered her next move. Suddenly, across the road, at number 24, she noticed an old man closing his front door. She checked the road for traffic and crossed quickly. The man was now pulling his gate closed.

"Excuse me," said Emma, when she arrived next to him.

"Hello, young lady, what can I do for you?" said the old man. He was pleased to be talking to such an attractive lady.

"I'm trying to trace the house where Alice Jarrett lives. I was told she lives in one of these properties."

"Arr, yep, that's young Alice, nice lady, lives across the road at 25. She should be in. Usually goes to work at about twelve o'clock."

"Thank you. You've been very kind."

The old man stood and watched Emma as she walked back across the road and up the pavement towards number 25.

Emma pressed the doorbell. A few seconds later an attractive middle-aged woman opened the door.

"Hello," said Emma. "I'm sorry to intrude. Mrs. Clare Bellamy suggested you may be able to help me. My name's Emma Caxton."

"Oh, Clare, yes, of course. Comedian, isn't she?"

"Yes," laughed Emma, "she certainly is that. I'm trying to find some information about Mrs. Lucy Charlton who lived at Riverview. I understand you and your parents lived next door, in Riverbank."

"Well, that's a long time ago. I think I must have been about eight when Mrs. Charlton died."

"Do you know of anyone who might still remember anything about her?"

"Not now. I reckon they must all be dead. My parents knew her best. My mum was often popping round but, of course, she's also dead."

"I'm sorry," said Emma. She felt she might be coming to another dead end – in more ways than one.

"I've got some old photos, black and white, of Mum and Dad at Christmas time. Just after the war. Mum and Dad were invited round to Mrs. Charlton's. It was their first Christmas in River Close. Dad was keen on photography. Would you like to see them?"

"Yes, please," enthused Emma. "That would be wonderful."

"Come in then. I've got to go to work at 12, but I've still got a few minutes."

Emma entered the hallway and followed Alice into the front room. It was bright, clean and very tidy.

"You sit yourself down over there, me dear. Me albums are in here, this cupboard."

Emma sat down on a two-seater settee and watched Alice bend down and open the cupboard doors.

"Now then," said Alice, "I sorted these out a couple of years ago. They're now all in date order. Ah, here we are,

Christmas 1946." Alice pulled the album out of the cupboard and stood up. She then walked over and sat down next to Emma on the settee. Alice flicked through the pages. There were four small black and white prints on each page.

Emma eagerly watched as each page was turned. When Alice came to the one she was specifically looking for, she pointed to a group of three black and white pictures and said, "Right, now these three photos were taken at Mrs. Charlton's."

Emma looked very closely at each photograph. Then she spotted it!

"Oh, wow," cried Emma, in amazement. "There it is!"

"What have you spotted, me dear?"

"That picture. The one on the wall. That's what I've been looking for."

Alice peered down to get a closer look. "Oh, yes, I remember that picture. Funny painting. Made up of lots of funny coloured dots. I'd never seen anything like it before… or since."

Emma lifted her mobile phone out of her handbag. "Do you mind if I take a photograph, please?"

"No, no, go ahead," said Alice, somewhat bemused as to why anyone would want to take a photograph of another photograph.

Emma quickly snapped two photographs of each picture in the album. "That's brilliant. Thank you so much."

"Can I ask why you wanted your photos?"

Emma explained and gave Alice a summary of the circumstances around her purchase of the painting. When she'd finished, she added, "I'm trying to trace this painting's history as far back as I can."

"I see. So, you've now got some evidence that Mrs. Charlton owned the painting in 1946. Yes, that's rather clever."

The Gamble

Emma initially smiled, but then with a more serious expression on her face she said, "The problem now is that I still have to find out about the period all the way back from 1946 to 1889."

"I think I can help there," said Alice, closing the album. "I do remember… I must have been about six or seven. I was in Mrs. Charlton's house, she sometimes looked after me when me parents were out at work. I was always fascinated by this weird picture. I could stand there for ages, just looking at it. Sometimes I tried to count the dots. The blue ones, then the red ones and so on. Anyway, this particular day, Mrs. Charlton was standing behind me, she was listening to me counting. Suddenly I realised she was there. She made me jump. But she then said that her husband, Billy, had bought her that picture just after they were married."

"Really!" exclaimed Emma, with eagerness in her voice. "I don't suppose you know when they were married do you?"

"No, sorry, me dear. But I'm sure you'll easily find that out. Aren't marriage certificates available nowadays on the internet? My husband's been tracing his family tree. I'm sure he found some certificates online."

"That's right. You've been such a help, Alice. Thank you so much."

"I'm pleased I was able to help, me dear. Now I don't want to appear rude, but I must leave for work in five minutes."

Emma quickly leapt up out of her seat and held out her hand. "Thank you again. I don't want to hold you up."

Alice stood up too, shook Emma's hand and showed her to the front door.

Emma walked back down Laker Street, towards 'The Hill'. She was happy with her morning's work, but was now feeling hungry. She decided she would treat herself to a sandwich and then, in the afternoon, visit the local library to use one of their computers.

It was just after 5.30pm when Emma arrived back at her parents' cottage. Her father was keen to know what she'd managed to find out. Even her mother seemed to be curious. Emma explained her conversations with Clare Bellamy and Alice Jarrett. She also described how comical Clare was.

"Then, this afternoon," continued Emma, "I visited the local library. Fortunately, it's one of the days when the library's open in the afternoon. However, I had to wait 30 minutes before I could access one of their computers. I could have used my mobile phone, but the screen on the library's computers is so much larger. It took me a little while to plough through the government's 'Births, Deaths and Marriages' website to find the surname, 'Charlton', but then I had the problem of Lucy's husband's name, 'Billy'. I tried to insert Billy, Bill, William, but these all failed. I tried several short cuts, because I didn't know Lucy's maiden name either. Anyway, to cut a long story short, I eventually managed to find out what I was looking for. They were married in St John the Baptist Church, Burford on the 12th July... 1908. I then went to the church to check their records, but, unfortunately, the church was locked. I'll call back there tomorrow, on my way home. Anyway, at least I now know that Billy bought the painting, probably sometime between 1908 and 1910. All I've got to do now is find out exactly when... and from whom it was purchased. Hopefully that will then open up the route back to 1889."

"You're becoming a proper Sherlock Holmes," said Bob. He had a large and affectionate smile on his face.

"But is all this time spent going to be worth it?" asked Diana, still concerned about her daughter's enthusiasm for this 'hobby'.

Emma held back her frustration and calmly explained, "If I can finally put together the complete provenance, going all the way back to 1889, then Ian thinks the painting could well be worth over three million pounds at auction!"

"Wow," cried out her father. He stared over at his wife.

Diana didn't say another word. She just gazed at her daughter, her eyes and mouth were wide open!

Chapter 46

Ian telephoned Michael Hopkins to arrange the meeting with Alexander. Viktor had given Ian four dates when he was definitely available. Ian offered the same dates and Michael said he would speak to his son and confirm one of them. An hour later he'd returned Ian's call. The date and time were confirmed and the venue agreed. They were due to meet at Alexander's house. It was located on the outskirts of Kingston upon Thames.

Ian and Viktor agreed to meet at 10.45am outside the red brick Kingston upon Thames railway station. Ian couldn't make their meeting any earlier as he had to take Robert to school. It was pushing it to be at their meeting with Alexander for 11.00am, but Ian was convinced it could still be done if they hired a taxi.

At 10.40am, Viktor exited the station and spotted a parked taxi. He walked over and asked the driver if he could wait a few minutes for his colleague to join them. The taxi driver asked where they were going and, after Viktor gave him the address, he said he could wait five minutes and flicked on the meter. At 10.44 Ian appeared and Viktor waved him towards the waiting taxi. Ian jogged across and they both got in. The driver started the engine and the vehicle sped off.

"The driver's got the address," said Viktor. "Everything all okay with you?"

"Yes, fine. The trains were relatively on time for a change. By the way, how's the gallery situation?"

"Both Mary and I are still looking for alternative premises. At the moment, nothing suitable is available, so we're carrying on as before."

Ian nodded. "Is the property consultant happy to wait?"

"Yes. I told Mr. Crawshaw the problem I was having. He said his client was keen on our premises, so was prepared to wait a little longer."

"Well, that's good news."

"Are we all set for this meeting?" asked Viktor, wanting to change the subject. The gallery situation was a bigger issue now, but he knew he had to be patient and bide his time. After all, he owed it to both Bob and Mary. He had no intention of leaving either of them in the lurch.

"I think we covered everything about our approach on the phone last night. Have you got any additional queries?" asked Ian.

"No. I guess we'll otherwise just play it by ear."

"Okay," said Ian. "I'm assuming Michael's going to be there. We can be pleasant, respectful and friendly to him, but remember, he's not our boss at Sotheby's anymore. We treat him just as he is, Alexander's father."

Viktor nodded.

The taxi pulled up alongside the driveway to a large, almost gothic style, house set in a large plot. The frontage to most of the house was hidden behind a well-clipped conifer hedge. Ian paid the taxi fare and the two men got out. They both stood in the entrance gateway and looked at the property.

"House clearing is obviously a very profitable business," said Ian.

Viktor nodded and they walked along the driveway towards the front door.

Ian rang the doorbell and, to their surprise, it was Michael Hopkins who opened the door.

"Hello Ian, Viktor. Come in. Alexander's on the telephone. We're in the lounge."

"Hello, Michael. Your son's business is obviously doing very well," said Ian, as he and Viktor followed him along a slightly dark and windowless corridor. At the end Michael opened a door on the left and the three men walked into a very spacious and well-furnished sitting room. The room was illuminated by strong rays of bright sunlight streaming through huge picture windows. The same windows gave a stunning view of the large and well-manicured garden.

Whilst they waited for whom they assumed was Alexander, who was still on the telephone, Ian and Viktor glanced at the five oil paintings hanging on the wall. Viktor then looked at Ian and raised his eyebrows slightly.

Michael pointed to a large settee for Ian and Viktor to sit down on. As they sat down, Alexander put the phone back on its cradle.

"Sorry to keep you, gents, but business is booming. What's bad for the country is good for us!" Alexander walked over to shake hands with Ian and Viktor, who'd both stood up again.

Michael made the introductions. "Alexander, this is Ian and Viktor. They both used to work with me at Sotheby's."

The three men shook hands and Alexander said, "Something must be wrong with Sotheby's for all three of you to jump ship!" He then laughed and sat down on a large armchair located immediately next to him.

Ian and Viktor smiled at Alexander's joke and returned to their seats.

"So, gentleman," announced Alexander, "I've arranged

this meeting for us to find out about each other and to see whether we all want to work together. Dad's given me a summary of your talents and roles at Sotheby's, so I suggest, firstly, I give you some information about my business."

For the next ten minutes Alexander outlined the details of his business.

Ian was impressed with Alexander's confidence and presentation skills.

"So, gentlemen," continued Alexander, "where do you come in? Well, for the last four years, we've had an informal arrangement with three London art galleries. One in the North, one in the West End and one in North Surrey. Before we clear the houses, we give the gallery details of all the paintings and artwork that we'll be collecting. They then give us valuations of what they're prepared to pay and we use these quotations when calculating our final offer to the client. We relied on these galleries' knowledge and their professionalism to give us an honest and reasonable valuation. However, we became suspicious when my wife spotted a Picasso for sale in one of their galleries. It was advertised with a 150% markup on their original valuation given to us. I gave the task to my wife to investigate some of the other previous pictures we'd offered them. The result? There'd been an obvious increase in their greed. I'm a fair man, aren't I, Dad?" Michael nodded. "I don't take kindly to people taking me for a mug or cheating me. Therefore, I've ditched them. I'm now looking for a new, trustworthy, professional person, or company, to deal with. That someone will have to be top notch. In return, I propose they'll get 50% of the profit when the painting's sold. That way I get a proper return and that person, or company, gets quality pictures to sell and a great incentive to sell at the best price. Now then, Mr. Caxton, Dad says you have all the qualities I require. What do you say?"

Viktor had concentrated on every word Alexander had

said. He was impressed. He couldn't see any immediate downsides to the proposition. The presentation was slick and positive. However, he also knew that Ian was bound to have some reservations and questions.

"It all sounds interesting, Alexander," said Ian, "but I do have a few questions."

"Alright," interrupted Alexander, "let's hear them."

"Firstly…"

Forty minutes later, Ian and Viktor were walking back along the driveway, heading towards the avenue.

"Well, Vic, what did you make of that?" asked Ian.

"It sounded pretty good. I thought Alexander had some okay answers to your questions. What do you think?"

"It appears more above board than I'd originally anticipated."

They arrived at the end of the driveway and stopped. "I think we came from this direction," said Ian, pointing to his right. "I don't think the main road's far away, so we may be able to get a taxi along there."

The two men walked towards the main road.

"Michael has obviously sold me well to his son," said Ian. "The ball really is in our court."

"We could give it six months and see how it goes," replied Viktor. He really wanted to try his hand at this new venture. He'd certainly have the extra time once he'd finished with the gallery. However, he knew it was far too big a job for him to do on his own. He wouldn't want to be involved unless Ian was fully on board as well.

Ian decided he needed more thinking time before he finally made his decision. "Let's sleep on it, Vic. Are you okay with a phone call tomorrow morning?"

"I have a meeting at ten o'clock, but should be free after eleven."

"Okay, I'll ring your mobile after eleven o'clock."

Chapter 47

As promised, Ian telephoned Viktor just after eleven o'clock. When Viktor answered the call, he said, "Hi, Vic. Ian."

"Hello, Ian. How's things?"

"Things are fine. Have you had any further thoughts about Alexander's offer?"

"Not really. I'm still convinced we ought to give it a try for six months and then review the situation after then."

"Having slept on it, I agree. Let's give it a try. I'm sure it could be rewarding and maybe a little exciting too. Who knows, we may unearth some special finds?"

"That's great, Ian, I certainly wouldn't want to be involved on my own at this stage."

"Well, actually, Vic, nor would I. I'm glad we're going to work on this one together. I'll give Alexander a call and tell him our decision. I then suggest we meet to work out the finer details and each other's roles."

"Okay. I'm really excited! This could be a great move."

After ending his telephone call with Viktor, Ian rang Alexander and informed him of his and Viktor's decision. Alexander was pleased and said he was looking forward to working with them both. Alexander explained that in two weeks' time his team would be visiting a large house on the Wentworth Estate, situated close to Virginia Water. He promised he'd contact Ian once again once he knew the exact date.

Just as Ian was ending his call, he heard a vehicle arrive in the driveway. He looked out of the window and spotted Emma climbing out of her car. He went outside to join her.

"Welcome home. How did your investigations go?" asked Ian. He then gave Emma a welcome home kiss.

"Fairly successful. I've got a lot to tell you. Let's discuss it later. How did the sale of the Lord Rye painting go?"

"All done and dusted," said Ian, with a smile on his face. "Toby arranged the transfer of our £1.2 million the day after Sir Edward agreed to buy it."

"Sir Edward?" asked Emma.

"A lot to tell you there too. We've got a lot of catching up to do. I'd better go. I've got a couple of jobs to do before I collect Robert from school."

"Okay," said Emma. She then watched as Ian got into his car and drove away.

Later that same evening, Emma was sitting on the large settee in the lounge. Ian walked in carrying two mugs of coffee. He placed the drinks on the small table in front of them and sat down next to Emma.

"Well, Mr. Caxton, you've made another million pounds. I could get used to this lifestyle!" said Emma, smiling and leaning forward to pick up her mug.

"Yes, it all went well," said Ian. He sat back in the seat and told Emma where Ferguson Hall was located and gave her a description of the house and the grounds. He also told her about Sir Edward, the huge hall and his fabulous art collection.

"It sounds wonderful… and just a weekend retreat!"

"It used to be. Now it's the main home of Sir Edward and his family."

"I wish I'd been there," said Emma. She was genuinely jealous.

"Anyway, how are your parents and what were you able to find out in Burford?"

Emma explained her stay with her parents and her mother's dig, again, at her career move away from accountancy. Then she summarised her day in Burford, including the funny Clare Bellamy, the very useful Alice Jarrett and the extra information she'd obtained by using a computer at the local library.

"Sounds as though you've made some serious progress. Well done," said Ian, placing his empty mug back on the table.

"I know, but the last part's going to be the most difficult bit. Establishing when Billy bought the picture and who from. Then, of course, I've still got to go all the way back to 1889."

"I still think you should stick to the Burford connection. My guess is that Billy was a local man and he bought the picture from someone in that general neighbourhood. The question is, was it a private purchase or from a dealer? Probably assume it was a local dealer to start with. I don't think you can go any further back until you've established those facts."

"Okay," said Emma, hesitantly. She'd already envisaged an historical journey.

"There's been one other development since you've been away," said Ian, leaning forward. "Remember I told you about Michael Hopkins and his son, Alexander?"

"Yes. You said you and Vic were going to meet him."

"That's right. Well, we did, and we've decided to work with Alexander for six months, initially."

"What exactly will you be doing?" queried Emma. She hoped it was not going to be another Andrei-like arrangement.

"Alexander's company specialises in house clearing for

the top end of the market. Bankruptcies, foreign nationals, older wealthy people having to move into a care or nursing home. Children whose parents have died and have no use for the family home or contents, etc. You get the picture." Emma nodded. "Well, Alexander wants Vic and I to assess the value of any painting collection that's part of the house's contents. He says he's been ripped off in the past and wants a better arrangement with me. Vic and I will go 50/50 with Alexander on the profit we make from the final sale price."

"But what about the current owners of these art collections, will they not be ripped off?"

"That's a fair comment, and one that I wanted to explore fully before we agreed to the arrangements. Vic and I will be responsible for valuing each painting before Alexander makes his overall offer to the owners. Alexander says he'll then build into his offer a quotation of 85% of our valuations. If the overall quotation is accepted, it'll be Vic's and my job to get the best possible sale price."

"Six months, you say?"

"Six months… initially, yes," replied Ian. He wasn't expecting Emma to be jumping up and down with joy, but at least she hadn't said no.

Chapter 48

When Viktor explained to Penny about working with Ian and Alexander, she was initially concerned, but then became more relaxed when Viktor emphasised that the agreement was for only six months to start with. He also told her that he wouldn't have agreed at all if Ian wasn't committed as well.

"So, what's involved?"

Viktor summarised Alexander's ideas and how he and Ian would end up with 25% each of the profits.

"You're not involved in purchasing any of the pictures?"

"No. We don't want that level of capital outlay, that's still Alexander's area. Our role is purely calculating the initial valuation and then achieving the best sale price."

"What happens if you make a loss when you sell?"

"Well, it's most unlikely as the outlay is 85% of the valuation, but, of course, if we cannot sell, or make a profit, we'll have to store the pictures until we can make a profit. I'm currently looking into suitable storage facilities. Alexander has his own warehousing unit, but it's not really secure enough for the value of the paintings we might be storing."

"On the face of it, it all seems okay."

"But, you're not totally convinced, are you?" asked Viktor, wondering what Penny might have spotted that he hadn't.

"Let's make that judgement in six months' time. Hopefully it'll all work out. After all, and as you say, it appears quite simple really."

After being fully convinced of the whole scheme, Viktor was not now quite so sure. Why was Penny not quite as keen or convinced as he was?

It was just after 7pm when Ian received a surprising telephone call from his father. "Hello, Dad, how are you?" asked Ian, a little concerned.

"We're both fine, Ian. We thought we'd let you know, we have a buyer for the 'The Willows'. Obviously, it's still early days, but it's a young couple and they seem very keen."

"That's a bit quick. Are they the first people to view?" asked Ian, who was genuinely surprised.

"No, the third. The other two couples are still interested, but they have to sell properties first. Our buyer, apparently, has nothing to sell. A cash buyer. They're renting at the moment. Even offered the full asking price."

"That's great, Dad. I presume you and Mum are pleased?"

"Yes. I was a little surprised. We haven't found anything ourselves yet."

"Have you been looking?"

"Yes, your mother was keen to get started immediately after you and Emma left the other Sunday."

"You're both very keen to move quickly then."

"We'd like to find a property before the summer's over. Then we can make any changes to the garden straight away, or shortly after in the autumn. When we do find a nice property, Ian, we'd like you and Emma to come and have a look yourselves, please… before we put in an offer."

"Of course, Dad, if that's what you'd like," replied Ian.

"You, and especially Emma, would look at the property with a far more dispassionate mind. As you know, it's been

The Gamble

over 40 years since we bought 'The Willows'. We're quite nervous about spending so much money."

"No problem, Dad. I'll tell Emma immediately."

"Thank you, Ian. Say hello to Emma and Robert from me and your mum."

"I will, Dad. Give my love to Mum. Bye."

Ian put the phone back on the charger. When he turned around, he found Emma standing nearby.

"You'll tell Emma immediately about what?" queried Emma. She'd heard the last few words of the conversation.

Ian summarised his chat with his father.

"Of course we should help them. It'll be interesting as well."

"You know, Emma, I've been thinking. I know in Mum and Dad's will that more or less everything's left to me, but I'd really prefer that they use their assets now and spend their money on themselves."

"Okay, but you say they're downsizing, so surely, they'll be releasing some of the equity from the sale of 'The Willows'. Also, you'll still inherit the major part of the assets, their new house and the contents."

"I know. That's what I've been thinking about. I think I should offer to buy 50% of their new house now."

"I doubt they'll agree to that."

"Their current will stipulates that, when the first one dies, their 50% share comes to me anyway. They own 'The Willows' on a 'tenants in common' basis. All I would be doing is pre-empting the first death."

"This all sounds pretty gruesome."

"Not my favourite subject either, but these things have to be faced. We also need to update our two wills as well. There's Robert to consider now. Anyway, that's for another day. Coming back to Mum and Dad, by me buying a 50% share now, it would free up further money for them to use immediately, like paying for any work on the new house and longer holidays. Also, it has inheritance tax advantages."

"I'm still not convinced they'll do it. You can talk to them, by all means."

"I'll have a chat with Dad first. If I can win him over, Mum's likely to agree."

Two days after returning to Antigua, Oscar had called in to catch up with Wesley Fredericks at the 'Shell Gallery'. This visit, however, was after he'd visited the large DIY store nearby. There he had purchased several tins of paint, rollers, trays, brushes and masking tape. He planned to be a very busy boy.

Wesley was pleased to see Oscar and welcomed him back from his long vacation. He was particularly delighted to see that Oscar's old spark and enthusiasm had returned. Oscar gave Wesley a brief summary of his holiday and Wesley updated Oscar on the local art market.

Over the next two weeks, Oscar spent most of his time at home, cleaning and redecorating the whole of the inside of his villa. He couldn't remember working so physically hard for such a long time. He and May also had regular conversations via email and video conferences. The only time May said she wouldn't be in contact was when she was back on mainland China.

May told Oscar about some of the pictures she'd recently traded and Oscar updated May on which room he was currently decorating. Occasionally, during video conferences, May could see splashes of paint still on Oscar's face. She teased him by suggesting he may be putting more paint on himself than on the walls!

Oscar was counting down the days until May's arrival. She confirmed she'd now booked her flights. Another incentive, thought Oscar, for getting the job finished… and as quickly as possible. After all, the paintwork would need to be completely dry and any lingering paint smells totally eradicated prior to her visit.

What he hoped for now was that nothing was going to go wrong and potentially scupper all their plans and arrangements.

Chapter 49

When Viktor arrived at the gallery, Mary had some interesting news for him. She told him that a property, just down the road in Old Bond Street, had become vacant and there was a sign in the window saying 'To Let'. The property was not far from their present location and, for Mary's benefit, it was closer to her Underground station.

Mary also said that she'd telephoned the estate agents and been emailed all the premises' details. She showed Viktor a printed copy of the email.

"All in all, Vic, I think this property might be just the right size for what we're looking for."

"Excellent," said Vic. He definitely needed to see this property. "Can you set up a viewing?"

"Already done," replied Mary, with a relaxed and self-assured look on her face. "We're due there at 2.30, later today."

Viktor checked his watch. It was 1.05pm. "Right, I've just got a few things to do first and then we can wander down and take a look."

At 2.20, Viktor and Mary left the gallery and strolled the short distance into Old Bond Street. Mary pointed to the large glass-fronted building, where, standing in the doorway, they noticed a young lady, smartly dressed in a navy blue suit.

The Gamble

"Hello, Miss Parker?" asked Mary, when they had both arrived at the entrance.

"Yes, you must be Mrs. Turnbull."

Mary nodded and they both shook hands. Mary then introduced Viktor.

After the customary greetings they all entered the premises.

Mary and Viktor stood together and looked deep into the room. It was a largely empty space except for two partition walls and a few items of mail lying on the floor. Miss Parker picked up the envelopes and fliers and placed them on the window sill.

"It certainly looks much bigger than our premises," said Viktor, breaking the silence.

"About 50% larger," responded Mary, "according to Miss Parker's square footage information."

Miss Parker opened her briefcase and gave Viktor and Mary a further printed copy of the premises' details. "Let me show you around and then we can go through any questions you might have."

For the next 20 minutes, Viktor and Mary were given the agent's tour. There was not a great deal to see, it was mainly empty space and they had to use their imaginations as to how they would use and divide up all the available space for the new gallery.

They were now back at the front door and Viktor re-read the premises' details. "I see the remaining lease is for 39 years. The lease and service charges seem rather high. I hope they're negotiable."

"This is a very exclusive and desirable area of London, Mr. Kuznetsov, and we think these figures are very reasonable. We also have two other companies interested in the property."

Viktor smiled. "Okay, I think that's it for now. Mary, do you have any questions?"

"Not at the moment," she replied.

"Thank you, Miss Parker, for your time. We now need to do some calculations," said Viktor. "We'll be in touch again very shortly."

Viktor and Mary separately shook Miss Parker's hand and then left the premises.

"Well, what do you think?" asked Viktor, as they made their way back towards New Bond Street.

"I think it would work really well. There's a lot more space for displays and potentially two nice size rooms for an office and for private viewings. The location too, I think, would be fine."

"It's quite expensive. I'm not sure Bob will agree to their charges. Let's chat a bit more when we get back inside the gallery."

After they both re-entered the gallery, Viktor started to speak, "There's a few things I would like to discuss with you, Mary."

"Do you want to do it now?"

"Yes, I think now would be good."

Mary walked over to her desk and sat down.

Viktor sat on the chair facing her and said, "Over the last few weeks, this potential move to new gallery premises has set me thinking. I'd really like to step away from my gallery involvement altogether and just concentrate on my outside clients. However, there's no way I'd want to leave you and Bob in the lurch, so I'm prepared to carry on the way we are until the dust has all settled on any new gallery. I've not mentioned any of this to Bob yet, so I'd appreciate it if you'd keep this discussion between just the two of us for the time being."

Mary nodded, but wondered what sort of impact Viktor's decision would have on her own job?

Viktor continued. "Both Bob and I have been impressed

with your involvement in this business. Since you joined, you've reorganised this gallery so much better than I ever could. This has resulted in an increase in the gallery's turnover and profit. I know Bob's very keen to continue his presence in London and I'm sure you'll have a big part to play in the gallery's future success. Anyway, the point I'm coming to is, I was wondering if you wanted a bigger role in the future?"

"This is all a bit of a surprise, Vic. I really need time to think about it. What bigger role are you thinking about?"

"Of course. I'm not looking for an answer right this minute, but obviously your answer would affect my own final decision. If you did want to take on the bigger role of 'Gallery Manager', then I'm sure I can persuade Bob to offer you a share in the business too."

"Really!" exclaimed Mary. She hadn't expected this.

"You deserve it. You've worked really hard. I can also help you with recruiting an assistant if you want me to."

"I do like working here, Vic. Mind, I'll have to discuss it with my husband as well."

Two days later, Mary gave Viktor her decision. "I've discussed your suggestion with my husband and thought very seriously about your offer. Yes, I'd like to be the full manager of the new gallery."

"Excellent. I'm really pleased and I know you'll enjoy the bigger challenge and responsibility. I'll need to speak to Bob and get his agreement, but I'm sure he'll go with my recommendation. Now all we need to do is finalise these two properties."

Mary smiled. She was really pleased with her possible promotion and to be moving to larger premises. She was now eager to get on with setting up the new gallery. "Have you heard back from the estate agents about your offer for the Old Bond Street premises?"

"Not yet," responded Vic. "But at least they haven't turned down our offer out of hand. Mr. Crawshaw's client has agreed to our terms to sell this property's lease to them, so I'm sure we're not too far away."

"Fingers crossed then," replied Mary. "What are you going to do if your offer's turned down?"

"When I discussed the new lease details with Bob, he suggested a 5% leeway, but I'm hopeful it'll not be needed. More profit and money for you in the future!"

Mary smiled again. She hoped Viktor would have similar success persuading Bob on her new role.

It was just 24 hours later when Miss Parker telephoned and confirmed that Viktor's offer on the Old Bond Street premises had been accepted.

Chapter 50

Emma had spent a lot of time trying to trace the history of Billy Charlton's early life. Her first success was finding out his date of birth, the 10th June 1882. This she'd obtained from the marriage certificate. This information then took her to Billy's birth certificate, which also named his parents as Harold and Ethel. Putting this information together, she calculated that Billy was married just after his 26th birthday.

Emma had noticed that at the time Billy's birth was registered, Harold and Ethel were living at 22, Almond Gardens, Burford. Therefore, they appeared to be a local family.

Emma then accessed the next set of ten-year census records. This was for 1891. She found that the occupants of 22, Almond Gardens were Harold and Ethel, Billy, aged nine, Mary, aged seven, George, aged five and Edward aged four.

From the 1901 census records, the occupants of 22, Almond Gardens were listed as Ethel, George aged 15 and Edward aged 14. The obvious absentees were the father, Harold, Billy and his sister, Mary.

Emma had become engrossed in the whole of the Charlton family history. However, her immediate attention was to concentrate on Billy, and at 19 years of age, where was he living and what he was doing in 1901? Was he still living in Burford?

Emma was convinced she was getting closer, but recognised there was still a massive gap. She checked back through her many notes and looked again at the photocopy of the marriage certificate that she'd had printed at the Burford library. Suddenly, she spotted another piece of vital information. At the time of the wedding, Billy's declared occupation was an engraver. Now what did that mean, she wondered? Engraver… it must be significant.

She switched her attention back to her computer and accessed as many websites that she could find relating to the history of Burford between the years 1900 and 1910. She looked at occupations, small industries and retail shops. Only one came up with any likely connection, a jeweller's shop but, unfortunately, it was not established until 1909. Another dead end. She decided to look further afield.

From the bookcase behind Ian's desk, Emma removed the AA road map of Great Britain. She found the page that included Burford and then searched for nearby towns or places where Billy could possibly have moved to. The two major populated places, Oxford and Cirencester, she temporarily dismissed as being too far away by early 20th century travelling distances. The only possibility, she concluded, could be the market town of Witney. She now looked at all the websites relating to the history of Witney between the years 1900 and 1910.

She eventually found two possibilities. 'Barrett's the Jewellers' and 'Parker and Son', art and craft suppliers. Both companies had been established well before 1900 and were still in existence in 1910. Okay, she thought, maybe, just maybe, I might be onto something here. She leaned back in her chair, removed her reading spectacles and rubbed

The Gamble

her eyes. They felt strained, so Emma decided to take a break and make herself a cup of coffee. As she stood up and stretched, she felt her back beginning to ache. She knew she'd been sitting for too long.

After a hot cup of coffee and early preparations for the evening's dinner, Emma went back to her computer. She started by looking at Parker and Son's website. It confirmed that they were still trading, but unfortunately, they appeared not to have any need for an engraver. She checked their 'history' section, but again, there was no part of the business that hinted that engraving had ever been carried out. Nevertheless, she decided to make a note of these details just in case she needed to make a telephone call. She hoped for better luck with Barrett's the Jewellers.

She found Barrett's website and was pleased to see they too were still trading today. After reading the business description, she was delighted to see that they did have a small engraving section. When she checked back into the company's history, it was all positive news.

Right, she thought, now it's time to find out if Barrett's had employed Billy Charlton at the turn of the 20th century and, if they had, was the painting linked, in some way, with their business.

Three days earlier, Ian had received a telephone call from Alexander. He'd informed Ian that his company had now been asked to formally visit 'Dexter's End' on the 12th to quote for the house clearance contract. He also explained that Peter Owen, OBE, had recently died and the house and all its contents were to be inherited by his only surviving relative, his grandson, Charles Owen.

Alexander also explained that Charles had informed him that 'Dexter's End' was now on the market for sale and he didn't have any future need for most of his grandfather's possessions. He was looking for a quick sale, for both house and contents, but was prepared to go down the auction route if need be.

Ian had established where the exact location of 'Dexter's End' was and had read up on the internet about the estate and nearby Virginia Water. In his notes he had written down:

The Wentworth Estate is an exclusive collection of very large and expensive houses intermingling with the three golf courses connected to the Wentworth Club. A number of notable sports stars and television entertainers have, sometime during their lives, called the Wentworth Estate their home. Virginia Water is one of the most expensive towns for property in the UK.

Ian knew it was a relatively short car journey from Esher to the Wentworth Estate. He'd told Viktor that he'd collect him at Virginia Water railway station, the nearest station to the Wentworth Estate. Viktor had checked the rail timetable and informed Ian that there was a reasonable rail service from London Waterloo. The pick-up time was then agreed.

When Ian arrived outside Virginia Water railway station, he immediately spotted Viktor waiting for him. Viktor jumped into the front passenger seat and Ian accelerated away.

"Trains were okay then, Vic?" asked Ian, as Viktor fastened his seat belt.

"Yes, good, it arrived a minute early."

"You got my email listing all the paintings we're going to see?"

"Yes," said Viktor. He'd done some of his own investigations and knew he'd be seeing some possibly expensive works of art. "Mr. Owen was obviously a very wealthy man, but not all that organised when it came to keeping records of when, and from whom, the paintings were purchased."

"We'll have to go, initially, with the information that

The Gamble

we've been given. There may be a lot of legwork later, if Alexander gets the contract."

Viktor nodded and glanced out the window. He was looking at the various properties they were passing. "You'd need to be very wealthy to afford to live in this area."

Ian drove along Christchurch Road and through the centre of Virginia Water. He was heading towards the junction with the A30. At this junction he turned left and headed south. After just a short distance, he turned left at the signpost saying 'Wentworth Estate'. They now entered Wentworth Drive and Ian paid closer attention to the car's satnav instructions. He was told to follow various narrow lanes, which were sheltered on both sides by predominantly high hedgerows of rhododendron bushes and pine trees. They did manage to get a few glimpses of one of the golf courses and partial views of some of the large properties, most of which were hidden behind large double gates.

Yes, thought Viktor, a very exclusive estate.

Ian slowed down as he approached a crossroads junction and looked at the satnav for further instructions. He turned right and, after about 50 metres, along a narrow lane, the satnav informed him that they'd arrived at their final destination.

Ian stopped the car but neither he, nor Viktor, could see any properties, just thick hedgerows. However, about another 20 metres further ahead Ian spotted Alexander. He'd just stepped into the lane and waved his arm. Ian moved the car slowly forward and Alexander pointed him towards the driveway. He drove past the large, ornate metal gates and a sign saying, 'Dexter's End'.

Ian got out of his car and looked up at the substantial, light-red brick building. Viktor walked around the car to join him.

Alexander caught up with them and said, "Hello, nice

location, isn't it? The house needs some serious modernisation though."

"Good morning, Alexander. Yes, but it has some nice external features," replied Ian. "Nice architecture and a mature front garden, although it looks a bit overgrown. Super setting though."

"My two employees are inside the house. They're checking out all the furniture and general contents. The grandson, Charles Owen, he's also in there… unfortunately," he whispered the last few words. "He's with two security guards and the estate agent. Lots of antiques and some nice paintings, but that's for the two of you to decide on. Come in, the security people are expecting you both."

Ian and Viktor followed Alexander through the front door, passing two uniformed security guards. The general lack of natural daylight was the first thing they noticed. The large amount of dark wooden panelling certainly didn't help.

They walked into the large sitting room. Again, lacking in natural light and with a hint of a musty smell.

"Help yourselves, guys. I'd better find out where my staff are. Take your time, we can chat later," said Alexander, and he then left the room.

"Okay, thanks," said Ian. He looked at Viktor.

"Bit gloomy isn't it?" whispered Viktor.

"Hello. I'm Charles," came a voice from inside the doorway that Alexander had just exited.

Ian and Viktor turned around and saw a well-dressed man, probably in his mid-thirties, walk into the room. As he walked closer, Ian noticed a harassed look on his face. Ian did their introductions and Charles shook their hands.

"I'm afraid the house is a bit dated," said Charles, unapologetically. "Probably needs knocking down and starting again. My grandfather lived here for over 50 years. When my grandmother died, he sort of just let it go. My father tried to convince him to move to something more manageable, but he wouldn't hear of it. He spent most of his time up at the golf clubhouse. Father died three years ago, so the pushing to get Grandfather to move, unfortunately, died with him."

"I see," said Ian. "Are all the paintings located in the house?"

"Yes, generally spread all around. My grandfather did have two valuable pictures but he gave those to my father about five years ago. Just wander around, please. I shall be here until you all go so, if you have any questions, I should be somewhere in the house."

"Thank you," said Ian.

Viktor smiled and nodded. Charles then left the room.

"Right," said Ian. "We'd better get started."

Chapter 51

At the end of their viewing, Ian and Viktor met in the sitting room. They were comparing notes. Viktor was more buoyant with his opinion, whilst Ian was a little more businesslike and level-headed.

"There are some good paintings here, Ian," said Viktor, excitedly. But then he was concerned about Ian's apparent lower key enthusiasm.

"I agree, there are a couple that could fetch a good price at auction and a few others that are okay. I was looking for the unusual, the painting that gives me an itchy scalp."

Viktor smiled and decided to follow his own opinion. "I totalled up a valuation figure of about £5.2 million."

Not bad, thought Ian. Viktor's coming along. "On the basis of the details on the listing and the poor provenances that we were given, I think you're probably about right. I'm happy to give Alexander that figure."

"Ian, you're not telling me something," said Viktor. He didn't like it when Ian agreed with him. Experience had taught him he was obviously missing something… and something valuable!

Ian scratched his head again. "Vic, you're right. We've seen 19 paintings and, on the basis of the current details we've been given, we'll tell Alexander £5.2 million. At that figure, everybody should be more than happy."

Viktor was about to challenge Ian for not answering his query but, at that moment, both Alexander and Charles Owen returned to the sitting room and joined them.

"Have you all finished?" asked Charles. He was now eager to lock up and relieve the security guards of their duties.

"Yes, I think so," replied Ian. He looked at Viktor.

"Me too," said Viktor. "An interesting collection." However, when he looked back at Ian, he had the distinct feeling he had made the wrong comment.

Ian looked from Viktor to Alexander. "We'll let you have our report by tomorrow evening."

"Okay. Well, I think we're all finished for today, Charles," said Alexander. "I can have our complete report with you within seven days."

"Thank you, gentlemen," said Charles. He tried to usher the group towards the front door. "I look forward to reading your report."

Viktor and Alexander headed through the front door and back into the daylight. Ian was a little slower as he followed them. When he entered the hallway, he became aware of the sweaty palm of his left hand for the second time. He looked up to the slightly grubby picture hanging on the wall. He rubbed both his hands together, trying to dry them.

Charles arrived and stood next to him. "Here's my business card, Ian," said Charles. "If you have any further questions or comments, you know how to contact me."

Ian gave him the briefest of smiles, took the card and pushed it into his jacket pocket. He then followed his colleagues back onto the driveway. He watched Charles as he switched on the burglar alarm system and locked the door.

During the car journey back to Virginia Water, Ian and Viktor discussed most of the paintings. Ten minutes after they'd arrived at the railway station, Ian's car was still parked and they'd agreed individual valuations on 18 of the

19 paintings. There was one painting, however, that Ian had not commented on. The one in the hallway. All he would say was that 'based solely on the facts they'd been given', he agreed with Viktor's valuation.

When Viktor exited Ian's car, he waved goodbye and headed towards the station entrance. He was anxious to get home to investigate item 14 on Alexander's original listing. The painting in the hallway. He was totally convinced that Ian knew something… something that he'd not yet discovered. He just hoped this was not going to be another Gainsborough moment!

Emma telephoned Barrett's shop, in Witney. She explained that she was trying to trace her family tree and wondered if the shop had records going back to the early 20th century.

Her call was transferred to a cheerful woman, who announced that her name was Jean Dixon. She stated that the company's records went all the way back to 1875, when the business was established.

"Excellent," said Emma. "I'm particularly looking for a person called Billy Charlton. A relative suggested that Billy might have worked for Barrett's in about 1905 or thereabouts."

Jean replied, "I'd need to look in the company's archives."

"I understand," replied Emma. "I'd be extremely grateful if you could check and let me know, please."

"I can do that for you, but it might take a little time."

Emma left her telephone number and email address. She also thanked Jean for her time. "Incidentally," continued Emma, "do you sell paintings?"

"Not now. We used to, some years ago, before my time though. It was only ever a very small part of the business."

Emma thanked Jean once again and ended the call. She

The Gamble

hoped the lady would come back with some positive news… and very shortly.

When Ian arrived home, he updated Emma with how his day had gone. He also described the Wentworth Estate and 'Dexter's End'.

"It all sounds rather grand and exclusive," said Emma.

"The Wentworth Estate certainly is but, unfortunately, the house and gardens at 'Dexter's End' have seen better days. The house has character but any buyer will knock it down and start afresh."

"That sounds rather sad."

"The house is quite dated and it would cost a lot of money to make it habitable and comfortable for the 21st century."

"Well, what about the paintings? Was it a good collection?"

"There are 19 pictures in total. Viktor's estimated a valuation of £5.2 million. He's about right… bar one thing."

"You've spotted something!"

Ian smiled and scratched his head. "There's a painting in the hallway. It's dirty and I think it must have been hanging there for quite a number of years. It's probably been forgotten about. I need to do some research, but, if I'm right, I think it could be worth well over £25 million!"

Chapter 52

Ian had just finished typing his report and was attaching it to his email to Alexander. He'd used most of Viktor's valuations and ended the email by saying he already knew of a couple of potential buyers for four of the paintings.

After sending the email, Ian closed down his computer, but then spotted Charles's business card on his desk. He picked it up and read the details again. He wondered why Charles had given him the card. Could it be that he wanted Ian to contact him? If so, why? Was it to do with the painting Ian was looking at when Charles spoke to him in the hallway? Or, could it be something completely unconnected?

"Ian," said Emma, as she entered the home office. "Can I have a word?"

"Yes, of course," Ian replied. His mind switched away from Charles Owen and he put the business card back on his desk.

"The 'Mademoiselle Chad' painting," said Emma, pulling a chair away from her desk to sit in front of Ian. "I recently telephoned Barrett's in Witney. I was trying to find out if Billy Charlton had worked for them and if they had any knowledge of the painting. I spoke to a very helpful lady called Jean. She's promised to investigate their old records for me. However, she did confirm that the shop did

The Gamble

once sell a few paintings, but they dropped that sector of business some time ago. Apparently, it was only ever a very small part of their business."

"Okay," said Ian. "That sounds promising."

"Well, the point is, I think I'm getting closer to establishing the final link in the chain. On Billy's marriage certificate, his occupation was described as an engraver. I spent a number of hours trying to establish who locally in 1908 might be employing an engraver. I eventually found two possibilities, both reasonably local to Burford. They were both in Witney. One was Barrett's the Jewellers and the other, Parker and Son, who were art and craft suppliers. However, I've largely dismissed Parker and Son. They never did have a need for an engraver. Barrett's, on the other hand, did offer an engraving service in the early 20th century and they still do today. Hence my telephone call to them."

"You have been busy," teased Ian.

"Yes, but I don't think I can do any more until I hear back from Jean. Is there anything else you can suggest that I should be doing in the meantime?"

"You could try to find out what happened to the painting after Seurat completed it. It's not that easy, I know, but he may have used an intermediary to sell his work. 'Mademoiselle Chad' might turn up that way, you never know."

"Okay," said Emma. She was a little doubtful that she would find anything but, nevertheless, she agreed to give it a go.

It was three days later when Ian received a strange telephone call from Alexander.

"Ian, hi. Glad I've caught you."

"Hello, Alexander." Ian recognised the voice. "I hope you're ringing to say you have good news."

"Partly," replied Alexander. "Charles has agreed to our quotation for the house clearance, but he's excluded all the paintings."

"Oh," responded Ian, with genuine surprise. "Did he say why?"

"No. All he said was that he wanted to discuss them directly with you. Did he say anything when we all met at 'Dexter's End'?"

"No." Ian wondered if it was anything to do with the business card. "We only spoke briefly and I think you were there at the time. I don't think he discussed anything with Vic either, because Vic would have mentioned it. I assume this isn't usual?"

"It's happened a couple of times before. The client often thinks he'll get a better price if he sells directly to a gallery, or by auction."

"I'm not sure about the gallery route. They'll want to make their profit. As for auction, well that's more of a gamble. He might do better, of course, but he could easily be worse off. Auctions are unpredictable and he'll still have expenses to pay. Sounds as though he's trying to be greedy."

"Have you got a pen handy? I'll give you his contact number."

Ian picked up a pen from his desk and wrote the telephone number on a piece of paper.

"Okay, Alexander. I'll contact him and let you know what he says."

"Thanks. Speak to you soon."

When Ian ended his phone call, he checked the number Alexander had given him against Charles's business card. They matched.

That same day, Emma also received a telephone call on her mobile. She was on the way to collect Robert from school

The Gamble

and was travelling along a country lane. She pulled into a farmer's driveway to answer the call.

"Emma Caxton speaking."

"Emma, it's Jean Dixon, from Barrett's, the jewellers in Witney."

"Oh, hello, Jean. Thank you for coming back to me."

"I've checked our records and we did employ a Billy Charlton. He joined us in 1898 as an apprentice engraver and left to join a new firm of jewellers in Burford, in 1910."

"Oh, that's super. Thank you very much."

"I'm really pleased I could help with your family tree."

Emma suddenly remembered that was the excuse she'd given for ringing Barrett's in the first place. "I have one other query, which I really hope you can help me with."

"I'll see what I can do," replied Jean.

"Just after Billy was married, he bought his wife a painting. I was wondering if your company still had records of paintings sold in about 1909 and if he might have bought it from his employers."

"1909, you say. If we still have the records, the picture should be easier to find. I can try and look it up for you. What was the name of the painting?"

"I've been told it's probably called 'Mademoiselle Chad'. A funny name and, apparently, it's also an unusual picture... painted with coloured dots."

"Yes, that does sound like a strange sort of painting to give to your wife. I'll have a look and let you know."

"I don't know how I can thank you enough. You've been so helpful."

"That's alright, but please don't tell my boss," whispered Jean and they both laughed.

It was two days later when Ian finally telephoned Charles Owen. After exchanging pleasantries, Charles came to the point. "I'm glad you telephoned, Ian. I knew you didn't remember me from five years ago."

Ian was suddenly stunned by this comment.

"My father and I met you at Sotheby's to discuss the two paintings my grandfather had given to my father," said Charles. "It was you who valued them and suggested they should be auctioned. Do you remember now?"

Since the time Ian had moved back to London from Hong Kong, he'd valued hundreds of paintings. Many of these he remembered but very few of their owners. "I'm sorry, Charles, but you'll have to tell me the details of the two paintings. It's the paintings I normally remember."

Charles gave Ian a summary of the two paintings and the artists. As the details were slowly revealed, Ian gradually remembered. "Yes, of course," responded Ian. "I think we even exceeded my valuations at auction."

"One and a half million pounds was achieved. My father was over the moon!"

"I do remember your father now. Didn't he want to buy champagne for everyone?"

Charles laughed at the other end of the telephone. "He did buy about 20 bottles, but they were consumed by my father, mum, grandfather and myself!"

"Sorry, Charles for not recognising you, but, as I say, it's the paintings I usually remember first."

"Ian, more seriously," said Charles, changing the tone of his voice. "Can we meet at my grandfather's house again please? There's something important I want to show you."

Chapter 53

Oscar had finally completed the decorating of his villa and rearranged his art collection to complement the new colour schemes. Gone were the previous owner's dated and bland hues. When he'd finally finished, he wondered why he hadn't bothered to change and freshen up the villa's decor before now. He tried to convince himself it was because he was too busy trying to establish his business connections on the island but, deep down, he knew it was simply mañana and a lack of incentive. Now he had a big incentive… to impress May Ling! She would be arriving in four days' time and he was pleased to be ahead of his self-imposed schedule.

Before finally packing away all his painting equipment, Oscar walked through the villa and meticulously inspected each room. The guest bedroom, and its ensuite, he had double cleaned. Finally satisfied, he hoped May would be similarly impressed.

Four days later, Oscar was standing in the arrivals terminal of the VC Bird International Airport, located just outside the capital, St John's. He was anxiously watching the exit doors as people arrived into the hallway after clearing passport control and collecting their hold baggage. He was feeling a mixture of excitement, apprehension and nervousness. He really wanted this visit to be a success.

He walked over and checked the arrivals board once again. Yes, the flight from Miami had landed, but there was still no sign of May. He started to feel anxious. Had she missed the connection? Surely if she had, she would have texted or telephoned.

The number of people now exiting had reduced to a trickle and Oscar was just about to check the arrivals board once again, to see if he had read the wrong flight, when May appeared. She seemed flustered and was struggling pushing a trolley loaded with two suitcases and a cabin bag. Once past the last barrier, Oscar joined her and they both kissed each other's cheeks.

"Are you okay? You seem a bit out of breath." Oscar was genuinely concerned. At the same time, he took charge of May's baggage trolley.

"I am now. It was a serious rush to get my connection at Miami Airport and I just hoped there'd been enough time for them to transfer my two suitcases. I was beginning to doubt they'd arrived here when I went to Baggage Reclaim. That was about 40 minutes ago. I breathed a sigh of relief when they did eventually appear on the carousel. I'm sure my cases must have been the last ones off the plane. Anyway, at least I've got them all now."

"The main thing is, both you and your luggage have arrived safely. It's so good to see you again, May."

May Ling smiled and kissed Oscar on the side of his face again. "I'm so excited and have been looking forward to this holiday for ages. I can't believe I'm finally here."

When they exited the air-conditioned building, the humidity and hot temperature suddenly hit May. "Wow, it feels like summer in Hong Kong!"

"Even by Antigua's standards, it's one of our hottest days. My guess is there'll be a thunderstorm this evening. Look over there." Oscar pointed to a group of black angry-looking storm clouds in the distance. "Hopefully, we'll get back to my villa in time."

Forty minutes later Oscar drove his Jeep into the driveway and parked under the carport next to the side entrance door to the villa. As they got out of the car, they could both hear the initial heavy raindrops landing on the carport's roof. Oscar unloaded the luggage and placed each suitcase by the door. He then unlocked it and let May enter the kitchen. Oscar followed behind and lifted both cases into the building, before taking a deep breath.

May turned towards Oscar and noticed he was sweating. She walked to his side and kissed him on the cheek again. "Thank you, Oscar."

"I think it's cocktail time," announced Oscar. "What do you say?"

May laughed. "I think I'd like to freshen up and change my clothes first. I feel a little grubby after two long flights."

"Okay. Let me show you to your bedroom. There's an ensuite in there too," said Oscar. He grabbed the handle of one of the suitcases and her cabin bag. "Follow me."

Both suitcases were on wheels so, as May followed Oscar, she pulled the second case herself, the wheels clicking over the gaps between the light grey porcelain tiles. They left the kitchen and entered a corridor, which was now painted in a light pastel cream colour. When they arrived at the last door on the right, Oscar pushed the door wide open and pulled the case through into the room. May followed.

"Here we are," announced Oscar. "I hope you like the coral colour. Being the guest bedroom, I wasn't sure what colour to paint it. Ella, my neighbour, suggested it."

"It's lovely and fresh. Very Caribbean. I love the bird pictures. Are they all local to the Caribbean?"

Oscar nodded. "Yes, the artist is a local man. He's quite young but I think he's captured the character and colours quite well." Oscar pointed to the far door. "The ensuite is through there. The towels and everything are in there too. It only has a shower, I'm afraid. If you want a bath, there's a separate bathroom along the corridor."

"I prefer a shower, so everything's perfect."

Oscar then pointed to a dial on the wall. "That's the air con control. It's quite simple, just turn it up or down."

"Thank you. It feels just right at the moment."

"Good. Okay, well I'll leave you to get settled in. I'll be in the kitchen when you've finished. I'm going to prepare a Caribbean version of sweet and sour pork for tonight's dinner."

May smiled. "That sounds intriguing. I shouldn't be too long."

"Right," said Oscar, leaving the room and gently closing the door behind him. He was still feeling a little anxious and nervous.

About an hour later, May reappeared as Oscar was just preparing the rice. When he looked up, he nearly dropped his jar of rice. May looked stunning!

"Wow, May. You look fabulous. I love the red Qipao," said Oscar. He could see she still had a wonderful figure to do the close-fitting dress proper justice.

"Why thank you, kind sir. Isn't that the correct English phrase?" said May. She'd made the impression that she'd hoped for. "Didn't someone say something about a cocktail?"

Oscar immediately put his rice jar down on the worktop and walked over to the fridge. "I hope you like my version of an 'Old Cuban'." Oscar opened the door and lifted out a pitcher containing a light green liquid, topped with mint leaves and just a few pieces of fruit for decoration.

"That's got champagne in it, hasn't it?" said May, walking over to join Oscar as he put the pitcher on the table.

"Yes, but don't worry, there's plenty more bottles of champagne for later."

May smiled and watched as Oscar stirred the pitcher's contents. He continued to explain the rest of the cocktail's ingredients. "It's also got some white rum, lime juice, Angostura bitters and mint leaves. I like it cold, but with no ice. I'm not keen on ice in my drinks. As I say, it's my version so I hope you like it."

Oscar poured some of the pitcher contents into two cocktail glasses and handed one to May.

She took hold of the glass stem and inhaled the aroma. "It smells very minty," she said, and then put her glass towards Oscar. "Gon bui!"

Oscar smiled. He pushed his glass forward towards hers and replied with the same words. They clinked their glasses together and May took a tentative sip. "Wow! This is really nice."

Oscar had a sip too. "It's certainly one of my better ones. I sometimes have a glass early in the evening, before dinner… out on the patio. Obviously, that's not going to happen tonight."

"I heard a really big clap of thunder when I was in the shower. I thought the roof was falling on me."

They both laughed.

"It's going to rain quite heavily overnight. Tomorrow morning it should be back to normal. I hope you've brought your swimwear for an early morning dip in the Caribbean."

"Of course. That's something else I've been looking forward to."

The next morning, and for several further mornings, they both walked the short distance to the beach for their early morning swim. Then, after returning to the villa, they enjoyed a refreshing and long lazy breakfast.

Oscar also took May into St John's and introduced her to the local shops and his colleague, Wesley, at the 'Shell Gallery'. They travelled around the island stopping at local bars and cafes. On the fourth day, Oscar took May to the area around English Harbour, located in the far south of the island. May decided this was one of her favourite spots to visit. Not only was she intrigued by the history of Nelson's Dockyard, but she thoroughly enjoyed a relaxing time picnicking on Shirley Heights. There they experienced the stunning panoramic views of the harbour and contentedly watched the many large and expensive yachts sail by. They tried to guess how much each yacht probably cost.

On their second picnicking visit to Shirley Heights, May confessed that she wasn't missing the noise, air pollution and the general hustle and bustle of Beijing, or, indeed, Hong Kong. She was enjoying the peace and tranquillity here and, for the first time in many years, a wonderful and relaxing holiday. Oscar, too, was thoroughly enjoying himself. He loved May's company and enjoyed spending their evenings together eating dinner on the patio. After the first night's storm, the weather had calmed down and they were taking full advantage of the warm evenings. Over the meals they discussed various topics and subjects but the conversations would inevitably drift back to the world of art.

It was during the middle of the eighth night of May's stay that Oscar was awakened by the sound of his bedroom door slowly being pushed open. It was totally dark in his room so he couldn't see the person quietly creeping in. He was just about to leap out of bed and confront the intruder, when he suddenly felt the sensation of a soft, naked female body slowly sliding up behind him and caressing his own naked skin.

Chapter 54

Emma's mobile phone rang whilst she was preparing dinner in the kitchen. She quickly wiped her hands and answered the call.

"Emma Caxton speaking."

"Hello, Emma. It's Jean Dixon, from Barrett's in Witney."

"Oh, hello, Jean. It's so good to hear from you again."

"I've checked our records again and, do you know, I've found your painting!"

"Oh, wow. Seriously?" replied Emma, excitedly. "That's wonderful. So, what exactly have you found?"

"Our pictures sales and purchases ledger for the ten years up to 1910 isn't very thick. As I said, it was only a small part of the business back then. Billy did buy the picture from Barrett's. On the 24th July, 1909. It cost him four shillings and sixpence."

Emma quickly scribbled down this information on a nearby scrap of paper. "Well, that's interesting because he was married on the 28th July, 1908. I wonder if this was a first wedding anniversary present?"

"Strange one if it was. I think I'd have wanted something a bit more romantic."

Emma laughed. "You've been so helpful, Jean. By the way, have you got the ledger with you there, right now?"

"Yes, it's next to me on my desk."

"In the purchases section, can you see when Barrett's bought the picture and are there any details of who they bought it from?" Emma held her breath and crossed her fingers. She heard Jean flick over some pages.

"14th November, 1902," announced Jean, reading the details as they'd been entered into the ledger. "Purchased at auction for three shillings. It was owned by a firm called Pickles and Co. Apparently, they'd stopped trading."

Again, Emma quickly scribbled down every minute piece of information. "Jean, you've been brilliant. There are two more things I would like to ask of you, please. Firstly, is there any chance you could let me have photocopies of these details and, secondly, I've got to come to Burford very soon, so I'd love to pop into Witney and meet you at Barrett's. I want to say thank you more properly. When would be a good time for you?"

The two women checked their diaries and agreed on a date and time. Jean said she'd have the photocopies ready for Emma to collect when she arrived.

After Emma finished the call, she shouted out loud, "Yes!" and went off to tell Ian the good news. She found him in the home office, sitting at his desk. He was surrounded by four reference books, all on the work of Paul Gauguin.

"I heard the scream. What's happened?" asked Ian.

"That was Jean Dixon on the telephone, from Barrett's," explained Emma, with a huge smile on her face. "She's found the records that take our painting back to 1902." Emma then gave Ian a summary of the new findings.

"Well, that's brilliant. Well done you… and Jean."

"I'm going to visit her next week. She's going to give me photocopies of the ledger entries. I'll also take her a huge bouquet of flowers to say thank you. Probably pop in to see Mum and Dad at the same time."

The Gamble

"Excellent," said Ian, genuinely pleased with Emma's just rewards for all her efforts. "I think the next step is for you to try and find out why this company, Pickles and Co, owned the painting in 1902... and where they got it from. That might be the last step back to Seurat."

Emma nodded and then noticed all the books on Ian's desk. "Paul Gauguin?" she inquired.

"Mmm," responded Ian. "I'm trying to identify a painting, I'm fairly sure it's by Paul Gauguin."

"Can I suggest we talk about it later. I was just preparing dinner when Jean telephoned. Will you collect Robert from school?"

Ian looked at his watch. "Yes, okay, I'd better go right away."

Later that evening, Ian and Emma were sitting in the lounge and Ian started to explain his situation. "I've found an interesting painting located in the entrance hallway at 'Dexter's End'. At first glance, it appears to be a fairly insignificant picture, not helped by its grimy condition. It's a still life painting of a bowl of fruit on a table. The artist has signed the name, 'Madeleine B'."

"Well, that's not Gauguin," said Emma. She wondered where Ian's story was going.

"Well yes... and no," replied Ian. "I'll explain more in a minute. Let me give you a little more background information first of all." Ian leaned back in his seat and continued. "Gauguin was a strange character. Most of his paintings were colourful but they often included a mystery, or sometimes a message he was trying to convey. However, the main surprise with Gauguin was that he'd never set out to be a professional artist in the first place. By the age of 33 he was married to Mette, a Danish woman, and she'd produced five children for him. He painted a little in his spare time, just a hobby really, because he made a very good living from being a successful stockbroker. He also had a part-time involvement with another business that bought and sold paintings."

Emma adjusted her sitting position and waited for Ian to continue. She was eager to learn more about Monsieur Gauguin.

"However, suddenly, at the age of 34, everything crashed, in more ways than one. It was 1882, the year that the Paris stock market crashed. At the same time the art market severely contracted too. Gauguin now found himself without a job and no regular income. Unlike most of his artist colleagues, Gauguin had not been to art college, nor did he have the experience of trying to develop a career in art at the same time as providing for his family. Eventually, he decided his only option was to become a full-time painter. Almost overnight the whole family had to quickly adjust to a new lifestyle, little income and all the challenges of Paul Gauguin's unexpected new situation."

"That's tough on the children," said Emma, with feeling.

Ian nodded and continued, "Mette, his wife, soon became disheartened and despondent from this lifestyle and announced she and the children were going to return to Copenhagen, back to her family. She had grown up in a middle-class environment and was not at all happy with this big step down in the family's income and reduced standard of living. Gauguin initially went with his family to Denmark, but he couldn't make a success of being a salesman, especially in a foreign country, so he returned to France to concentrate on his painting. He struggled to make a living and constantly needed to move to different accommodations. Although he wrote many letters to Mette, essentially the marriage was over. From being happy, wealthy and with a loving family, he was now in a critical and desperate situation."

The Gamble

"But his paintings sell for millions today. Surely he made some money?"

"Gauguin was a French post-impressionist artist and was largely unappreciated until after his death. Yes, today, he is much more recognised for his experimental use of colour and the 'Synthetist' style, which was distinctly different to impressionism. However, back in the late 19th century, his work often seemed to have a slightly darker edge. I wonder how much of his mental anguish was filtering through to his work. He often depicted scenes of 'good v bad' or included questions or suggestions that make one wonder what extra message Gauguin was trying to convey. Anyway, in 1888 he turned up in the village of Pont Aven, where a number of other artists were also living. He rented a room in a small hotel called the 'Pension Gloanec'. I'll come back to this hotel in a few minutes. I need a glass of wine. Do you want one?"

"Just half a glass, please," said Emma. She was impatient to hear how this story related to Ian's picture at the house in Wentworth.

A few minutes later Ian arrived back with the two drinks. He sat back down and resumed his story.

"You mentioned earlier about Gauguin's paintings now selling for millions. Well, in 1891 he moved on again, this time to Tahiti, where he spent the rest of his life. There he concentrated on painting young and beautiful local women, people working in fields and views of the tropical countryside. His paintings gradually became more interesting and tempting to buyers. He'd managed to capture the exotic… creating an image of a tropical paradise."

"Sounds idyllic."

"Two of these paintings, 'Otahi' and 'When will you marry', sold in 2013 and 2014 for US$120 million and $210 million respectively!"

"That's absolutely staggering! And you say he had very little money himself from this sort of work during the time he was alive?" asked Emma.

"As I said earlier, his paintings only became seriously appreciated after his death. His work became more influential later, especially to the French avant-garde and many modern artists, such as Pablo Picasso and Henri Matisse. The reason Gauguin's art became popular after his death was mainly from the efforts of an art dealer called Ambroise Vollard. This man organised exhibitions of Gauguin's work very late in his life and he also assisted with organising two important posthumous exhibitions in Paris."

"That's so sad, Ian. That stock market crash obviously had such a long lasting and devastating effect on the man's life."

Ian nodded. "Ironically, without it, we wouldn't be sitting here now talking about him! Anyway, let's go back to Pont Aven in 1888. Gauguin was now in his 40s and because most of the other artists in the village were much younger than him, he became a sort of father figure. He fell in love with the sister of one of his fellow artists. However, she was half his age. Madeleine Bernard was her name and she became a close friend and posed for a number of his paintings. Gauguin also got on very well with his landlady at the 'Pension Gloanec', and, on her birthday, he painted a still life picture called 'Fête Gloanec'. He gave this picture to her as his birthday present. He signed it, not as Paul Gauguin, but as 'Madeleine B'!"

"Oh, my goodness. So, you think this picture in Wentworth is the same painting?"

"It's not quite that easy. There's already an authorised version of 'Fête Gloanec' and it's definitely signed 'Madeleine B'. I think it's being displayed in the Musée des Beaux-Arts d'Orléans, in France."

"Oh," said Emma, a little deflated. "So now what? Is the Wentworth painting a copy or a fake?"

"I'm not sure, but my sixth sense tells me the Wentworth version is the real work. My challenge is to try and buy the painting at 'Dexter's End' and then prove that this picture is the original and the one in France is, well… a fake!"

Emma laughed. "The French will love that."

Chapter 55

Emma now felt she was so close to solving the last leg of the 'Mademoiselle Chad' provenance trail. She was also convinced that the final piece in the jigsaw lay with Pickles and Co. Who were they, where were they based and why did they own and then sell her painting? Did they have any sort of French connection?

Emma, once again, accessed the wealth of information on the internet, but she was struggling to identify a company called Pickles and Co. was existing at the end of the 19th century. She rechecked the notes she'd written down when talking to Jean. Suddenly a spark of inspiration came to her. Pickles and Co. had ceased trading! So, she thought, when did they actually cease trading? Surely there had to be a record of that event.

On the following Tuesday Emma arrived at Barrett's the Jewellers complete with a large bouquet of flowers. The shop assistant rang Jean and told her that Mrs. Caxton was in the shop to see her. Two minutes later Jean arrived in the shop from her office upstairs.

"Hello, Mrs. Caxton," said Jean, with a welcoming smile. Emma guessed she was probably about 60, but had obviously kept herself quite trim for her age. "It's so good to put a face to the voice."

Emma smiled. "You've been so helpful, Jean. I thought I must thank you properly. Here, these are for you." Emma pushed the bouquet towards her.

"Oh, they're lovely. That's really kind of you. Come upstairs to my office. We can then have a chat and I can put these lovely flowers in water."

Jean led Emma out of the main shop area and upstairs towards her office. At the top they turned right and walked down a narrow corridor, passing two doors. At the end, Jean stopped and pushed open a door which had a sign on it saying 'Office'.

Jean laid the flowers down on a cupboard. "I'll put those in water shortly. Please, Emma, do sit down. It's a little cluttered in here but, well, it's usually only me."

Emma sat in front of the desk as Jean returned to her own seat.

"Now, where's my manners," Jean said, reproaching herself. "Would you like a cup of coffee or tea?"

"No, no. Thank you, I'm fine," replied Emma. She didn't intend to stay too long.

"Here we are," said Jean, passing Emma a large brown envelope. "These are the photocopies you asked for. It's all been rather exciting looking into Billy Charlton's life and career at Barrett's. Our old records make quite interesting reading."

"Thank you so much," said Emma, pulling out and looking through the six sheets of paper. Suddenly she stopped and focused her attention on one particular sheet. It was a photocopy of the invoice for the purchase of the 'Mademoiselle Chad' painting at auction, dated 14th November 1902. Printed at the bottom of the invoice the address of Pickles and Co was revealed. '12, Cornmarket Street, Oxford'.

"Is everything you wanted there?" asked Jean, concerned that Emma had suddenly become quiet and very focused.

"Yes, yes. Again, thank you so much." Emma's mind was now buzzing. She had an address!

"Well, I hope it all helps with your family tree," said Jean, relaxing again.

Emma smiled. "Yes, it's all been such a fascinating journey." She didn't want to tell a lie, but decided not to reveal the truth either. "I think I've taken up enough of your time, Jean." Emma stood up, in readiness to leave. "It's been really nice to finally meet with you."

Jean stood up too and walked around her desk to stand next to Emma. "I'm so pleased I was able to help... and thank you so much for the flowers. I must put them in water before I take them home. Come, I'll show you the way out."

Emma followed Jean back along the corridor and then down the stairs. This time they didn't go back through the main shop, but towards a side door.

"Here we are, Emma. Turn right in the alleyway and you'll be back on the High Street."

Emma passed by Jean and through the open door. Stepping into a narrow access lane, which led to a small car park, she turned back to Jean and held out her hand. "Thank you, for everything."

"It's been a pleasure. Goodbye," replied Jean, after shaking Emma's hand.

Emma walked the few steps along the lane and back on to the High Street. She had a very big smile on her face!

Later that evening, Emma was eating dinner with her parents. She'd just explained why she'd been in Witney. Her mother was unusually quiet, but her father was fascinated with Emma's detective work.

"So, what are you going to do now that you've got that Oxford address?" her father asked.

"After I left Barrett's," replied Emma, "I called in at

The Gamble

the Witney local library and used one of their computers. I eventually found out a lot more information about Pickles and Co.'s history. They were not only an art shop in Cornmarket Street, but they also ran an agency from their offices upstairs. The agency was involved with purchasing and importing paintings by some of the post-impressionist artists in France. Unfortunately, the company ceased trading in 1902, so I'm not sure if I can prove how or when they purchased my painting. Georges Seurat, he's the artist, died in 1891, so, I'm assuming the purchase was probably not directly from him, unless, of course, they bought it before he died. Maybe Ian will come up with a few better ideas."

"Do you think this is likely to change the painting's value?" asked her mother.

"To be honest, I don't know. Ian's still very positive and he's the expert. It's so frustrating though, to be so close."

"I know you'll get there in the end," said her father, with an encouraging smile on his face. "Hard work often reaps rewards in the end."

After dropping Robert off at school, Ian drove the relatively short distance to the Wentworth Estate. Most of the commuter traffic had long gone, so his journey was quicker than he'd anticipated. He'd now arrived at the entrance to the estate and, although he'd reset the satnav on his car, he largely remembered the route and the various turns and the lanes. It was only about eight minutes later when he arrived at the entrance to 'Dexter's End'. The large ornate metal double gates were locked and he noticed the intermittent flashing blue light of the alarm system at the side of the sign, 'Dexter's End'. He checked his watch. He was ten minutes early.

After switching off the engine, he stepped out of his car and stretched his arms. He could already feel the warm sunshine beating down on his face. The only noise was the local bird life and in the distance the sound of a lawn mower. Probably on the golf course, he thought. Leaving his car in front of the gates he walked onto the lane. Directly opposite the driveway was a mixed holly and hawthorn hedge. He spotted a small gap which gave him a glimpse of the neighbouring property. He walked closer and peered through the gap. He could see part of a lovely white-painted house and the side garden, which not only contained an array of shrubs, but also a hard-surfaced tennis court.

Ian's attention was suddenly interrupted by the sound of an approaching car. He stepped back and watched as a taxi drew up and stopped directly behind his car. Seconds later, Charles Owen got out and the taxi drove away. Ian crossed the lane to join his colleague.

"Sorry, I'm a bit late," said Charles. "There were no taxis available at the railway station when I first arrived."

The two men shook hands and Ian replied. "I was early so I thought I'd enjoy the warm sunshine. This area is a nice part of the world."

Charles removed a small electronic device from his pocket and pointed it at the gates. He then pressed one of the buttons. The blue flashing light immediately stopped and the two gates slowly opened. "Drive your car in, Ian." said Charles, and he stepped aside.

Ian returned to his car, drove through the gates and parked on the gravel driveway, about 20 metres from the front door. In his rear view mirror, he saw Charles following him briefly, before stopping, turning around and then pointing his device at the gates. The gates slowly closed.

Ian got out of his car and waited for Charles to join him. "It wouldn't be a good idea to lose that device," joked Ian.

Charles smiled. "There's a keypad on either side of the gates… just in case."

The Gamble

Charles walked to the front door and unlocked it. He then switched off the burglar alarm and Ian followed him into the house.

Although it was very warm outside, Ian decided the house still felt cold and possibly smelled of damp. Definitely unlived in, he thought, and, once sold, the building will certainly be knocked down and replaced by something much more contemporary.

Ian followed Charles, and the two men walked into the sitting room. Charles then headed straight towards an old oak sideboard. Ian watched him and, when Charles opened the end door, Ian spotted there was a safe built into the wall at the back.

That's clever, thought Ian, but when he saw Charles start to enter the coding, he walked away to the south-facing window and stood absorbing a shaft of sunlight.

Charles retrieved a brown folder, relocked the safe and shut the wooden door. He then walked over to join Ian. "When you were last here, I saw you, several times, looking at the painting in the hallway. Alexander's report had a valuation of £34,000. What made you think it was only worth that amount of money?"

Ian was a little stumped and didn't really know what to say, so he began to waffle until he could think more clearly. "Viktor thought it wasn't a very exciting painting. The provenance paperwork you provided was a bit vague and didn't reveal any detailed history or when it was purchased. If it's not a copy, then it's probably late 19th century. Viktor had never heard of the artist."

"But you know better don't you, Mr. Caxton. You know exactly who the artist is and also its true value. I'm not an idiot, Mr. Caxton, so don't treat me like one."

"The truth is, yes, you're right. I do know the real artist and I've a fair idea of its value... if, of course, it's authentic... and not just a fake."

Charles smiled and glared at Ian. "It's not a fake!"

Ian continued. "You gave me your business card for a reason. My guess is that you only provided paperwork that was sufficiently vague to give the impression your grandfather was not very organised. Just enough information to obtain lower valuations. I think you also have a fair idea of the correct value… if it's authentic, and that you had no intention of selling your grandfather's art collection, especially just via a house clearing firm. Your grandfather didn't own any valuable furniture items, but he had a very good eye, and more expensive taste, when it came to his painting collection. Once you realised you recognised me from our dealings in the past, I'm certain you planned this meeting from that very moment."

Charles continued smiling and then gently applauded Ian's comments. "Very good, Ian. Yes, you're right," he said, in a more relaxed tone of voice. "I'll be frank with you, as long as you promise that the following information goes no further."

"Okay," said Ian, hesitantly.

"The paintings in this house, excluding our friend in the hallway, I reckon, will fetch about £50 million at auction."

"Only with the correct and undisputed provenances. Certainly not with the paperwork you've provided so far," interrupted Ian.

Charles tapped the brown folder he was holding. "This folder contains copies of all the undisputable provenances."

It was Ian's turn to smile and raise his eyebrows. I'm dealing with quite a shrewd cookie here, he thought. He knows the art world.

Charles continued. "We both know that that painting in the hallway is titled, 'Fête Gloanec' and signed by 'Madeleine B'. We both also know that this pseudonym was used by Paul Gauguin, in about 1888. Mr. Caxton, I think it is worth about £30 million!"

The Gamble

Ian smiled again. "Maybe not quite that much, but, well... you might be correct... at the right auction, but obtaining that sort of price can only be achieved with an undisputed provenance. By the way, did you know there's already a painting being displayed in a French museum, called 'Fête Gloanec' and it's signed, 'Madeleine B'?"

Charles shrugged his shoulders. "Maybe, but we know which painting is the authentic one, don't we, Ian?" He once again tapped his folder. "These are just a copy of the original paper records of the real provenances. I have several copies both on my computer and on various back-ups. The originals are in a bank depository."

Ian nodded. "So, Charles, what do you need from me? Why am I here?"

"I have a problem, Ian, and I'm fairly sure you'll be able to help," said Charles, now with a much more serious expression on his face. "If my grandfather's art collection is valued correctly, at a total of about £80 million, and that becomes public knowledge, then Mr. Taxman is going to seriously slam me for inheritance tax. I want you to prove conclusively, Ian, that the value of all these paintings is worth only... what? Shall we say, about £10 million."

Ian raised his eyebrows and a tiny smile appeared on his face.

Charles continued. "I can then pay Mr. Taxman a much lower figure, obtain probate and get on with the task of selling 'Dexter's End'. In return, Ian, I have a proposition, which I'm hoping you'll be seriously tempted by. Achieve all this for me and I will then give you... totally free, the 'Madeleine B' painting. Yes, the one in the hallway. By your very own considered valuation, a snip at maybe between £25 and 30 million! So, Ian Caxton, what do you say? Do we have a deal?"

The story continues in

'The Result'

Volume 5 in the Ian Caxton Thriller series

DISCOVER THE FIRST THREE VOLUMES OF THE IAN CAXTON THRILLER SERIES.

'THE OPPORTUNITY'

Ian Caxton is a senior manager at Sotheby's. After successful career moves to Sotheby's branches in New York and Hong Kong, Ian is now based in London and earmarked for the top position. However, following a chance meeting with Andrei, a very rich Russian art dealer based in Monaco, Ian suddenly reassesses all his plans and ambitions. Even his marriage is under threat. The Opportunity charts the tumultuous life and career of Ian Caxton as he navigates the underbelly of the art world, one of serious wealth, heart-stopping adventure and a dark side. The big question is, will Ian take The Opportunity? And if he does, what will the consequences be, not only for him, but also for his wife and colleagues?

'THE CHALLENGE'

The art world is full of pitfalls, mysteries and risk. It is a place where paintings can be bought and sold for millions of pounds. Fortunes can be made… and lost! For those whose ambition is to accumulate wealth beyond their wildest dreams, expert knowledge, confidence, bravery and deep pockets are certainly needed! Ian Caxton is being tested by fake paintings, a financial gamble on the artwork of a black slave, his wife's life-changing news and a series of mysterious emails that suggest he's being watched. More dramatic events, mental conflicts and soul-searching decisions. How will Ian cope with all these extra demands?

This is the big question, that is The Challenge.

'THE DECISION'
A worrying letter from a dead colleague, a Gainsborough painting downgraded by the experts, a new partnership opportunity, an unexpected statement from his boss and his wife's announcement of her new ambitions. These are just some of the new challenges we see Ian Caxton having to grapple with this time. The answers and consequences of which lead ultimately to his bold life-changing decision!

In Antigua, Oscar joins up with a new business colleague, but soon discovers a world of fraud, deception and murder. Penny experiences unforeseen changes to her life and Viktor is informed of an amazing surprise.

Another page-turning tale of adventure, intrigue, greed and risk, where millions of pounds routinely change hands. Welcome to the exciting, mysterious and sinister happenings that continue to occur in the art world!

Ingram Content Group UK Ltd.
Milton Keynes UK
UKHW010632120523
421641UK00004B/110